Toss *the* Bride

Toss *the* Bride

Jennifer Manske Fenske

Thomas Dunne Books
St. Martin's Press ⚐ New York

THOMAS DUNNE BOOKS.
An imprint of St. Martin's Press.

Chapter three originally appeared, in slightly different form, as
"In the Okefenokee," in *Nantahala* (Spring 2003).

www.stmartins.com

Library of Congress Cataloging-in-Publication Data

Fenske, Jennifer Manske.
    Toss the bride : a novel / Jennifer Manske Fenske.
        p. cm.
    ISBN 0-312-33981-X
    EAN 978-0-312-33981-4
    1. Commitment (Psychology)—Fiction. 2. Weddings—Planning—Fiction.
3. Atlanta (Ga.)—Fiction.

PS3606.E57 T67 2006
813'.6—dc22

                                                      2005050101

First Edition: January 2006

10 9 8 7 6 5 4 3 2 1

For my beloved husband, Jonathan,
keeper of the secret language

Toss *the* Bride

1

The Horse Bride

My experience with horses comes down to this: When I was fourteen, my best girlfriend, Savannah, invited me to spend the week with her at Camp Sugar Dale near Atlanta. Savannah was sleeping away at the horse camp all summer and she could bring one friend for a week, just to try it out. It was probably a brilliant marketing campaign designed to breed another hundred girls begging their parents for a summer of riding overstuffed ponies and swimming in the mossy lake. I knew my parents could never afford to send me to Camp Sugar Dale for a day, let alone a whole summer, but I went anyway.

Wearing my beat-up tennis shoes and jeans instead of fancy jodhpurs, I rode with the best and brightest of Atlanta girlhood. We were on those ponies all day. After breakfast, after lunch. We even had a trail ride and campout one night with the horses tethered nearby. I could hear them rustling and stomping all night while I tried to get comfortable with the marriage of my sleeping bag and a twisted tree root.

I am reminded of Camp Sugar Dale because in the intervening

twelve years, I have not been around horses to smell their horsey smell and breathe in their wholesome type of friendliness. That, and the way a horse's eyes can look you up and down and sort of pass an equine judgment. Those Camp Sugar Dale ponies had us little girls figured out, and from the look in their sleepy eyes, half-closed in the suburban sunlight, they weren't too impressed.

Francie is giving me the horse look now. She spies my white linen dress with the pretty eyelet shoulders. She searches over the borrowed white pearls and the slightly scuffed open-toed sandals. She marks my bare legs and takes note of the Band-Aid covering one knee. With a roving brown eye, Francie tells me she does not like what she sees. Heaving out her chest, shaking out her mane of blond hair, she steps back and snorts. Then she whirls around and heads back toward the barn at a trot.

Francie is the bride.

It's two hours before her wedding at the Cumberland Valley Botanical Gardens. The hydrangeas are wilting, the groom is late, and Francie's bridesmaids look like they need maids of their own to attend them. They lounge nearby in a converted historic barn with green awnings. No one is dressed, ready, or even slightly concerned that a major event is taking place in 120 minutes.

So far, I have been on the job three hours. My first task was to arrive at the barn and check the rooms where the wedding party would dress and wait. Are the embroidered linen handkerchiefs set out for the men? Is the silver monogrammed brush waiting on the bureau for the bride? Breath mints? Mint julep pitchers? My boss, Maurice, says never to trust anyone *ever,* and I've found more often than not, he's right. Take today, for instance: When I got to the bride's room, a fancy-schmancy hotel-type room with huge gilded mirrors and a large hook hanging from the ceiling for heavy wedding dresses, I almost fell over. The trendy Black Magic roses Francie wanted were there all right, but from the looks of the wilted petals and gummy stems, they needed some black magic about two days ago. I placed a frantic call to the florist, a local floral celebrity who is a bit on the touchy side. Once, when Maurice complained about a botched centerpiece, the florist pitched a box of two-hundred-dollar bridesmaid bouquets onto the floor.

Flowers can get pretty ugly.

Talking into my combination phone-wristwatch-calendar—a gift from my boyfriend, Avery, who recently went to Japan—I told the florist's assistant that the Magics were past their prime. The bride would be here any minute and if she saw her bride's room decorated with dead roses, it would not sit well. Right then, I pictured Francie in my head and got a shaky, sweaty feeling. Francie always looked past me when she met with Maurice, like my singleness and need to work for a living were catching.

I managed to solve the crisis by dumping the sagging blooms and stalling until the florist's assistant arrived with fresh Black Magic roses. I placed the vase on an antique sideboard, dodging the gaggle of bridesmaids lounging here and there. The afternoon marched on.

Sometimes, in my quiet moments, I reflect that my existence has come down to groveling at the feet of overpaid florists so that a mean-spirited bride can enjoy some expensive flowers for about twenty minutes. It really seems like there's something else I could have done with my life. If I could ever drag Avery to the altar, I would do it in the dead of winter, without flowers. There would be no doves, no clinging jasmine, and no powder-blue skies.

A wrinkled-looking boy of about ten or so walks by listlessly. Kicking at a stone on the path, the boy looks up. Two bumblebees drone near my right ear.

"Hey," I say to him.

"Hey, can I go down to the swan pond? My mom's saying I can go."

I recognize the boy from the rehearsal dinner the night before.

His name is Granger. I remember him because he stayed close to the dessert table all evening. "It's Granger, right?"

The boy's eyes widen. "You know me?"

"You were there last night. The party at the Magnolia Room?" I like this kid. He has round green eyes and hands that look like they would rather be climbing a tree. He grabs at his little-boy tie.

"Yeah. I had to go to it because my sister is getting married. My mom said I had to."

"Is this the same mom who won't let you go down to the swan pond?"

Granger drops his tie and looks up at me with a smile. "How did you know she wouldn't let me?"

"Let's say I had one guess and I knew it had to count," I say and smile back at him. Granger slides away, back toward the barn. I keep my eye on him until he walks behind a tall hedge of azaleas.

"Wedding party, party of wedding people," hisses the loudest and softest of voices. "I need you to crack to it, step with it!" It's Maurice. As a really big-deal wedding planner, he can do what I cannot. I'll find out later he has just been to the barn and whipped those lazy attendants into shape. Dresses are flying and lipstick is being applied. This wedding might happen after all.

You don't get in Maurice's way. Not with the money these people are paying him. The higher his fee goes, the more they seem to do what he wants. But Francie's wedding party is clearly pushing him to the limit.

"Macie," Maurice says, pushing down his creased sleeves from his elbows. "I need you." It's a hot day, and Maurice will change for the third time right before the wedding. His first outfit of the day, jeans and a T-shirt, was hours ago. His microfiber pants and crisp cotton shirt are for now, and his ultraslick, costs-more-than-I-earn-in-three-months suit is in my car. I've stopped looking at the labels when I pick up his dry cleaning. Maurice is in his own fashion league. I once asked his wife who had the bigger closet, she or Maurice. She just smiled at me like a woman who has given up the fight. I found out later that when they remodeled their house last year, half of the bedroom space went to Maurice's clothes. His wife uses a closet down the hall.

"What do you need?" I ask. Maurice praises me for organization, so he'll probably want me to check over the distribution of wedding favors. The bride selected little sacks of chocolate for the 416 guests who will be here in 110 minutes. The chocolates—imported from Paris—are cooling in a refrigerated truck attended by a bored college student. Sometimes I wonder whether my life would be easier if I had nothing to do but order chocolates from overseas. Francie spent a good month hounding me about what she should give as a favor. I finally found the chocolates when Avery returned from a trip to France. Francie popped one in her mouth at Maurice's office and that was it. I pointed out to her that the chocolates were a good idea because of her name. She stared back, licking her lower lip with a swift stab of the tongue.

"What? Huh?"

I sighed patiently. "Your name? Francie? France."

"My real name is Lydia Jane. I don't understand what you mean."

I gave up. Francie is just one of those brides we toss who will go out of my mind in a few weeks. "Tossing the bride" is Maurice's lingo for getting a bride married and out of his hair. When she's good and married off, it's not our concern anymore. Of course, I secretly want to conduct an informal poll someday to see how many of our brides are still married one or two years out.

"I don't know how to say this, Macie," Maurice mumbles, looking past me to the wedding area. White wooden chairs with soft satin bows are arranged in an arc all the way to an altar that is arrayed with heaps of white freesia, lilies, and scented stephanotis. Combined with the sunlight, the effect is almost blinding. I hope the guests bring sunglasses.

"You don't know how to say what?"

Maurice pauses. He's a good boss, as far as bosses go. I know I'm fortunate to have this job. It pays way more than my gift-wrapping stint at Luck's department store. That's where I was working when I met Avery two years ago this month. I gift wrapped crystal bowls and china platters, making sure to tuck in the silver Luck's gift card. I was good at it, but mental gymnastics it was not.

Avery introduced me to Maurice and convinced him he should give me a try. I've been with Maurice for more than a year, and I've seen my share of weddings. It's time I had my own, I say to myself. In my head. Not out loud.

"Francie wants you to change," Maurice says quietly.

"What? Lydia Jane wants what?" I have to struggle to keep my voice down. Nearby, a groomsman loafs about, trailing his fingers through a camellia bush. At least he's dressed in his suit.

"Francie thinks your dress is too, uhm, formal for what you have to do in the ceremony." Maurice's eyes are still trained on the wedding area. He seems embarrassed, poor thing. But I want to run up the aisle, knocking over chairs as I go. I love this dress. It's gorgeous. Avery bought it for me from a little store near Lenox Mall I never even knew existed. And he was only one size off, so when I exchanged it, I saw how much it cost. It is not only "formal," as that doltish bride suggested, it is—

"So, you hear me?" Maurice asks.

"What am I supposed to do, then? Would my bra and panties be a little more, oh, I don't know, informal?"

Glancing around, Maurice grimaces at me. "Okay, so I think it's stupid. I mean, your dress is very nice. Avery must have picked it up because I've seen your taste and—"

"Thanks, Maurice. Appreciate that. But I'm still walking down the aisle with nothing on unless you fix it." I cannot believe the nerve of this bride. It is too late in the wedding parade to find something else to wear. I'm the horse wrangler. This is the dress I've picked.

A little background here: When Francie approached us about her dream of riding down the aisle on the back of her favorite horse, Rhubarb, we tried to talk her out of it. "Think of the horsehair flying everywhere," we said. "Think of the chance of a horsey accident on the crisp green botanical garden grass." It didn't matter. This is what Francie wanted. And Francie was going to get what Francie wanted. She even rented a special white leather sidesaddle from some rodeo in Tennessee. Her dress will cover its chunky rhinestones, thank goodness.

Maurice invented my role in the ceremony because somewhere in his memory he had stashed a story I told him about Camp Sugar Dale. I don't even remember what it was, but that's Maurice. His mind traps things for when he needs them again. I've seen him pull out the scientific name of a rare orchid that a bride was trying to recall. I've been there when he remembered the perfect Brazilian vegetable dumpling sauce for a puzzled caterer. It's amazing, really.

Francie was delighted to know that Maurice had a "horse person" on staff. I got the job of wrangling the horse—bringing Rhubarb down the aisle with Francie Lydia Jane on board. When we get to her fiancé at the end of the aisle, he's supposed to help Francie down from the saddle, and I'm supposed to lead Rhubarb off to the waiting trailer. He doesn't get to hang around for the reception. Poor Rhubarb.

I'd picked out the dress Avery gave me because Francie wanted me to wear white, just like herself and the horse. I kept my end of the bargain.

Maurice has snapped on his earpiece and is rattling some directions into his phone. "Size eight? Hold on—" Maurice eyes me up and down. "No, make that a six. A little scrawny. Not much in the bust. Okay." He clicks off abruptly. "Your dress will be here in thirty minutes."

"Who in the world?" I say, once again impressed with Maurice's ability to get the right thing in the right place. The botanical gardens are plopped in a little rural town miles from Atlanta shopping.

"That was Melanie from Melanie's Boutique over on Main Street. I ordered the most exquisite little pin there last year for a bride. Remember Alinda?"

I shudder and nod. Best to let that memory slip away to sweet oblivion. It's been my experience that brides whose names start with *A* are more trouble. It's a pet theory of mine. I also have this other theory that there are a limited number of faces in the world, which is why people say, "You look just like so-and-so." There are only so many faces to go around and they get recycled. I haven't met my face yet, but I'm waiting.

"Macie, are you listening?"

I nod. Maurice tells me to keep a lookout for Melanie's minivan. For the next thirty minutes, I extinguish a number of small wedding fires. A bridesmaid has forgotten her strapless bra. I show her a thing or two about masking tape. One of the groomsmen is hitting the mint juleps a little too enthusiastically. I send out for strong coffee, "light on the soy milk." He actually tells me this with slurred speech, and then tries to kiss the bride. It is not a brotherly kiss. I walk away because there are some things for which I just don't get paid.

A few minutes later, I get a chance to chat with my best friend, Iris Glen, when she stops by the gardens to make one last check on the wedding cake. Iris is also in the wedding business. She is a pastry chef and the owner of Cake Cake, *the* place to snag an Atlanta wedding cake.

"Swamped?" Iris asks. Her assistant dropped off the towering white cake a few hours ago, and Iris wants to make sure every icing rosette is still in place.

"Yeah, but what else is new? You would not believe this bride and her crazy demands." I make a face.

"I've worked with Francie for eight months, too," Iris laughs.

"She originally wanted her name spelled out on the cake in big, shimmering letters. I suggested that might not be the best plan."

We share a brief laugh in the middle of wedding chaos. I adore Iris for lots of reasons. She is loyal, kind, and a blast to be around. We work together frequently because our brides naturally want to order the best, and Iris is absolutely the best.

My dress replacement arrives, so I bid farewell to Iris. When I finally wriggle into the white size-six Melanie dress, I feel like giving off a Francie snort. The cotton dress drops to my knees and is balanced on top with a big boat collar. A huge bow, stuck square in the middle of my chest, teeters back and forth with each step. I look like an overgrown eight-year-old girl from 1936. I creep out of the women's bathroom in the barn and look for a place to stash my real dress, my beautiful dress. I try to avoid the bride's room, but Francie catches sight of me and drags her enormous wedding dress—the train is ten feet long—out into the hall.

"Ah, that's better. You look like a nice southern girl." Francie licks her pink lips. A bit of color sticks to her perfect front teeth. I don't bother to tell her. "Maurice and I thought that other dress was a little"—she pauses for effect and glances back down the hall toward the men's changing room—"trashy. If you know what I mean."

I nod and lower my head. The bow on my chest swings dangerously. "I know what you mean. Exactly."

Francie gathers the sides of the dress in her manicured claws and swings back around, glaring at me while she turns. She thinks I have insulted her, but she can't be sure. The train of her dress knocks over a ceramic umbrella stand, and I scramble before it dashes to pieces. Maurice arrives dressed in his suit, gives the new dress and me the once-over, and motions me outside. It's time for Rhubarb.

Back in the garden, well-heeled guests are escorted to their seats by the languid groomsmen and ushers. The heat is heat; it's something you get used to in Atlanta. My dress is a bit starchy, and I rub at the boat neck where it touches my skin.

"Don't do that," Maurice hisses at me. We're stalking Rhubarb. He's supposed to be behind the two-hundred-year-old boxwood hedges. We turn and turn again, traveling deeper into the maze of green and brown. A sparrow skitters along the path, a twig resting in its beak. We finally find the white horse dozing and tethered to a sullen stable hand.

"Rhubarb don't want to do this today," the horse handler informs us.

Maurice stops short in his leather loafers. I sense his persuasive charm gathering like a thundercloud for this final challenge. He wants that stable hand to lead me to the back of the garden. He wants Francie hefted up on top of the horse's broad back, and then, he wants to toss her like a sack of rice.

"He just don't want to," the stable hand says mournfully. A small man, he stands beside the horse, one hand on the lead rope.

"What, exactly, does that mean?" Maurice asks with the politest gloss of rage. The sound of strings soars over the boxwood. The musicians have started the prelude without the signal from Maurice. I watch his fingers clench and release.

"Maurice, go on. I'll take care of this." I motion for him to leave. The bow swings wildly. To my relief and shock, Maurice walks away. But not before he gives the sleeping Rhubarb a nasty look.

I eye the stable hand and decide to take a gentle approach. "How long have you been with Rhubarb?"

"It's been about four years," he says, relaxing his grip on the lead rope. "Ever since Miss High and Mighty went to college."

"He's a thoroughbred, isn't he?"

Rubbing his lined face, the stable hand nods. "That's right. His racing name was Cherries Jubilee. He retired at five. Won a stakes race at Pimlico."

I take a step closer and put a light hand on Rhubarb's white neck. The warm skin twitches under my fingers, but the horse doesn't move. Over the hedge, the strings segue into another piece. They sound slightly sour and slow. It's hard to keep stringed instruments tuned in this humidity.

"You know, we'll all be in a lot of trouble if we don't get this horse down that aisle," I tell the stable hand.

He nods and gives Rhubarb's rump a playful slap. The horse's brown eyes open and look around. They size me up, childish white dress and all. "You ready, Rhubarb?" The stable hand gives the horse a knowing look, and I realize they are two of the few genuine creatures in this sprawling garden.

Rhubarb then does something that makes me think I am correct. He winks at me. He really does. I know it sounds crazy, but I was there. I follow the horse and the stable hand back through the maze.

"You know, it wouldn't be so bad if she would just visit him once in a while. He misses her. I think he was her fourteenth birthday present. These horses have a long memory, you know." The stable hand stops talking, lost in thought.

I watch the horse, his head dipping up and down as he walks, feet sinking into the loamy path. I wish I had a horse like this, waiting for me behind a stall door. Must be nice to be missed by such a beautiful animal. The stable hand reaches up briefly to pat Rhubarb's neck.

I move to take the lead rope. Rhubarb's eyes widen as Francie appears from behind the hedge. She waddles to his side, her dress billowing out behind her like a melting wedding cake. The horse takes an uneasy step forward. His caretaker, with the help of a handy stepladder, hoists Francie up and into the saddle. Rhubarb shifts uneasily, but I would, too, if layers and layers of crinoline, silk, and beading were poured over my back. The music turns serious, the guests stand, and I know it's our turn now.

"Take me up there," Francie screams. Her voice sails out over the last two rows. A few black-dress-wearing women give Francie polite, frozen smiles. I pull on Rhubarb's halter. It's crafted of smooth leather and topped by a brass nameplate. We start down the grass aisle. Behind me, I can feel Francie pitch and sway. The fabric of her dress spills onto my arm. Some of the netting is nudging my big, fat bow. I feel it tug at my breast.

I think about Francie up there and wonder if she feels any sense of joy. I wouldn't know it to look at her. Not at all. When I mull over the Francies of the world, I ask myself the question, What is her fiancé's name? What I mean by that is most of the women we work with are obsessed solely with the perfect wedding. They want foreign chocolates, humongous diamonds, honeymoons in paradise. Running me ragged, and Maurice insane, these brides hawk over every detail until I dream about them way past their wedding dates.

But I never know the fiancé's name. Of course, we *know* it. It's in a file somewhere. Peyton or Drayton or Tad somebody. He (or his father) has a lot of money. The bride (or her father) has a lot of money. But when she talks about the day, the bride tells me about how wonderful it will be, who will be in the audience, why her dress is the best one ever made. The man who stands at the end of the runner is nowhere to be found. Unless she is joking about how inept he is with wedding planning, the bride doesn't bother to talk about her intended.

Avery wonders why this bothers me so much. He tells me not to worry about people who are vapid or petty or mean. I know he's right, but deep down, I wonder if he is on their side. He just might be.

For most of our two years together, I have been happy to be Avery's girlfriend. We play tennis, grill steaks and fish, take walks, and generally amuse ourselves with the numerous trappings of a big city like Atlanta. There is always a festival, a free movie on the park green, or a new restaurant opening. I have never, ever been bored with Avery even though he comes from a family that is totally different from mine.

Mr. and Mrs. Leland (I haven't yet brought myself to call them Jack and Babs) are quite a pair. They live in the type of house that makes you slow the car down to get a better look. She has glossy black hair cut into a little bob that seems hip and timeless at the same time. Fond of manicures, pedicures, and facials, Mrs. Leland is always telling me over cocktails about the latest new spa with hot gravel treatments and bouncing stone massage. Mr. Leland is friendlier. He grills for us, talks about the stock market, and maintains an intimidating collection of periodicals. As a result, Avery's father is incredibly well versed on every current event. You name it—hurricanes, Middle East politics, poverty statistics—Mr. Leland knows something about it.

I like sitting on the Lelands' veranda, sipping a drink and glancing over at Avery while his father talks about the new critical biography of Shakespeare or an award-winning German documentary. It is a life unlike anything I have ever known, but I have learned to adjust. Sometimes, on nights with Avery's parents, I watch my boyfriend. Lately, as I have begun to think more about the future, I have noticed something about Avery. I think he's just waiting. On something.

He's certainly not waiting for a wedding. But Francie is, so I keep the horse moving. The standing guests smile grim little smiles to Francie and Rhubarb as we walk past. I imagine there is a groundswell of sympathy for my poor dress. Maybe not. As we approach the end of the grassy aisle, Rhubarb stops abruptly. I urge him on as he swings his gentle horse face toward me. I feel a shiver go through the wiggling mound of fabric draped over my right shoulder. I cannot imagine how Francie is going to dismount gracefully. I hear her give a little cry. I stop tugging on the lead rope. Rhubarb is not going anywhere. Before I can think to move, the horse's big teeth protrude from his mouth, and he takes a huge chomp out of the front of my dress. I stumble backward, caught in yards of white fabric. I can't get away. But as I struggle, I realize Rhubarb has liberated me from the blasted white bow on my dress. A guest to my left gasps.

Glancing up and back, I see that Francie is many things: wilted, furious, embarrassed. Rhubarb tosses the bow around his gums, his long pink tongue assisting him with pleasure. Finally, the horse spits the soggy piece of fabric onto the immaculate grass beneath his feet. I seize the moment to lead him up to the waiting minister and groom. Somehow, they get Francie off of the horse and I pull Rhubarb away and back to his handler. The ceremony goes on.

Rhubarb doesn't wink at me again, but I could swear that as I lead him away from the crowd, he laughs like only a horse can. I pat his strong, white shoulder, and we make our way back through the boxwood hedge. Bride tossing is not always clean and pretty, but it's what I do.

2

The Restless Bride

Avery takes a shiny silver fork and reaches over to my plate, tines hovering, ready to pounce. I give my plate the once-over to see what he wants. It must be the tuna. Actually, Avery's father called the fish something else, but to me, it's pretty much tuna.

"Are you gonna eat that?" Avery asks as his fork descends. He swoops in without waiting for an answer because he knows what I will say. Mr. Leland always piles way too much food on my plate. It's Friday and dinner is almost finished; we are relaxing on one of the verandas on the back of Avery's parents' house. Avery lives there, too, in a three-room suite on the first floor.

"You like that, Macie?" Mr. Leland asks and pours more white wine into his wife's glass. Mrs. Leland hums a little tune under her breath and then eyes the driveway. She is waiting for her masseuse or manicurist or some other attendant. So far, in my time with the Lelands, I have figured out that Mrs. Leland is rarely without a pampering appointment. She also asks what time it is frequently. Avery told me a long time ago that she refuses to wear a watch. She genuinely seems to be grateful when you answer her. She asks, "Do you have the time?" in a small little-girl voice, and then when you produce the hour and minutes of any given day, she acts delighted, even overjoyed.

I nod to my now-empty plate and tell Mr. Leland that I enjoyed the fish.

"There's a secret to grilling the perfect fish," he says mysteriously.

Avery and I wait, expecting more. Mr. Leland returns to his grill. It's a shiny stainless-steel number built into a little alcove on the veranda. To the side is a wood-fired brick pizza oven. A French door leads to the real kitchen inside.

"Avery," Mr. Leland says, "remember that chef we had out to the house when you were, oh, I don't know—how old were you?"

"You'll have to be more specific, Dad," Avery says, a smile on his face.

"The guy who liked fish with every meal? Chef Pack-a-something."

"Packanac. He was written up in all the foodie magazines," Avery says. "He taught Dad how to grill and sauté every type of fish. But if he didn't like the way something turned out, he'd toss it into the bushes. Plop! Over the edge of the veranda."

"We were picking rotten fish out of the azaleas for weeks," Mr. Leland says. "You were just in high school, right?"

"Dad! I had already graduated from college when he was here."

"Ah, well, it seems like you're still our little boy, Avery," his mother says idly.

A welcome breeze moves across the veranda. I tap my toes on the wooden planks under my feet. I'm restless tonight.

Sensing my mood, Avery puts down his napkin and smiles at me. Right then, I love him in one of those perfect moments you have when you're really lucky. His green eyes are kind and his hair lifts up a bit in the late-afternoon breeze. I think: I want to be with this man. But Avery does not talk about this kind of thing. Tennis, fish, even architecture, Avery will gab about all night long. But get him to discuss the future? Of us? Forget it.

"Let's get out of here," Avery says. "Want to walk in the park?"

We love Piedmont Park. It's Atlanta's version of Central Park. Tall office buildings, condos, and hotels surround the playing fields and trails. It's hard to believe I live here sometimes. In my hometown of Cutter, Georgia, a five-story office building is a big deal.

We zip down to the park in Avery's convertible. From his neighborhood in Buckhead, it takes about fifteen minutes. We park on a side street and enter the park through one of the stone gates off of Piedmont Avenue. Since it's summer, it's still light out. Too late, I realize I should have sprayed on mosquito repellent. It's getting on toward dusk, and my arms and legs will become a feeding ground. Avery's wearing pants, so he's less likely to be bothered.

"Dog park?" he asks me, and I nod. We turn toward the old bridge.

Piedmont Park has an off-leash area for dogs and their owners. I love to walk in through the double gates and watch all the dogs play with one another and with their humans. Poor Avery has stood in there with me for hours. I seriously want a dog, but I figure there's no point in getting one until I'm married. I want to pick one out with my husband. Avery has never owned a dog. I find this to be a serious flaw. I grew up with them, like they were furry brothers and sisters. In fact, the last two years are the longest I've ever gone without a dog in my life.

As we walk, I play a little game and count the number of weddings Maurice and I have had in the park. There, over by that fountain near the gazebo was a nice small one. I like those. Small-wedding brides usually have a sense of decency. There are no celebrity singers or hand-embroidered cocktail napkins. The outside brides are, on the whole, a little more reasonable. Sure, they have money, but they want to put it toward their honeymoon climbing in the Alps or camel-trekking in Africa. I've never climbed a mountain in another country or ridden a camel, but it sounds like a nice way to spend the first few weeks with your husband.

Avery is always traveling somewhere. He doesn't exactly work, per se, but he does explore. I've never asked to go with him—not even once—although I used to think I would be thrilled if he offered. But lately, I have begun to consider our future. Traveling together to foreign lands is starting to seem like something I would rather do as his wife, not just his fun, happy-go-lucky girlfriend.

I guess I'm also touchy about traveling with Avery because I know that he would have to foot the bill for everything, right down to the cab racing down the Champs-D'Élysées or the gondola ride on a canal in Venice. In some ways, I do feel like I travel to exotic places with my boyfriend. He takes pictures of himself next to volcanoes and marble statues and sends them home to me. He buys gifts of coral necklaces and leather boots from faraway markets and then tells funny stories about shopkeepers when he returns.

At about the time I'm bored of counting wedding sites in the park—I'm up to twenty-two—Avery and I pass under the old stone bridge and arrive at the dog park. Inside, I spot my favorite breed and migrate toward them. There's something I love about a German shepherd. The regal head, the loyal brown eyes—it's the perfect dog for me. Alongside the chain-link fence that surrounds the dog park, three German shepherds romp with one another. Their big paws turn over the wood chips, making little clouds of dust pop up here and there. I sit down on a rock to watch. Avery stands beside me and plays with my hair.

"So, I guess you have another one tomorrow?" Avery asks, even though he knows that Saturday is my big workday. We're only together tonight because there's no rehearsal dinner for Darby's wedding tomorrow.

"You got it. It's the restaging."

"Ah," Avery says, nodding. He knows about this one.

Darby was one of our biggest clients. Her father owns a ton of radio and television stations up and down the East Coast. Darby is a puffy-haired blonde who works as a news anchor in Atlanta. Her remarkable talent for mispronouncing the names of famous people and major capitals of the world has brought her some fame and even a few fans. When it came time for her to marry, she chose Maurice before she chose the groom.

Darby's wedding was actually three months ago. Big affair—splashy ceremony in a huge cathedral off of Peachtree Street, even bigger reception at an exclusive Midtown club. Guests took home baby magnolia trees as favors. Horse-drawn carriages brought the entire wedding party to the reception—not an easy thing to do on Atlanta's overburdened city streets. I worked for months on this wedding. When I say we tossed her, I mean we tossed her. Maurice took a week's vacation after that one. He even turned off his cell phone.

I pet a shepherd who trots over to me, pink tongue practically dragging on the ground. "You're playing hard, aren't you, boy?" I rub his big, friendly head. Dogs tend to establish cliquish play groups at the park. The bigger dogs run with one another, while the little guys, like Jack Russell terriers and poodles, form a protective club near the front gate. Occasionally, a dopey boxer will try to crash the small dogs' party. When that happens, one of the small fries sends the bigger dog running off with a whimper. Those small dogs are a tough lot.

"So, what time's the restaging?" Avery asks, rubbing another shepherd who has jealously arrived on the scene. Their owner, a middle-aged woman, smiles at us from a few feet away.

"I have to be at the church at 10:00 A.M. That's the earliest they would let us do it. And we have to be out by one because a real wedding's coming in."

When Darby's wedding pictures came back from the New York photographer (who had been flown down to Atlanta on Darby's father's jet and was put up in a rented private home for the wedding week), I was told she almost hyperventilated. Apparently, the tall photographer got a few too many shots of the much shorter Darby's dark roots cresting out of her blond curls. "He was looking down on me!" she wailed to Maurice. She compared her stripe of dark roots to a skunk or a zebra. Now, according to my unscientific count, about every second woman in Atlanta dyes her hair some color of blond. It's a southern thing, which doesn't necessarily mean it's tasteful. Most women let their roots show way too long before they trot into the salon for a touch-up. One would think Darby would have taken care of a little detail like this prior to the wedding.

Other minor picture snafus ruined Darby's "whole wedding experience," she told Maurice, who enjoyed telling me about it later over lunch. "She wants the whole thing redone," he said, attacking his arugula salad.

"What does the 'whole thing' mean?" I was horrified. I never wanted to see this woman again. At the reception, she cornered me in the bathroom and demanded I check her honeymoon luggage in the waiting limo to make sure her kiwi face cream was packed. When I found the monogrammed luggage and the favored face cream—which I did open and sniff, nice stuff—I also found a peculiar book tucked under her makeup case. *Fixing the Loveless Marriage* seemed a bit premature, but I'm not nosy. Anyway, when I reported that the face cream was packed and ready to go, Darby screwed her face into a picture of long-suffering resignation. "Oh that, I know that's there. What I really need you to do is make sure my last broadcast is cued up on the DVD player in the limo. I want to surprise Trey when we pull away from the reception. We can watch my last interview together."

Darby "retired" from the news business when she married, to

much ado. Before the wedding, she confided to Maurice that the retirement was a staged thing—"designed to encourage adoration of the talent," she helpfully supplied—and after her first child, she would return to a morning show and tell stories about her offspring to an eager Atlanta public.

Now it's three months later and Darby has quietly returned to the air. There is no pregnancy, and Maurice has two different home numbers for the couple. Regardless of this, the "wedding" is rescheduled for tomorrow.

I take Avery's hand as we wind our way out of the park. He has great hands—strong and soft at the same time. I ask him if he would like to restage our time at the dog park, just to get it right. "I can have that woman bring her dogs back at exactly the same time. I'll even tell her to wear the same outfit, if you'd like." Laughing, Avery pulls me closer to him, and I wrap my arms around his back.

"I'm so glad you're not like those other girls you marry off," he says. "That's one of the best things about you. You're real and different and not stuck on, I don't know, material stuff."

"You like that about me?" I look up toward Avery's face. A mosquito whines near my ear, and I swat at it.

"Yup. And I like that you don't hold what I have against me."

I assume Avery's referring to his family money. "It's not your fault that your great-grandfather made a fortune. You're kind of my charity project. 'Be Nice to Rich Boys, Inc.' I do this out of the goodness of my heart."

Avery gives me a kiss, sighs, and leans down and whispers in my ear. I hold my breath and hope that I don't smell like fancy tuna. There is the sound of a jogger softly padding by on the asphalt trail. I try not to move. Avery is about to ask me something.

"Would you like to get some ice cream?"

Darkness is falling in the park. The day is ending. I nod and slap at another mosquito. We walk quickly to the car, dodging other couples strolling at dusk.

I first met Avery in a neighborhood not too far away from the park, on a hot Atlanta morning. I was moving into an old apartment building off Ponce de Leon. It was my first big-city move, just me and the U-Haul all the way from Cutter, Georgia. Mom and Dad had to work, and couldn't make it up to help me. To tell the truth, I think they were relieved. Heavy traffic and parallel parking are not their favorite things.

My new apartment was on the top floor of one of those old antebellum houses that had been chopped up into a zillion little odd-shaped living spaces. I rented it over the telephone, trying desperately to sound like I knew what I was doing, and talking with a clipped accent that was definitely not Cutter, Georgia, USA. The landlord told me later that she thought I was from England.

I wedged the U-Haul into an empty spot in front of a Dumpster and turned off the engine and the last blasts of air-conditioning. By the time I got the key from the landlord and said good-bye to a month's rent, my shirt was soaked in sweat and I was dying for a shower. I opened the truck and started pulling out boxes of clothes, books, and CDs. I decided to make a little pile beside the truck and then trek up and down the interior stairs of my new apartment building.

On my second trip down to the truck, I noticed a cute guy watching me from the veranda of the house next door. This home was gracious and broad—and definitely not chopped up into apartments. Its glossy white clapboards were adorned with green painted shutters. Immaculate plantings of salvia and vinca set off the perfect southern mansion. By contrast, my new home was a big, sagging thing, with a broken pot of geraniums out front and NO PARKING signs tacked onto the listing pine trees surrounding it. A mailbox with six boxes was bolted to the front porch. Still, it was home, and I was determined to learn something about big-city life.

The cute guy kept watching me. It did not make me nervous, because he had a friendly, as opposed to a creepy hide-'em-under-the-stairs, type of look. I figured it couldn't be me he was checking out. After all, my faded red T-shirt and old hiking shorts were not the highest in Atlanta fashion. I decided to give him a smile the next time I emerged outside to grab another box.

I was heading down the uneven stairs back to the truck when I looked through the glass front door. Next on the list was bringing up my computer, a gift from my aunt who always hoped I would head to community college. That's when I saw the cute guy pulling the computer box out of the truck as he balanced a bit dangerously on the edge of the tailgate. I stared for a second, too angry too move. This was my welcome to Atlanta? A handsome guy stealing my stuff? A yell started somewhere in my throat, and I pushed through the glass door and ran across the front porch. I leapt the front stairs in one bound, heading for the back of the truck. Dry pine needles crunched underfoot.

"Hey! Get out of my truck!" I stood at the end of the tailgate, looking up into the U-Haul. My voice, never very forceful in most situations, sounded pretty wimpy.

The guy glanced up, startled, and looked into my eyes without blinking. He held the monitor box in both hands, and that's when I realized he was not alone. A grizzled man with a gray beard and hair wrapped in a bandana crouched inside the truck, trying to pull the box loose. I looked at both of them, confused.

The two men struggled harder, each pulling and pushing on the monitor box. After one aggressive shove, the cute guy nearly fell off of the tailgate. The other man grunted, then made a low growling noise.

"Let go. It's mine," the man cried, breathing hard. A stain of sweat soaked the bandana on his forehead and he bared his teeth. "I saw it first."

"This isn't yours," the cute guy said.

Things were starting to make sense. I smelled the sweat and dirt of the man, who I assumed was homeless. I immediately felt stupid for leaving the truck open and unlocked. This isn't Cutter, I chided myself.

"Look, give the police a call, miss. I'm sure they will see our side of things," the cute guy said, addressing me for the first time. I noticed his face was tanned and lined just enough to let me know we were about the same age. I also noticed he had really nice manners for a man wrestling with a computer and a homeless guy.

"The cops?" I said. Where was I going to find a phone? I didn't even have electricity in the apartment yet. A few cars drove by on the street, a few feet from my truck, but none seemed to notice that we needed help.

"Yeah," the guy said, grunting a bit this time as the would-be thief tried again to push him off of the truck's tailgate. "Use your cell."

"Um, yeah, my cell," I said, patting my pockets as if I weren't sure where my nonexistent cell phone could possibly be at this moment.

The guy was quick, because he picked up on my confusion. "Here, take mine." He reached into his front pants pocket and pulled out a silver phone with one hand, while keeping a grip on the computer box with the other hand. Then he tossed the phone to me. I was impressed. "I'm Avery, by the way," he said.

I was feeling really weird but happy to have someone sharing my moving-day disaster. Since he was looking in my direction, I tried to give Avery a smile. I hoped he wasn't too disgusted by my independent-girl sweat. "Hi. My name is Macie."

"Ah, dial 911," Avery said. Back to reality. There was a crime in progress here.

I tapped some buttons, too nervous to see if I was dialing correctly. That, apparently, was enough for the homeless man, because he let go of the box and hopped off the tailgate and ran down the street. When he got to the corner of Virginia Avenue, he yelled back at us, "I saw it first!"

Avery laughed and set the box down on the wooden floor of the truck. I wiped the sweat off his phone and handed it back to him.

"You know, I was watching your truck all morning. I could tell you'd left it open," he said.

"Apparently not a wise move."

"Not in this neighborhood." Avery nodded.

"Guess I stick out just a bit?" I suddenly felt self-conscious in my wilted summer outfit. Avery, in comparison, looked like spring in a pressed cotton shirt, crisp pants, and leather sandals.

"Nah," he replied. "You're just a trusting soul. Not much is wrong with that, unless you like giving away nineteen-inch monitors."

I laughed a real laugh, the first of my big-city life. And, just like that, Avery Leland galloped into my life. He spent the rest of the day helping me move in, carrying all the heavy things. He sent out for sandwiches and fruit juice; he even returned the moving van so I wouldn't have to drive it downtown. When my phone was hooked up two days later, the first call I received was from Avery.

It has now been two years. I'm still nuts over him, and he says he feels the same way about me. I'm not the girl who pulled up in a rental truck, too naïve to know to lock it against thieves. I have changed a lot. I am now thinking about the future, a husband, the rest of my life. The question—the question I ask myself daily—is, Is Avery changing, too?

The morning after our walk in Piedmont Park finds me at the cathedral. Right away, I know Darby is going to be unhappy. In the intervening months since her first wedding, the cathedral has taken on an ambitious construction project. The front lawn is torn to pieces, and construction fencing surrounds the property. The lawn pictures of Darby and Trey will not be restaged—not unless they like Georgia clay and construction orange.

Inside the church, I try to be friendly to the wedding director. She works for the cathedral, and I've heard she is upset that we'll be using the house of worship for such a vain reason. I can't blame her. Darby's father probably pulled some strings, maybe donated an orphanage or something. Whatever the reason, here we are.

"Bridal people, bridal people," Maurice says, running into the bride's dressing room. He stops short and shakes his head. It's just me and the wedding director in front of him. Maurice is all out of sorts. He's used to a room full of people listening to his instructions. The other people in the wedding party won't be here today. Darby at least had the tact not to invite them to the restaging.

When the bride enters the dressing room forty-five minutes late, I feel as if I have been thrown back in time. Darby's hair, makeup, dress, and flowers are as I remember them from March. And her hair is a perfect shade of blond with no pesky dark roots showing. For the record, I think she would look better as a brunette, but she's not asking me.

I am pretty sure that Maurice is making a nice bundle off this day. His services were long since paid for when Darby called him, crying, a few weeks ago. We'd had a bride cancel when she found out her fiancé was visiting strip clubs twice a day—for lunch and dinner—so Maurice made room in his calendar for the restaging. I am earning time and a half, something that makes Darby's demands just a little bit more bearable.

"Gracie, come get my veil. It's very heavy, so don't drop it."

"It's Macie, Darby." Maurice looks at her disapprovingly. He can do that.

Darby shakes her perfectly stiffened curls—"Macie, sorry"—and runs over to check her appearance in the gold-framed mirror. I hang up the hand-beaded veil, which probably took two months off the life of some poor Italian woman, and settle in to wait. The photographer and groom are missing, but that's not my problem.

"So, how's married life?" I ask for my own amusement.

Not turning around, Darby says, "Well, it's been a blast, really.

We go out to our property almost every weekend. Trey likes to hunt. And I throw these rustic dinners down there. He thinks I'm just the best cook."

I picture Darby in an immaculate kitchen, ordering servants around while Trey drags in a still-warm beast. It's a far cry from the celebrity restaurants Darby used to frequent.

"That sounds nice," I say. "The country must be very relaxing."

"Are you from there?" Darby says, dabbing at her lipstick. I've noticed she keeps eyeing her cell phone on the ottoman.

"What?"

"The country? Are your people down there?"

I do one of my inward, nondetectable sighs that I've learned to perfect. Because I work for a living, some brides think I must have scratched my way out of a chicken coop, kissed my brother-husband good-bye, and made my way to the Big City.

"Yeah," I say with a bit of a twang. "We're from the country."

"I thought so," Darby says, and throws her used tissue onto the floor.

Maurice wanders by at about the same time and gives me a puzzled look. I know this means the photographer is here, but not the groom. I nod to him and turn my attention back to Darby. "So, is Trey on his way?"

"He's stuck in traffic."

This is a good Atlanta excuse. Traffic is a way of life here. But it's a Saturday, the Braves aren't playing in town, and there's not a cloud in the sky to slow travel. I get an uneasy feeling and excuse myself.

I find Maurice in the narthex of the cathedral. "I don't think the groom's going to show," I say gravely. Being inside churches always makes me lower my voice.

"Me, either. He hasn't returned my phone calls all week. He probably doesn't want to see her. Or do this ridiculous restaging.

Well, we have about one hour to get him here or the church people are going to toss *us*."

We start with the cell numbers. Those prove useless, so I call the house where we think Trey is staying. A woman with an accent answers and I tell her who I am and what I want. I can tell the woman—probably the housekeeper, because she calls him "Mr. Trey"—is covering for him, so I try to keep her on the phone. I confide that it's my job to strongly encourage the appearance of Darby's husband. Taking a chance, I even infer that if Mr. Trey would just make an appearance, maybe he could talk Mrs. Darby out of this asinine display of wealth and vanity and—

There's silence on the other end of the phone. I hear rustling.

"Macie, it's Trey." His booming voice comes over the phone with a note of sadness or frustration; I'm not sure which.

"Hey, Trey. Sorry to bother you. It's just that I have this little problem."

On the other end of the line, Trey inhales sharply. A dog barks, and I hear him shush it. "Let me guess, your problem is about five feet tall and wearing a wedding dress."

"Oh, she's no trouble, Trey. Really." The lie is so bad, I wince. Maurice has appeared at my elbow, straightening his tie and smoothing back his hair. He gives me a threatening look but I don't take it personally.

"Look, Macie. You don't have to fake it. I know what my wife is like. That's why I'm not down there. She's just got to have everything her way. I mean, have you ever had to restage anyone's wedding?"

I admit that this is a first for me. A popping sound comes over the line. I think Trey has just opened a beer. I try another tack. "I don't suppose that you would come down here and let us have the pleasure of your company one more time, would you?"

To my relief, Trey laughs. "No, there's no chance, Macie. I liked you and Maurice all right, but that was probably the worst day of my life. Well, actually, the worst day came later." He pauses, takes a sip. "But the wedding was pretty horrible. Do you remember the Rhett Butler impersonator at the reception? I wanted to hit him. I still can't believe Darby hired those people."

I decide not to bring up the actress dressed as Scarlett O'Hara who tried to dirty dance with all of the married men. Lowering my voice, I go for the honest approach. "Trey, I think if you don't show up, Darby will just camp out here and wait for you. She seems very determined."

"That's my girl," he says with a nice flourish of bitterness. "I'm going hunting. Sorry, Macie." He clicks off.

I hold the silent phone in my hand. I've given it my best shot and now Maurice is pacing the room, nodding, chin in his hand. I know that he doesn't give a fig about Darby, but he does care about her rich and connected friends. We can only hope that Darby will be so mortified she won't tell this story at parties.

"So, that's it? Trey is history?" Maurice pats the front of his jacket and sighs heavily. Too late, we hear a rustling in the hallway outside the narthex. Then a door opens and closes. We see a flash of white.

"Darby!" Maurice bellows and then gives chase. I am a little in shock. I didn't know Maurice could run. He's always so in control. I decide to get in on the action and push through the double doors in the front of the church.

Outside the cathedral, I catch sight of a woman swathed in white, veil flying out behind her, running with her dress bunched up in her hands. Maurice is just steps behind, his bow tie jiggling. His handmade leather loafers don't look like a good match for the grassy lawn that slopes down to Peachtree Street. I start running when I see what lies ahead.

Darby is headed for the road.

I realize then that Maurice and I aren't dealing with a vain bride or a spoiled bride; we are dealing with a deranged bride. And she's going to cartwheel into traffic because her new husband likes dogs and hunting more than he likes her.

I'm hopelessly behind the chase, but I try. The grass bends under my hasty feet. From the corner of my eye, the construction fencing that borders the long lawn is just a streak of orange plastic. To my right, a few people on the sidewalk have stopped to watch the running bride. I play tennis with Avery, so I try to summon the muscles in my legs that let me return a wicked crosscourt shot.

Maurice isn't doing too badly. As they close in on the sidewalk spanning Peachtree, he dives for Darby and misses. Her bouncing veil bobs mere inches from his fingers. The road is just steps ahead, and that's when I close my eyes. I can't believe I'm about to see a bride get hit in traffic.

I hear honking and brakes squealing, but no thuds, so I look. Darby is lying down in the road, layers of satin organza and silk georgette billowing around her while traffic idles in four lanes. She slaps at the pavement, crying and throwing a very public tantrum. Maurice will later tell me that Darby plunged right into the moving swell of Saturday shoppers and errand runners and every car stopped without harming one blond hair on her freshly dyed head.

Maurice leaves the safety of the sidewalk and rushes to her aid. But the driver of a furniture truck has already climbed down from his cab to Darby's side. She sobs and the driver offers her what, from my viewpoint, looks to be a very clean hankie. When Maurice draws closer, the driver snarls, "Don't you think you've done enough?" I think he even calls Maurice a pretty boy, but I can't be sure. I'm not leaving the sidewalk. I don't get paid to wade into traffic.

"I'm not—I'm not, surely you don't think—" Maurice is, for once, speechless. "I'm a married man!"

"That's even more disgusting. You could have gotten her killed, moron," a woman standing beside her minivan says. "You don't need him, sweetie." Darby wails like an animal.

Maurice backs away from Darby as the crowd grows. We stand

there for about five minutes watching people get out of their cars to offer Darby advice, food, and sympathy. Sirens make their way down Peachtree. I motion for Maurice to get going. He doesn't need this kind of publicity, and Darby is obviously fine. Well, she's not fine and her dress is ruined from wallowing in road grease and dirt, but she's alive.

"This day could not have gone worse," Maurice says when he joins me on the sidewalk. Someone heaves a soda can our way.

I point to the first news van careening up the sidewalk. Maurice decides to slip on his shades, and we make a retreat to the edge of the lawn. Several cathedral staffers who have come outside to see what the fuss is about give us the eye. This won't help Maurice the next time he has a wedding here.

Eventually, the police coax Darby off to the side of Peachtree, and when she won't talk to Maurice, we leave. By this time, a few reporters have tried to shove microphones in our faces, but their real target is Darby, fallen-from-grace news reporter. Maurice seems like a footnote and as soon as he can, he splits. I clean up the bride's room, carefully packing Darby's cosmetics case. I wonder what kind of self-help guide she'll read after today's episode.

It really doesn't matter; we've tossed her—two times—and it's time to move on to the next bride. I turn off the lights to the bride's dressing room and close the door.

3

The Museum Bride

So far I have seen a giant sloth's matted belly and the delicately crossed paws of a fox. If the fox had a say in the matter, my guess is he would rather be running through a damp forest glade instead of crouching stuffed and perpetually foppish-looking in an air-conditioned museum exhibit. I have also had two lattes from the museum coffee shop. The shop is helpfully tucked next to the museum store.

Maurice is running this way and that, measuring the museum's Great Hall. We have a wedding and a reception here next week, and there's something wrong with the width of the hall. Maurice is threatening to pull the whole shindig from the museum because their measurements are off by ten feet, but I know he won't do it. He's simply having an especially high-strung day.

May is a particularly trying time for professional wedding planners—and their staff. The heat hasn't sunk in yet for the summer, and the days are balmy and perfectly well behaved. And, of course, every gal in Atlanta gets it into her head that she must be married during the month of May. I've grown to hate May and all its chirpy, springlike trappings. Part of me knows this is a twisted way to enjoy the loveliest season of the year, but I promise it's the job.

I leave Maurice and wander through the museum. If he notices I am gone, he will take a guess that I am inspecting the fire exits and valet parking options for next week's event. I love to organize, make lists, and cross off items. I carry folders, three under my arm right now, in three different colors. I'm wearing another gift from Avery—a rose brooch that contains a tiny digital camera—and before the day is out, I swear that Maurice will show it off to someone. "Look," he'll coo, "it takes real pictures!"

With the Great Hall to my back, I climb the white stairs, heading for the entrance level. A spooky dinosaur looms over the entire hall. I noticed earlier that the dinosaur's head is glaringly small for the rest of its body. This makes me think of the dinosaur's brainpower. I wonder if it was sort of a slow creature, prone to making mistakes and stumbling toward extinction.

I enter the exhibit area that details the various areas of Georgia. I've lived here all my life, but I couldn't tell you where these places are. The Piedmont. Springer Mountain. The Cumberland Valley. I didn't much pay attention in school. Mostly, I had boyfriends and we had a good time—now, not in the way a person would think. It was more like a fun season when I didn't have to do anything but brush my hair and pick out a cute pair of sandals. Now that I'm twenty-six, I see that there was probably more I could have done with my life.

More and more, I find myself thinking about settling down. It makes sense. After all, I'm surrounded with all the trappings of love: pricey sit-down dinners for five hundred, bead-encrusted dresses from Paris, and strolling minstrels who take requests. At least, that's what these brides think is love.

With Avery and me, love is often wrapped in keeping up with his odd but strangely endearing family. The Lelands tend to get excited about some interesting stuff. Last week, Avery's dad brought home an outdoor ceramic beef-cooking stove called the *Vite*. The cooking directions were written in Czech or Polish, so Mr. Leland just guessed. The fillets ended up curling, blackening, and eventually catching fire. As the two laughing men threw water on the smoking meat, they yelled, *"Vite! Vite!"* I stood a safe distance away, pouring lemonade into tall glasses.

"See there, son," Mr. Leland said with tears in his eyes, "it pays to learn a foreign language."

Other times in the Leland house, Mrs. Leland plans the evening. She likes to pick out a movie for all of us to watch, although I learned pretty quickly that she talks all the way through the flick. She enjoys asking questions such as, "Who is that? Is he the killer? Is he going to kill someone?" until Avery says, "Watch the movie, Mother! We don't know yet!" I like hanging around the Lelands. They are very different from my family, but not an awful different.

To be perfectly honest, though, I don't know if his mother is all that happy. She has sad eyes sometimes. If I really think about it, it seems like having scads of money actually gives you more headaches, not fewer. For me, I knew I had to go to work when I was done with high school. My grades really weren't much to write home about, so college was a dim, vague dream. Avery, on the other hand, had a lot more choices. Half of the time, I believe he's still trying to decide what road to take. At least, I think so.

I pass another dinosaur, this one with an eager college-age worker standing under it. The worker is holding a large bone. He looks nervous, poor guy, like he knows he should approach the small knots of parents and kids wandering through the room and offer them some sort of dinosaur demonstration. Maybe wave the pitted bone around, giving the kinder a mouthful of facts. But the poor kid looks scared, totally whipped and nervous. I think about going over to him and asking a lame question about the dinosaur whose crotch he's standing under. You know, give him a boost.

Instead, I realize I am tired. I have spent all day keeping up with Maurice and his demands. He's all right, but sometimes, blast it, I grow tired of helping other women get married. I'd like to toss the whole lot of them out of the window, to tell the truth. I sigh, remembering I would have to go back to waiting tables or gift wrapping at Luck's.

Thinking too much about Avery makes me clench my jaw, so I duck out of the dinosaur room and head into the Okefenokee Swamp. The exhibit is set up, like all of them, to imitate a place. It's a hard thing to do, and I think the museum pulls it off as best as it can. The birds aren't moving, though, and the water is stiff Plexiglas, and all of a sudden, I am deep down sad. The swamp's birds were real once and now they are stuck on sticks that jut up out of cattails. Really, it's no life that I can appreciate.

I pause on the swamp boardwalk that snakes through the exhibit. A red-shouldered hawk hangs above me, frozen on a wire with a snake in its talons. Herons and other birds I think I should know are crammed into the space to my right. A bullfrog pulses a deep-throated warning. I read a little about the swamp. I learn that the swamp's cypress trees will eventually take over because that's what cypress trees do. They'll make a thick, knitted space where earth can form and then the swamp will be out of business. Just like that, it will be gone.

While I'm standing there, the bullfrog music gets louder. And the lights start to fade. At first the lights dim slightly, then freefall from color to a darkness that tells me night is on. I almost feel the rush of a night wind in the wet swamp. A mosquito hums near my ear. In the other room, the dinosaur is forgotten by bored children. Then, without a skip, the lights turn up and it's morning in the swamp. More birds join the looped audiotape. It's bright and pink, the way a sunrise always is when you're looking right into it.

A group of tourists enters the room. They have noisy children. I read the rest of the swamp information. It seems the only way the poor Okefenokee can get out of its predicament is to have a good ol' fire. Apparently, when the fire destroys the cypress trees, the spaces of earth between the trees collapse, and all of the water is free to be swampy again. The lights start to dim again, and I realize I'm in for my second night in the swamp. A kid steps on my foot. I decide to leave.

It's not that Avery wouldn't marry me. Or that I haven't, well, you know, hinted. Looked at rings. Threatened in my own way. But Avery, he's working on some other level. Like the battle of the swamp bottom back there. There's stuff working down in the depths that no one knows about. And you might think it's sad and sorry to get hung up on marrying someone, but when you're not twenty-one anymore and you're working for a man named Maurice who paid more for his imported dog than you made last year, sad and sorry starts to work itself over pretty good.

I think about that swamp as I drive to Maurice's favorite jewelry store. The bride we're tossing later in the summer is named Isabel, and she wants to give all her bridesmaids platinum *I* pendants. Subtle nudges that perhaps they might want to receive pendants with their own first initials have gone unheeded. So, here I am, in Barrclere, inspecting and then ordering fifteen *I*'s in Gothic script. They will be ready in ten days. Isabel will be thrilled, I tell Maurice into my wristwatch.

"Are you using it?" he screams to me. He thinks the volume is low because the watch is so small.

"Yes," I reply. The saleslady at Barrclere points to me. The other salesgirls stop to look. I feel like Judy Jetson.

"So Euro. See you tomorrow."

I nod and sign off. The time flashes at me: 5:25 P.M. It's almost time to meet Avery. We're playing tennis before dinner. He likes to work up an appetite. Before I go to meet his convertible, I order a pendant for myself. I'm in luck; the *A*'s are in stock. I wear my purchase outside into the spring air.

• • •

Tennis is no simple affair at the Lelands'. For one thing, Avery's father might join us. That's always tricky because Mrs. Leland told us Mr. Leland feels he is losing his youth, and winning at tennis is one way for him to "pull back the hands of the time-clock," as she puts it. Mrs. Leland never joins us, even though she played tennis at Vandy and a few trophies up in Nashville have her name on them. Then there's Avery, a really decent player, and me.

Avery and I start with a few ground strokes. I enjoy warming up. It's something about the rhythm of the new, yellow ball bouncing toward me and then away. Occasionally, the rhythm stops and starts when I toss one into the net. Avery rarely makes mistakes. Unless his mind is on something big, he can hit winners by me all day long.

This is a source of tension between us. "Avery," I'll say when he hits a particularly evil shot to my backhand when he knows full well I am recovering from diving for his previous return. "Avery, give me a break. That's not fair."

"Fair? What's fair?" he'll reply without breathing hard.

This is where I pout and refuse to play anymore. In my mind, an opponent who picked up a racket for the first time two years ago is not to be tortured with a constant volley of winners. Especially when said opponent is the girlfriend.

But Avery, of the summer tennis camps in some European country and custom-made leather tennis shoes, does not subscribe to my way of thinking. I am reminded of this when a wicked slice drops in front of me and thuds out of my reach. The warm-up is over.

We play hard for thirty minutes and then relax for a bit at the net. Avery leans over the webbing and gives me a quick kiss. "You seem distracted today. What's going on?"

"Oh, well, you know, it's the job. I just live for those bridal gals," I say.

Avery laughs, showing his pink tongue and white teeth. I smile back, feeling the spring sun on my face.

"I'm thinking about telling the next bride who asks for those tiny autumnal flowers they saw last month in *Atlanta Wedding* to jump off Stone Mountain," I say.

"Why?"

"Because that magazine is printed months in advance, so those flowers were available, like, eight months ago. I cannot get them for a May wedding," I reply, starting to get worked up.

"Okay, easy. I was just asking." Avery flips his racket over in his hands, examining the strings. He's ready to play again. But I'm not. I go on.

"You'd think that one of these perfectly intelligent and rich women would take the time to notice that flowers called 'autumnal joy' would not be sitting around their chichi florist in early May. It's just not going to happen!"

Backing away from the net, Avery stops turning his racket over. He glances toward the veranda, where his father is reading *The New Yorker*. He can't hear us because he's a good quarter of a mile away from the courts. I can make him out, just barely. He's a tiny speck wearing a V-necked sweater.

"So, that's what I get worked up about. Every day. And Maurice has 'absolute confidence' in me because I can alphabetize folders while wearing a telephone watch. Believe me, when I get married, I will not be wearing this watch and I will not order flowers that don't exist naturally!"

A trickle of sweat runs down my chest and lodges in the band of my sports bra. Without looking at Avery, I know that I've gone too far. Avery hates conflict, and I don't really like it too much, either. My parents don't fight, and neither do his. Mom teaches thirty second-graders, so when she gets home, the last thing she wants is a noisy house. Dad delivers mail and is alone all day, riding the rural routes around Cutter. He is usually fairly quiet; I've heard him raise his voice maybe a dozen times in my life.

"Ah," Avery starts to say.

"No, I'm sorry. I shouldn't take out my day on you."

"Well, that's okay. I guess." Avery's face is stretched tight with some sort of decision. I figure he wants to get back to the safety of the veranda, or, at the very least, away from me.

We walk toward the house, Mr. Leland, and some sort of awaiting cold plate. I'll find out later that it is smoked salmon, a dish I'd never had until I started dating Avery. I wonder, if we ever break up, will I like the taste of salmon ever again or will it just be a fish I knew once, a long time ago?

Maurice calls me in early on Saturday. Katie Anna, our bride, the one with the natural history museum reception, has cold feet. Maurice tells me loudly over the phone that she isn't sure she wants to be Mrs. So-and-So for the rest of her life. The parents of the bride are pressuring her to go through with it. The creamy engraved invitations alone set them back eight thousand dollars. The wedding is in seven hours.

I arrive at the museum, where the tables and candle globe centerpieces are being set up. Museumgoers wander along the perimeter of the Great Hall, looping around to tour an exhibit about ancient Syria. Mentally, I try to place the country on a map, but I draw a blank. I was never that great with geography.

"There she is," Maurice whispers dramatically as I skirt the caterer's helper laden with white wooden chairs. "You've got to get on this, and I mean fast."

Maurice is worked up. He reminds me constantly about referrals and reputation and publicity. If this bride bails—and from the look in her dazed and sobbed-out face, I think she's close—Maurice will be damaged. I'm usually sent in to save the day. I'm supposed to talk about babies and white wedding dresses. If that doesn't work, I'm to go for the you'll-be-lonely-until-you-die jugular. The sad thing is, I kind of believe in it all. The white dress, the honeymoon in Belize, the procession of infants in short pants. Standing in the Great Hall with that tiny-headed dinosaur towering over the entire show, I'm not sure how anyone can escape where they're going.

Katie Anna agrees to go for a walk with me. She is a pretty blonde with a thin nose and the peppy gait of a gym fanatic. Even though it's her wedding day, she looks sad and confused. I know immediately where to take her. We go to the Okefenokee Swamp. On the boardwalk, I point to the frozen thrushes and plastic water. Her blond hair, recently done up in a cascade of curls and twirly French knots, has become a bit unhinged. I touch one sprung curl and tuck it back into the rest. As the pink lights of morning come up on the swamp, Katie Anna lets me put one arm around her shoulder as she cries.

She tells me that her fiancé is really, well, she says apologetically, there's no other word for it, an ass. He works all day and then expects her to put on a black dress and entertain clients. He likes wrestling and drinks beer with every meal. She envisions a parade of expense-account dinners and low-brow weekend sports that never ends, yet she can't think of life going forward unless she marries him in six hours.

Katie Anna and I stand in the swamp for about a week of up and down lights, cooing birdcalls, and mating deep-voiced frogs. She cries a little bit, and I explain the wonders of the swamp I had never seen before last week, even though it's in my home state. I tell her about the trees knitting together and the sorry chance the swamp has to make it out alive. She stops crying and lifts her head just slightly, all the while working her two-carat ring off her left hand. When I get to the part about fire helping the swamp get back to what it's supposed to be, Katie Anna has the beginnings of a smile that no cypress tree, small-headed dinosaur, or ass-faced fiancé can take away.

And so we leave the swamp at sundown, but not before Katie Anna takes that ring and drops it into the water. Of course, it bounces right off the Plexiglas and rolls over to rest beside a dusty white heron, and her father will retrieve it later because he is mad and wants to cash it in to make his daughter pay for her treachery.

But for now, the only one wearing white is the heron, and as we leave the swamp, Katie Anna turns to blow her a kiss. I would have put the ring on the dead bird's beak, but I can tell that Katie Anna is the type of person who respects the DO NOT TOUCH signs posted here and there. My cell phone rings, and I know it is Maurice begging me to save the day. I know I did not.

Later, Maurice and I will make the calls that pull the plug on something as big as a fancy-schmancy wedding and reception. It's no easy feat. I could go on and on about all of the details: food, swan handlers, antique china rental, jewelry security. In the end, it really doesn't matter. The caterers throw out thousands of dollars of food, the heirloom tiara is returned to the safe, the bridal programs are discarded. Everyone has been paid, so they have a night off. I wander around the Great Hall, watching the men load up the white chairs and tables. Iris arrives with the wedding cake and then turns around to take it back to her studio. I'm busy on the phone canceling the honeymoon reservations, so all I can do is give Iris a weary look. "Come over later," she whispers. "We'll eat cake."

Maurice is still in his first outfit of the day. I wonder what he will do with his evening. He looks really down.

"One of our potential clients—Lila Stall—was going to come by tonight and check this place out for her wedding next year," Maurice says with a weary note to his voice. He leans against a palm tree the florist has not yet removed.

"Oh, who's she marrying?" I sit on a folding chair. It strikes me that this is the first time I have ever sat down in a wedding rental chair. Usually, I'm working. It's not too bad, a little on the stiff side.

"Do we ever know their names, Macie?"

He's right. For most of the brides, it's all about the day. Come to think of it, Katie Anna never even mentioned her fiancé's name. I wonder what he'll do tonight. Probably watch wrestling. I get a quick chill, thinking of Katie Anna's narrow escape.

I really hope she will be all right. Katie Anna seems like the kind of woman who is on her way to figuring out what she wants. I like that. Maybe the swamp can work its magic on me, too. I say good-bye to Maurice and head back toward the Okefenokee exhibit. I think I will stand on the boardwalk and beg the water—that deep, black water with the power to conjure a swamp-saving fire—what in the world will happen to a girl like me.

4

The Pink-Haired Bride

I probably attend at least three weddings a month, and while that may sound like it's all party-party, it actually is not. Besides the behavior of the brides and their families, there is the inevitable same slate of songs, readings, and bridesmaid dresses I saw last week. At the reception, the chunky pork tenderloin is going to rub shoulders with the same Caesar salad. Once in a while, someone will really shake things up and order a fish topped with mango salsa, but for the most part, every wedding tends to feel or look depressingly, unavoidably, exactly the same.

I am hanging out in Iris's studio, watching her work on Gwendolyn's wedding cake—a cake that promises to be very different. I'm also swiping bits of cake she's trimmed and slapping on a little of her trademark butter-cream icing.

"This is amazing," I say, my mouth full of cake and icing.

"Glad you like it," Iris says, smiling. She never gets to see people enjoy her cake because she drops it off hours before the reception. Turning her attention back to an intricate design on the bottom layer, Iris gently pipes a feather-light line of icing on the curves of the cake round. Layers two through six are lined up behind her on a stainless-steel table waiting their turn.

Iris runs Cake Cake out of a studio filled with baking pans, cookbooks, and bins of flour. I should also mention it smells like heaven. She found the space in a converted factory that now houses hip tech businesses and restaurants. A scrappy ensemble theater operates next door, and sometimes actors come over and buy cupcakes or pies, whatever she has on hand. Iris will bake anything, anytime. She says baking is good for your heart, and I believe her. Her best customers found her for their weddings and they keep coming back. For these folks, Iris will do anything. I've been out with her at a bar, and at midnight she'll say, "Gotta go bake" because one of her favorites wants a fresh kuchen by noon.

Iris is having fun with Gwendolyn's cake. For starters, it's completely unlike the white, genteel, fondant icing cakes that most brides want. Not Gwen. For her, everything has to be different. She's a pink-haired, budding fashion designer who has her own ideas. Brainstorm number one: a pink cake. I even found a little punk-rock couple to go on top of the sixth layer. Gwendolyn loved it. She said, "It's so out, it's in." I think I beamed a little bit.

"This color is really, really pink. It seems very Gwen," Iris says, stepping back to examine her art.

I have to agree. The cake will be pink, the bride's hair is pink, and her wedding dress—well, that's as pink as can be. Gwen designed the dress herself and thinks it could be a big thing next year if her wedding gets a little press in one of the local magazines.

Gwendolyn's mother has a bit of a problem with all of the alternative wedding arrangements. I've seen her go after her daughter like a yippy dog, but so far, Gwendolyn has not backed down. I can see it's wearing on her, though. When her mother wanted to serve mimosas in crystal champagne flutes at her bridal luncheon, Gwen wearily said yes. And the bridesmaids—artists, musicians, and models, all—will be wearing bras under their dresses, thanks to Mom. I even had to order the strapless undergarments so no one could claim they had forgotten to pack them. Those were fun calls—asking complete strangers for their cup size.

"I think this wedding will actually be exciting," I say to Iris. She's adding little black sugar dots in and around the pink icing curlicues. So far, the cake looks, as they say, good enough to eat. I am actually starting to look forward to the reception. Maurice is having a new Thai restaurant cater the sit-down dinner. Avery introduced me to Thai food, and now I'm a total snob about who has the best basil rolls in town. I've heard this new place is great.

"How's the bride's mother doing so far?"

I play with an empty icing bag. "She's coming around. Little bit by little bit."

"I think it's sad how brides' mothers get in the way. I won't do that to my daughter when I have one," Iris says.

"That's assuming you have a daughter. You could give birth to nothing but sons. And you would have to bake gorgeous cakes for their snippy, mean wives-to-be."

Iris looks up from the bowl of pink icing. "Since when have you become so cynical, Mace? Not all brides are like the ones you and Maurice handle every week."

I fall into a canvas director's chair near the counter. "Remind me again? How do normal brides get married?"

Iris resumes piping. "Well, let's see," she says, a wicked smile coming over her face. "First, they set a budget."

Feigning a yawn, I say, "What's that? I don't know what that is. It sounds common."

"Well, a budget is something that tells a person what she can and cannot spend."

"Hold on, Iris," I drawl in my most southern accent. "My hand is hurting from the weight of my four-carat diamond."

"Rest it on that shelf over there. You poor thing."

I sigh dramatically. "Go on, you were saying something amusing about restricting my spending?"

Iris chokes back a laugh. "Yes, it's true. You will have to set a budget. There is a limit to what you can spend."

"I would rather die."

Iris looks at me and makes a funny face. I start laughing so hard that my stomach hurts. Or maybe it is all the cake I have been eating. Iris has to put down her icing spatula for the next layer because she can't keep her hand steady. She walks around the counter and sits down beside me.

"Sometimes I don't like what I do," I tell her.

"I know, I know."

"I envy you, Iris. You have a gift and you go and do it. I wish I knew what it is that I'm supposed to be doing," I say softly. "Satisfying every spoiled bride's whim is not my idea of contributing to society."

"You think I contribute to society?" she asks. "Please. Maybe people's waistlines. But not the building of government, the arts, or religion. I'm just a baker." Iris gives a nod toward the counter with the cakes.

Rolling my eyes, I pat her icing-caked hand. "Just a baker. Yeah, that's why you were on the cover of *Atlanta Bride* last summer. And why there's a six-month waiting list for your Christmas pies, and people fly your cakes in their own private jets to Bora Bora."

"That only happened once, and it was to Hilton Head Island, not Bora Bora. You're stretching things. Just a bit."

I glance around the studio. Iris's pans stand neatly stacked on stainless-steel racks. Her huge sacks of flour wait in plastic bins near the white and brown sugar. Black-and-white photographs of her wedding cakes hang on the plaster walls in black metal frames. I like this space. She has it all together. I know that I do not.

"So, speaking of weddings, when am I going to bake for you?"

This is Iris's favorite question. She teases me because she knows Avery is no closer to walking down the aisle today than he was six months ago. I get tired of explaining my boyfriend to my family—which is safely in Cutter and, thankfully, not in town to harass me—and to friends like Iris. About the only person who doesn't hassle me is Maurice. He has enough brides on his hands, I figure.

Just the other day, I found a brochure for a pricey Italian resort in Avery's car. I picked it up and read about the sandy beaches and lagoonlike pool and all of the spa treatments. I put down the brochure and got very quiet. Avery will probably go there with his parents or by himself—he likes to travel alone (which I think is strange)—and I just decided to have a pout about it. It might sound a little weird, but lately, as I get closer and closer to wanting to marry Avery, I imagine us traveling together. And when I do, it's as a married couple. Jetting off in our current boyfriend/girlfriend status holds little attraction for me. I want things to be permanent with Avery. It's daring but I'll say it: I want to be his *wife*.

But when I get right down to it, I'm not even his fiancée. We don't plan vacations together. Plus, the trip would have to be on his tab because wedding director's assistants can't afford lagoon pools. So, with all that said, I guess I just wanted Avery to gush, "Macie, guess what? I found this great resort and I want you to come with me. We'll get married by the sea and honeymoon to the sounds of the ocean. Where's your wedding dress?" Harrumph, I groan to myself. That will be the day.

"What are you thinking?" Iris asks. She is the nicest friend I've ever had, and I know I am lucky to have her. In high school, I never really ran with a gaggle of girlfriends because I was always clutching a boyfriend. It's nice to be more grown-up and have a woman friend with whom I can talk about issues bigger than lip gloss and good brands of hair product. I met Iris at a wedding, right after I started with Maurice. I had to go to a country club outside of the Perimeter—that's the highway loop around Atlanta—and I was lost. I was driving on a traffic-choked side street and starting to panic when Iris's van cut in front of me. I was steamed at first. There I was, lost, and edgy because I wanted to make a good impression on Maurice, when this big, white van marked "Cake Cake" cut me off. Driving poorly in Atlanta is a public art, and I was turning that over in my head when it hit me: Cake Cake. That was the wedding-cake baker for the wedding I was trying to find. I figured the odds were good that the van was going to the reception site, so I followed it through fourteen yellow lights and in no time was at the door of the country club, exactly one minute early. Iris drives like a maniac, but I didn't tell her that when I met her.

The sunlight in Iris's studio, combined with the smell of cake, is making me sleepy. I try to give her the "I don't want to talk about Avery" look, but that doesn't deter Iris. Nothing does. When she was applying for a business loan for Cake Cake, the bank turned her down. Not at all ruffled, Iris returned to the bank the next morning, dressed in a cute purple suit, and passed out cake to all of the employees and bank customers waiting in the lobby. A few minutes later, a vice president invited Iris back to her office and Cake Cake was officially launched.

"Don't give me that look. I'm just concerned about you," Iris says, and I know she is. Her brown eyes are kind, and I soften just a bit. Maybe I can tell Iris about my Avery concerns. I just don't know if they will make sense. I've joked about Avery with Iris, but I probably have not been too honest. It's hard to talk about the things in life that aren't going exactly the way a person would like them to go. She is my best friend, though, so I give it a try.

"You know how Avery is kind of sweetly drifting through life?"

Iris nods in a noncommittal manner. I think she is warily agreeing.

"Well, I feel like I've been caught up in that. Like a tidal pool and, oh, I don't know, the moon or something."

"That's a lame nature simile," Iris says with a smile.

"You're not helping."

"Sure I am. I like Avery, even though he lacks a certain sense of direction. Well, you can thank that boozy mother of his." Iris will never forget the Lelands' first Christmas party she attended. Mrs. Leland was a bit soused and started reciting poetry no one had ever heard. Avery was mortified, of course. She's usually sort of dippy, but that was extreme.

"Iris, it's not his mother. Well, it could be. She is kind of bizarre." I pause for a moment. "Avery is so nice and funny and loyal—all qualities that I love about him—but he's never really had to think about the future. No one ever really pushed Avery to do something or be anything."

"How so?" Iris says and rubs her face. She still has a lot of work to do today. I should wrap this up.

"Okay, name three jobs you had by age eighteen," I say.

Without missing a beat, Iris ticks off landscaper, waitress, and stationery-store clerk. "So?"

"I was a baby-sitter, worked in a ham store, and I did a stint as a knife seller. That didn't last."

Iris says, "And your point?"

"My point is, you and I were asked to do something, be something. Whether we wanted spending money or more freedom, whatever—we went out and got jobs. My mother waited in the car when I walked into the ham store right before Thanksgiving to apply for the job. I told the manager, 'I'm honest and I will work hard for Holiday Hams.' "

"You really said that?"

"Back off." I laugh. "They paid one whole dollar more than the other part-time holiday jobs in town, and I got a free ham for my Christmas bonus. My mother was thrilled.

"Anyway," I go on, rushing my words a bit, "Avery never had that experience. If he wanted something, he had an allowance. When it came time for him to drive, a butler or some type of servant taught him how, and then his father bought him a brand-new car."

"My first car had a rust hole in the floorboard, but it was great," Iris says.

"Exactly. Avery wasn't asked to do anything or be anything. No wonder he has no plans. And that includes me." I cross my arms and shut my mouth. I've probably said enough.

"Macie, do you love Avery? I mean, really, really love him?"

I turn the question over in my head. I do love him, like I've loved no one else. And I like him, too. I like the way he adores gum-ball machines and always carries an extra quarter or two for a sour-apple surprise or a tropical blast. I like going to restaurants with him because no matter what I get, he will have to try it and declare it tastier than what he ordered. I like his eyes and the way they laugh when I say something that is only kind of funny.

"Yes, I do," I say. It's more of a sigh.

"Well, then, I think it's time for Avery to decide what he wants. He needs to be a man, make some decisions, and plan for your future. You would do that for him, so he needs to do that for you—if he loves you as much as you love him."

Exhaling, I give Iris a tight smile. I want to be mad and try to explain Avery to her in another way, but she is right. Avery needs to make some decisions. I have made mine, deep inside, to this man who makes me laugh and smile. I want him to propose. I guess I could do the asking—plop down on one knee and offer to spend the rest of my life with him, but I don't want it that way. I want Avery to want me, and for it to be real and serious and perfectly right.

Iris stands and stretches. She has a big pink cake to get out the door. I give her a hug, say good-bye, and make my way home.

Gwendolyn's wedding is set for 10:00 A.M. Saturday. While I adore morning weddings in theory, because of the freshness of the hour and the whole garden-party theme that brides go for these days, it's a beastly thing to get together. For Gwendolyn's wedding, I had to wake up at four in the morning. I have been at the church for what seems like ages. Gwendolyn has been with me, too. I like her a lot. I would make a fervent wish that all brides were like Gwen—easygoing, funny, and real—but I know it's not going to happen.

We're in the bride's room arranging little pots of beaded flowers that Gwen made herself. She created several eye-catching items for the reception, such as the large scarf that will be draped around the pink cake. She also made the party favors each guest will take home: delicate little pillows filled with lavender. When I asked her if she dried the lavender herself, Gwen just smiled. I think that means she did. I guess these things come naturally to a fashion designer.

Gwen's dress hangs on the big hook in the bride's room. Even with the opaque garment bag covering it, the bright pink of the satin comes through like a low-wattage lightbulb. She was going to change into a kimono for the reception, but I think Gwen's grouchy mother absolutely refused even to consider it. I imagine it would be a pretty nice kimono, since I love Gwen's clothes. She wears cute skirts with bits of lace sewn on the edges and embroidered sweaters with touches of ribbon. All of the things she wears—sometimes paired with a floppy hat or chandelier earrings—are funky and feminine.

Maurice sticks his head in the room, not bothering to knock. It's so early that he knows no one will be changing clothes. In fact, the three of us are the only ones here so far. The church janitor let us in and then relocked the front doors. We're in a Midtown Lutheran church just blocks from the famous Fox Theatre, a restored 1920s movie palace. When the wedding is over, the guests will walk down the street to the Fox for the reception in a ballroom that has a huge Tiffany glass skylight. I'm looking forward to this one. I've already been down to the ballroom this morning to make sure the caterers did their thing. Two hundred white chairs are ringed around white tables decorated with pink tablecloths and set with antique china. The entire room looks lovely.

"Macie, can you come with me?"

I give Gwendolyn a smile and move quickly to the door. Following Maurice down the hall, I wonder what has gone wrong. I can tell he is perturbed about something. Usually when I'm with a bride, he leaves us alone. But this is different.

He leads me toward the sanctuary. We step from the hallway through the red wooden doors, and I gasp. I cannot believe what I am seeing. "No, no, this isn't right!" I wail.

The neo-Gothic interior of the church has been transformed. Ivy and white roses—the most traditional wedding flower combo ever—are pinned to the end of each pew. Big white looping ribbons top the staid flowers, and brass candlesticks encased in glass globes top the pews. Brass candelabrum loom from every perch near the front of the church. Ferns sit in white wicker baskets on the steps up to the altar. It is perfectly, numbingly, just like every other wedding I've helped arrange.

I am having trouble breathing. The church is decorated in every way the opposite of what Gwendolyn had ordered. In fact, this is the exact nightmare of what Gwen—my funniest, most creative, and favorite bride ever—did not want at her wedding. All over Atlanta today, brides will walk into churches and rented halls just like this one. They will love it. Gwendolyn will not.

"Where are the tropical flowers? You know, those imported hothouse blooms with the sticky thingies?" My words are coming fast. I'm not making much sense. "And the sari scarves for the ends of the aisle? The light pink candles on silver sticks?" I look at Maurice, but he seems to think I know the answer. "And who in the world put these ferns in here? There's no room for the wedding party to stand near the altar!" I forget my usual whisper-in-church voice, and my words bounce off of the stone walls. I stalk up and down the smooth, polished center aisle.

"Macie, I have no idea of what happened here. While you were with Gwendolyn, I was minding the caterers over at the Fox. At least that room looks correct. But this, this is going to push Gwendolyn over the edge."

I stand, mouth open and heart racing. I simply do not know what to do. Gwendolyn's offbeat sense of style was going to make her day unique. That's what every bride seems to want, but few follow through with it. They say they want it to be different, but in reality they desire ferns and rented candelabrum and the fancy caterer who was written up in *Atlanta Magazine* last month. I know they will pick the same readings, hymns, and Bach tunes as the bride before them.

I've often thought that someone should open a wedding consulting business called Textbook Weddings. Brides would have a limit of three alterations to the preset schedule. Straight out of the box, each wedding would be the same. How perfect! This sanctuary would be the perfect one for Plan C—A Classy Wedding. I get chill bumps up and down my arms and look over at Maurice.

"I simply don't know what happened," he is saying, more to himself than me.

"I confirmed everything with Stella's Blooms last week. They even told me how the tropicals were coming in on their own plane." Gwen may be different and unique, but she is still wealthy.

"What are we going to do, Maurice?" I say, glad that he's the boss, not me.

"Well, I'm going to get on the phone with Stella and raise some—"

Maurice stops in midsentence, not because we are in a house of God, but because Gwen's mother has arrived. From the way she tilts her head and gives a sparse smile from the back of the church, I would say she is triumphant.

"Of course," Maurice says to me softly. "Here we have our answer."

Gwendolyn's mother has ruined her daughter's wedding, and it hasn't even started yet. I inhale and turn to face this woman who obviously loves common ferns and tacky bows more than her almost-married daughter.

"Hello, Camille," Maurice says, stepping into his smooth wedding-coordinator role. Although he is wearing his casual wedding-day outfit of a cotton shirt and pants, he acts as if he has donned the most elegant suit paired with custom loafers. Maurice oozes grace under pressure.

"You like what I've done with the place?" Camille asks in low tones. Her mouth curls around the words, reminding me of a bad television villain.

Maurice asks, "Where are the flowers we ordered for Gwendolyn? The sari scarves? Her pink handmade candles?"

Camille pulls at the lapel of her beige jacket. Her mother-of-the-bride dress hangs in the bride's room near the pink wedding dress. "I've made it no secret that I do not share my daughter's penchant for shocking displays. I decided that I simply could not afford to have the family embarrassed by her—what would you call it?—unwashed bohemian tastes."

Nodding, Maurice crosses his arms. "But don't you think you might have discussed this with us beforehand? Or perhaps with Gwendolyn?"

"Oh, Gwennie won't even notice. Look, you can hardly tell the difference in the white roses versus some other spiky thing she selected."

"Her tropical flowers were red and orange," I say through clenched teeth. "I'm guessing she'll figure it out."

Maurice gives me the most withering of warning looks. Since I think I might say something else, I slip away. I need to get to the bride before her mother does any more damage. I walk out of the sanctuary, and that's when I hear the scream. It's Gwendolyn.

Gwen is racing down the hall toward me, holding a billowing white wedding dress in one hand. The lengthy train drags on the floor. A woman with a blow-dryer is giving chase. I follow them to the sanctuary. I can hear Gwendolyn screeching at her mother. She really gives it to her. I stand beside the red wooden doors to the sanctuary, unsure of whether or not to enter. Finally, I walk in just a few feet and pause under a stone arch.

"You cannot expect me to wear a dress that you have picked out, Mother!"

"You certainly will," Camille says, eyeing the white dress draped over Gwen's arm. Even though I'm some distance away, I can tell the dress is something Gwen would try on to humor her mother, but she would never, ever wear it. It has mounds of tulle and lace and bows and oh, it's really dreadful. Gwendolyn's pink dress may be loud to some, but she has designed it herself and it is brave and different and beautiful.

"I will not wear it!" Gwendolyn's short pink hair bobs as she says angrily, "Get rid of this now."

"You'll do it like this or there will be no wedding, dear."

"You're kidding, right? Since when did my wedding become your own personal bridal fantasy?"

Camille is cool as she gives Maurice an apologetic look. "I'm sorry you have to see this, Maurice. Sometimes Gwendolyn is a little passionate."

"Don't condescend, Mother."

Maurice clears his throat. "If I may offer a compromise."

The women glare at each other and ignore him. Gwendolyn says, "If you don't take this dress away and get rid of that evil hairdresser you sent over, I will not be responsible for how this day turns out. Don't push me, Mother."

It is then that I realize the hairdresser is in the sanctuary, a few feet behind Gwendolyn, clutching her blow-dryer. She looks pained, as if she were wishing she could be transported about three thousand miles away. "I could do a faux French twist," she says in a whisper.

Gwendolyn ignores this and then seems to notice the sanctuary decorations for the first time. A shade of rage passes over her face. I've never seen someone so angry but not angry. It's like she's moved past angry altogether. I really feel for her. If Avery and I ever get married, my mother would be involved, of course, but she would content herself with the reception menu or the bridesmaids' dresses. She would not remake the entire thing. Of course, I know Mrs. Leland would be heavily involved. Mr. Leland would probably insist on paying for it, too. Not as an insult to my parents, but because he and Mrs. Leland would invite so many society-type people. A quaint, country wedding back home would not be the type of shindig the Lelands would go for, no sir.

I watch as Gwendolyn touches a stiff little white rose hitched to one of the pews. She fingers a stalk of baby's breath and then turns to leave the church.

"Gwendolyn! Don't you walk away from me! Get back here right now!" Camille's voice echoes throughout the ornate sanctuary. I can almost see the stained-glass images of all the saints frowning down on us.

Gwen stops and turns, the white dress still in her arms. "I'm sorry you've had to waste so much money, and I really wish I could have enjoyed the flowers I ordered and that someone presumably paid for. But since I can't, because of you, I am not going to show up here today in a few hours. I'm going to call Jake and we're going to get married elsewhere."

Camille inhales so deeply I fear she will turn purple and fall to the floor. I picture her mean heart breaking onto the unyielding Lutheran tiles of the sanctuary. "You are being ridiculous, Gwendolyn Leigh. Your father and I have worked very hard to give you all of this and you will show up like a good girl and get married here."

"Mother, I have never been a good girl."

"You will not do this to me," Camille says and presses her lips tightly together. "Think of what people will say."

I take a second and picture Jake, the fiancé. He's probably at home, getting ready to get out of bed. I see him there, scratching his shaggy hair, wondering what time he should get showered and dressed and when exactly it was that Gwen wanted him at the church. Jake is an artist and a die-hard trail runner. If you want to find him, you have to check out his studio behind his house or his favorite park, Sweetwater Creek, a few miles west of town. He refuses to own a cell phone—something I find courageous in this town of people just panting to communicate—so he can be hard to track down. When Gwendolyn tells him what has happened, I know he will back her up. He probably will not even care where they get married, as long as they do. He's that kind of guy.

My watch beeps the hour: it's 8:00 A.M. I get a queasy feeling because the bride is not dressed, she's redefining the word *angry,* and there's this little problem of where the actual ceremony will occur. At least the reception is taken care of, thank goodness.

"Mother, if you could just see that I'm different and accept that, this day could have been very nice. As it is, it's over for me. But I am going to get married to Jake today, even though I know you think I could do better to marry a lawyer or a bank president," Gwendolyn says.

"How is that artist going to support you and children? Have you thought about that?"

Gwendolyn drops the white dress to the floor. Her mother makes a little whimpering cry and grabs for it. "That's a Marie de Valledor!"

"And my dress is a Gwendolyn Coldren. If you would just take a second not to be such a snob, you would see that it's very nice. I've already had one order for the exact dress from an Emory student for her wedding next year."

If this bit of information changes anything in Camille, I can't tell. She looks as uncompromising as she did when she walked into the sanctuary. Gwendolyn turns and rushes out, her pink hair making a streak through the solemn room of stone statuettes and stained-glass saints. I follow her. If she wants to change the wedding location, I will have a lot of work to do.

In the bride's room, Gwendolyn is crying just a little as she holds her cell phone up to her ear. "Jake, just come get me. My mother has really—I can't explain it right now. Please come."

I walk in slowly, giving her space.

"No, we're getting married, but just not here. You should see the place. It looks like something every Atlanta bride would die for," she says, rolling her eyes over at me. I nod in agreement. "And there's this horrible dress. And a hairdresser. And who knows what else. She's taken over my wedding—on my wedding day!"

Gwendolyn hangs up and turns to me. "We've some details to work out. Are you up for it, Macie?"

I say I am. This day is getting stranger by the minute. I wonder if Maurice would approve. He's no doubt smoothing things over with Camille. With someone as prickly as she is, though, I think even Maurice will have a hard time making a dent.

"Okay, okay," Gwendolyn says, pacing back and forth in the overly floral-patterned bride's room. Large vases of flowers crowd the antique dresser. "We have two hundred people arriving in less than two hours. We have the pastor, the wedding party, and the programs. Everything is perfect except for the fact that the church is decorated for the wrong wedding and my mother has a really big mean streak. I refuse to get married in that place."

"Do you want to have the wedding outside?" I ask. I don't know why I think of it. It just comes to me. If she doesn't like the way her mother took over the wedding, why not just get around it by moving outside? It's hot out there, but it is nothing Atlanta people can't handle. Plus, the ceremony is fairly short. Within no time, the guests will be in the air-conditioned beauty of the Fox Theatre.

Gwen shuts her eyes and thinks for a moment. A lock of pink hair falls over her forehead. I hold my breath. I really want to be helpful.

"I like it!" Gwendolyn says, her eyes opening wide. "But where? We have to use the parking we've reserved here at the church, and we can't ask the guests to walk down to Piedmont Park. It's too far, especially in the heat."

I think of the Midtown area. There are shops and bars and trendy eateries, but no secluded parks. Then I remember: The church has a little slice of manicured grounds near the main parking lot. It even has a fountain and clumps of begonias and impatiens. I tell Gwendolyn about it and she claps her hands. We decide the wedding party will walk down the outside main steps of the church and over to the impromptu wedding area. That way, she still gets an entrance. It will be sweet and dramatic.

My next job is to find the pastor and let her know about the change of plans. Luckily, she's in her study and agrees to it. I think the reverend is secretly rooting for the fashion designer/artist takeover of the wedding. I've heard this pastor has a tattoo, so I'm not surprised. She's a rebel at heart.

With the official stuff out of the way, I find Maurice and tell him what Gwen and I have worked out. He looks relieved and actually thanks me. This is a first. It turns out that Camille has gone back home to regroup, but she knows her time is running out. What can she do? She can't stop people from coming at this point, and everything is paid for, so Gwen and Jake can get married if they want to.

Maurice and I split up, he to make sure the little piece of park property is free of homeless sleepers, and me to make sure the programs are unboxed and that the musicians know the new plan. I find the flute player downstairs in the music hall and ask her to spread the word. She is tall and thin, in that languid musician way, and I think she gets it. You never can tell with those people. They always seem to be playing notes in their head.

I make a dash upstairs to the bride's room and happily see that Gwendolyn is getting hugs from her just-arrived bridal party. Jake is there, too, helping her into her dress. I think this is sweet. They are one of those couples who couldn't care less about the "don't see the bride" rule on the wedding day. It seems sad that Camille is not there to help her daughter, but that is her choice.

Maurice makes one last check down at the Fox to make sure the reception has not been tainted by you-know-who. He says that everything looks perfect. Is Iris's cake there, and is it pink? I ask. He assures me it is. My guess is that Camille was impressed with the cachet of having a cake from Cake Cake. After all, Iris *is* exclusive.

By the time the guests arrive, the ushers have done a good job setting up chairs in a semicircle around the fountain. A lot of people will have to stand, but at least those who need a seat will have one. The programs flutter in the guests' hands just a tad because a perfect summer breeze is making the warm morning very comfortable. Maurice stands across from the parking lot, keeping an eye on his watch. He has changed into his suit, and I might be a little off, but I think his heart is beating like crazy. I believe we're going to get away with this one.

At the very last minute, a chauffered car pulls up to the curb and Camille and a man whom I assume is Gwen's father step out, both dressed for the ceremony. A van stops behind them and out jump six or seven men who look as if they were just pulled off of a construction site. Camille waves them into the sanctuary. All of the guests turn, talking stops, and we wait. Maurice grimaces and takes a hesitant step toward the church. He probably senses this is beyond him by now.

Within minutes, the burly men reappear carrying the decorations from inside the sanctuary: candelabrum, ferns, and stiff little roses trailing white ribbons. They haul them down to the little park, squeezing past guests, and dump decorations in little heaps here and there. The poor fountain gets the brunt of it. I can hardly see the delicate burbling arc of water because of all the ferns piled on the edge. By this time, the guests are thoroughly puzzled and people start talking about the bizarre decorating scheme. Camille stalks down the center aisle to prop up a huge arrangement of gladiolas that has fallen over in the grass.

"Maybe it's a performance art piece?" I hear one woman ask another. Finally, a guest can't hold back his laughter. Another one joins in, and then everyone has the giggles. I look around, wanting to laugh myself. Even the older folks are in on the joke. Everyone knows this is Camille's crazy idea of a wedding, not Gwendolyn's.

Camille hears the laughter and looks around. I notice her coiffed hair is a bit wispy from the exertion of moving flowers. She breathes deeply and tries to smile, but she can sense that everyone is looking at her like she has lost it. Finally, she sits near her husband, who plainly wants to be invisible.

Taking advantage of the moment, the miniorchestra begins the unfamiliar strains of a classical piece that I've never heard. I love it. I don't know what it is, but it's not Purcell or Wagner, and that's good enough for me. The construction workers find their places at the back of the crowd and stand, arms crossed. One man still wears his banana-yellow hard hat.

The bridesmaids, escorted by the groomsmen, walk slowly down the limestone church steps and cross the little park area. Due to the candelabrum stuck awkwardly in their path, the women each have to do a little dip and sway when they get to the fountain. It's unorthodox, but it works. Traffic swooshes past on Peachtree Street, but it just seems to fit the occasion. The music changes and the guests stand. They turn around toward the church in time to see

Gwendolyn and Jake walking hand in hand down the church steps. When they reach the bottom, they look at each other gently and pause. I know they do not hear the rattling of delivery trucks or the squeaking of brakes. They seem only to have this moment together. The construction guy wearing a hard hat gives a low catcall when he sees Gwen in her pink dress.

Then, just as quickly, the couple walks forward, shaking hands and hugging guests who are crowded into the little park. I see Gwen checking out the wilted gladiolas and the pesky ferns, but she just sighs. She and Jake, too, have to sidestep the candelabrum and a few white flower arrangements. But after that, Gwen just gazes at her fiancé and they stand beside the fountain. I know she has decided to move past what her mother has done. I admire her.

Everyone smiles and leans forward to hear what the pastor says. It is a lovely ceremony, and I am proud to have helped make it happen. Later, I will even save the program and a pink napkin printed with the couple's initials. I will also tuck away a picture of the bride with the construction workers after the ceremony. The guy who made the catcall apologizes. Gwen tells him she loved it, but she is a married woman now and off the market.

The reception at the Fox is divine, and the cake is scrumptious. Gwendolyn even gives me a little gift. "It's a velvet flower pin made from vintage material," she says with a smile. "I think they are going to be hot this year in the new store I'm opening in Midtown."

"Congratulations!"

"Thank you. It's a wedding gift from my dad. My mom will come down there after she reads about it in *Atlanta Magazine,* I guess." Gwendolyn shrugs, but I know she is hurt. Later, I will overhear her mother bragging to a guest, "Yes, she made the dress herself and already has quite the following with her design business!" I am glad to hear it for Gwendolyn, and I hope her mother says it to her before too long.

Maurice ends up leaving the reception a bit early. I tell him to go, that I will make sure everything wraps up perfectly. I wave good-bye to Gwen and Jake as they leave the reception a few minutes later. She leans on her new husband's shoulder, a little tired, while he shakes hands with well-wishers. They are happily in love and seem grateful their friends have stayed to see them off.

I am filled with a desire to see Avery, so I speed dial him on my cell. We have the whole night to look forward to, and I think I will take him a piece of pink wedding cake. He should love it as much as I do.

5

The Naked Bride

I climb into Maurice's silver sports car. Luckily, the air-conditioning in the tiny cockpit is going full blast. It's a scorcher out here. I direct a little plastic vent toward my face. The Atlanta summer sun fills nearly every day with hot waves of light that hit your eyes, then skin, then lungs with humid persistence. Air-conditioning is vital to life.

"So, what does Carolina want now?"

Maurice taps his fingers on the leather steering wheel and tilts his head to the side. "Oh, I don't know. How about a wedding dress, for starters?"

This day cannot get any wackier. We're tossing Carolina in four days, and everything was pretty much under control until yesterday. As far as brides go, Carolina has been no worse than the rest. She's hard to get on the phone, flaky about making decisions, and pouts when she doesn't get her way. The biggest request she had was to allow her Aunt Gretchen to sew the wedding dress and bridesmaids' dresses. Maurice was against it—he's a hound for labels—but eventually caved in to pressure from Carolina's family. They own a chain of local appliance stores, all indicators of a handy pile of money and referrals for Maurice.

Aunt Gretchen was supposed to have been a big-time couture designer in her day. Carolina had a million stories about her aunt's prowess at the sewing machine. "Every garment I wore as a child was made with her hands in her Parisian studio," she was fond of telling me. I would just nod. My parents outfitted me at the local Kmart in Cutter. Some people have charmed lives.

Carolina's wedding-party dresses have been a major ordeal. Patterns were obtained and fabric ordered with no problem, but Carolina's attendants—there are five women in all—live out of state. They have sent Aunt Gretchen their measurements and will cram their one-and-only fitting in right before the wedding. This plan seemed to worry everyone except for Carolina, who assured us that Aunt Gretchen was one of the best.

I told Avery about this plan over supper last weekend. He was in a mood, a bit on the tense side. I figured he was just tired of hearing wedding stories. After all, it's a lot of what I talk about because I am immersed in weddings all day long, and sometimes into the wee hours of the morning. Avery, on the other hand, can chat about the latest art-house movie, a new tennis grip he's trying out, or the Bulgarian cheese trade. He knows a lot about a bunch of things. "Jack of all trades, master of none," he is fond of saying with a grimace.

"So, this bride, Carolina, doesn't seem to be nervous that her wedding is a week away and ole Aunt Gretchen still won't let her see the dresses," I said to him over a dinner of spinach salad and grilled tilapia at our favorite bistro, Tang.

"What?" Avery says, lost in thought.

"Never mind. It's just another story from the Bad Bride Files."

Avery looked at me, really looked at me. He wiped his mouth with his napkin and said, "I think you need a vacation."

"Yeah, try telling Maurice that in the middle of the summer bridal season," I said, rolling my eyes. I took a sip of sweet tea.

"Well, I just happen to know of a place where we could go, and if you get Maurice's blessing, maybe we can take off for a little bit," Avery said, pulling a folded brochure out of his pocket and placing it on the table between us.

It was the Italian lagoon pool brochure that I had found a few weeks ago. There on the glossy pages was my fantasy vacation, complete with dazzling pools, sandy beaches, and exotic villas, nicely creased down the middle from the trip in Avery's pocket. A hopeful pitter-patter revved up inside my chest—was this going to be an engagement trip?—and then just as quickly turned to a cementlike thud. There was no way Avery was ready to propose. I just felt it deep inside.

"What's wrong? You look like I just asked you to help me pick up trash on the highway, rather than fly to Italy."

"It looks wonderful, Avery, it really does."

"But?"

"I can't possibly afford a vacation like this. With what Maurice pays me, I would be lucky to buy a glass of wine at this little pool-side bar," I said, poking my finger at one of the glossy pictures. Deeply tanned women and men hovered around a stone hut, lofting glasses into the air. It was hard to see in the small picture, but I was sure everyone had perfectly straight teeth.

"Ah, I had a feeling you would say that," Avery said. "So, I wanted to tell you this trip would be a gift. From me to you." He waited for my response.

If Avery had asked me to go away with him two years ago, and I'd had some money saved up, I would have said, "Where's my pass-port?" But now I am twenty-six years old, two years have passed, and we are no closer to making things permanent. Sure, we could jet off to an exotic locale, but when we came back, we would be no closer to marriage. Call me old-fashioned, but I want to travel the world with Avery as my *husband,* not my boyfriend. Is that too much to ask?

I love Avery, and I know he loves me. We play together, laugh together, so perhaps we can plan our lives together. I've never said it just like that to Avery, but maybe now was the time to try.

"Well, you know how we're tossing Carolina next weekend?"

"Can we talk about us, and not your robot brides?"

"Just listen," I said. "When she is married off, Carolina's husband is going to whisk her away to some French island for the honeymoon, and then they are going to start their life together."

Avery took a long sip of tea. "Is this before or after she walks down the aisle naked because Aunt Gretchen can't get her act together?"

I know he always listens to my bride stories, but sometimes I forget. "After," I said, smiling a bit for the first time. Avery can make me laugh. I thought about this for a moment and then put on a more serious face. The face of someone who wants to get married to her true love. In this decade.

"So, what I mean is, Carolina is going to jet off to a perfect French island with her husband"—I leaned on the word for emphasis—"and then come back to Atlanta and start her perfect life. You know, married and all."

Avery stared over at me before glancing down at the brochure. "I see. You want to go to France."

"Avery!" I threw my black cloth napkin across the table at him, a gesture that fell on the less dramatic side.

Avery's mouth opened to give me a look of faux horror. "Oh, wait. That's not what you meant," he said.

"Forget it." Somehow we've moved from the glossy stiffness of an Italian beach vacation brochure to Other Big Life Questions. But it was not my idea, right? I was minding my own tilapia.

"Macie, Macie, listen to me. I know what you are saying. I really do. I was just playing around."

I stirred my now-warmish iced tea. "What did I mean, then?"

Avery looked uncomfortable at that moment. I waffled on the edge of feeling sorry for him. But the feeling was short-lived. In Avery's mind, Italy was just a country. For me, a trip like that had to mean something, like we were moving toward more than just next Friday's date. I considered a big trip to be one with all the trimmings, like the vacations I read about in travel magazines: packable clothes, a wide-brimmed hat, a slim silver camera to record memories. As grown-up as it was making me sound, I wanted a guidebook for the future: Avery and me against the world. Or something like that.

"You feel as if a vacation like this one is for married people," Avery said, looking into my eyes. "Real couples with plans and dreams and other important things like that. If we go just as we are now, you think we'll never get serious—we'll just keep coasting along. Am I right?"

I stared at Avery and leaned forward. He got it exactly right. This might be the moment where we settled it once and forever. Where we were going, what we would do. I could open my mouth, say the words. It would be a first, but he was worth it. I looked at Avery across the table.

Wordlessly, our waiter glided up to the table with the evening's dessert tray straddling his outstretched arm. "Who wants some chai flan?" he asked, mouth stretched into a wide grin. "Or perhaps the chocolate torte. It is, let me tell you, to die for."

Avery asked for the check with a few terse words. We rode home quietly, neither one of us mentioning the Italian trip or anything else that mattered. The brochure was tucked back into Avery's tidy pants pocket. And I was left with thoughts darker than the richest chocolate torte at Tang.

With seventy-two hours to go until the wedding, Maurice decides that today will be the day we force dear Aunt Gretchen to show us the goods. We have actually spoken to her once by telephone, and she assured us the sewing was coming along nicely, thank you, and didn't we know that genius was not to be rushed? Carolina backed her aunt up, insisting that she has been to her home for fittings.

I meet Maurice at his home in Druid Hills. The tree-lined neighborhood is filled with handsome Tudors and stone mansions. Maurice and Evelyn live on a street across from a lush park. Evelyn's family goes back generations. Her maiden name used to be on a department store downtown and is carved onto more than one building over at Emory University. The house is hers.

"Macie, so good to see you." Evelyn greets me at the door. I walk through the enormous antique wooden door and remember for the hundredth time that the foyer is bigger than my apartment. Quite frankly, the house dwarfs Evelyn. She is a really small person. Small hands, small body, short little hairstyle. I feel oafish next to her. We chat a little about our current bridal disaster.

"These brides today. They leave everything to the last minute," Evelyn says. "I mean, Maurice is really worried about this one. He was making calls until eleven last night."

"And we've got quite the work to do today if the dresses aren't ready," Maurice says, walking into the foyer. He kisses Evelyn goodbye and nods to me. "Ready?"

Aunt Gretchen lives across town in an area genteel people refer to as "declining." Her neighborhood, once proud and vibrant, has been swallowed up with rentals and occasional fits of crime. We find the house—a sagging bungalow with a sturdy hydrangea bush out front—on one of the better streets. Maurice parks the sports car out on the curb. "Ex-couture stars don't get much in the way of a pension, I guess," he remarks.

We push through the picket fence and step over cracks in the front walk. Maurice knocks on the door. No one answers. We stand there, unsure of what to do.

"Maybe we'll be really surprised," I say with a dose of enthusiasm. "Maybe she's a genius and this is her swan song." I trace the outline of a dress in the humid air, one arm clutching the file folder on Carolina's wedding.

"Maybe Aunt Gretchen has been hitting the sauce," Maurice says, peering through the windows into the front room. Leaning over his shoulder, I look into the dusty Craftsman windows and gasp.

A woman whom I can only guess is Aunt Gretchen sleeps in a recliner, her mouth open and a beer can tucked between her legs. Her chest rises and falls rhythmically, so we know she's alive. Cats glide by, shaking their tails at each other. A fan rotates slowly, stirring the pattern pinned to a dressmaker's dummy. Other than that, there is nothing else in the room except hundreds of bolts of fabric. They are crammed into every available space. The television cart. On the couch, six or seven deep. Lining the walls. I see every type of fabric possible: wild prints, velvets, plaids, and florals.

"She's a fabric junkie," I breathe out loud.

Maurice groans out loud. "Check out the dummy."

I did not notice it before, but the pattern pinned to the mannequin is for a bridal gown. A heap of white material lies nearby. One of the cats performs an impromptu bath among its folds. I wince. That embroidered silk was pretty darn expensive.

Maurice straightens up and stretches his arms over his head. "Well, at least we know our answer. Give Carolina a call. Tell her to meet us at O'Dell's House of Bridal."

My cell is halfway to my ear when I pause, arm extended. "Meet us where?" O'Dell's is a one-stop bridal chain our brides—and Maurice—despise. The dresses are (horrors!) bought off the rack. The bridesmaid dresses are last season's. They even have dresses for pregnant brides. There are dark bridal haunts into which our brides just do not venture. O'Dell's is one such place.

"Macie, Carolina doesn't have much choice. If she complains, remind her that old Auntie was her idea and that she wouldn't listen to me when I said we should go another route."

I really hate getting stuck with the hard stuff, but I make the call. A bride without a dress who is getting married in three days is not inclined to be nice to the wedding planner's assistant. I long to dial up Avery instead, ask him how his tennis game went this morning, but I remember we parted awkwardly a few days earlier after our dinner at Tang. We've spoken a few times since then, but I don't feel very keen about him. He obviously knows that something is wrong, but I stubbornly refuse to bring it up again.

"Carolina? It's Macie."

"Who?" The bride's voice comes on the line and she already sounds cross.

"Macie, Maurice's assistant."

"Oh. What's up?"

I take a deep breath. Carolina is like all brides. She must be treated with extreme caution if something is going wrong. In this case, wrong would be an upbeat way to describe the situation. Crappy, awful, disastrous—all of these are better words. I decide to speak slowly, like I have everything under control.

"Maurice would like you to meet him at a local store to select some dresses—just in case we get in a jam with, well, you know."

"Aunt Gretchen will have the dresses ready," Carolina shrieks. "I'm tired of everyone questioning my judgment on this! Why can't I have a few people who believe in me?" A few sobs come through the line, and Maurice hears them clearly since he is standing next to me. He whips out his cell, punching buttons furiously.

"Hold on, Macie. I'm getting another call." Carolina says.

I hang up and step back. Maurice looks ticked.

"Carolina, dear, Maurice on the line." Maurice is all smoothness, although I can see the bulging vein on his forehead. It's beastly hot today, even in the shade of Aunt Gretchen's sad front porch. I glance back to the front room. She's still sleeping. A third cat arrives on the scene.

"Darling, you're going to have to meet us at the O'Dell's shop out near Perimeter Mall. I'm sorry, but that's just the way it's going to have to be. Really. That's right. No, I don't believe so." Maurice nods and shakes his head in a regretful manner that I wish Carolina could see. He is the picture of sincerity.

I cast a tired eye around the porch, wishing for something on which to sit. My legs hurt a bit, either from cramming myself into Maurice's sports car or from walking around tense all week with this wedding on my mind. Finally, I plop down on the low stone wall on one end of the porch. I try to imagine fixing this house up a bit. Maybe scrape off the old paint, tear off the rusted awnings, plant some flowers. Back in Cutter, my dad always took care of our brick ranch on Tupelo Street. The yard was small, but it was trimmed with a white fence covered in climbing roses.

A man on a bicycle glides by in the street. He wears a fast-food uniform and carries a bag of groceries under one arm. He eyes Maurice's sports car and gives me a nod as he passes.

"Well, Carolina, if you must know, I think your aunt has had one too many," Maurice says, his voice rising.

This gets my attention. It takes a lot to get him riled up on the outside.

"How do I know? Because I'm standing on her front porch and I have an armchair view of Auntie sleeping in her armchair. From the look of things, nothing has been sewn in this house for twenty years!"

I think that Maurice is going for bridal shock value. Instead of shielding Carolina from the worst of it, he's embracing the debacle and trying to force the bride to act. It's risky; I've never seen it work.

Carolina must be giving it to him. Maurice closes his mouth, nods repeatedly, and brushes a piece of lint off of his pants. Finally, he stands up straight and starts walking toward the car. I follow him.

"Now, get your mother and meet us at O'Dell's. We are going to pull this thing together, darling. I mean it. I'll see you in an hour." Maurice's face is tense.

"What did you say? What did she say? She's coming?" I ask Maurice in the car as we speed away.

"It seems that Carolina knew all along Aunt Gretchen wouldn't be able to finish the job. In fact, everyone did except Gretchen. Her battle with the bottle has made her a bit, shall we say, overconfident. Carolina just got more and more desperate and started inventing fittings that didn't take place, just to protect her aunt. It's the most bizarre thing."

"I guess she really loves her," I say.

"I'd say," Maurice nods, turning onto the expressway. "Now, are you ready to find this bride some dresses?"

O'Dell's is a huge white store built to live beside other huge white stores in a shopping center near the mall. Large posters featuring beautiful brides tossing bouquets, laughing at secrets, and kissing flower girls decorate the store. One entire side of the place is taken up by wedding dresses hanging from oversized racks. Some gowns are in plastic. Still others have fallen from their hangers and slump, defeated, on the mauve-colored floor.

Our goal is to walk out of here with a dress that looks like it took four European seamstresses four months to create, using really tiny stitches and pricey trimmings. I start pulling at fabric, fingering necklines, and flouncing skirts. Maurice takes over in a way only Maurice can.

"Donna, yes, that's the one. This chair will do." Maurice waves to a woman with a name tag that identifies her as the manager. She lugs a satin chaise lounge over to a raised platform near the back of the store. "Put it down there, please."

Next, another employee trots up with satin shoes and a strapless bra in Carolina's size. She disappears and yet another woman arrives on the scene with coffee and scones. "All I could get was raspberry from the coffee shop next door. I hope that's okay," she says to Maurice and almost drops a curtsy. I roll my eyes and get to organizing the dressing room.

By the time Carolina slinks into the store with her mother—both wearing dark glasses, I kid you not—I have lined up several not-too-awful dresses. I will admit that spending the last year dealing with high-end silk doupioni and satin charmeuse has changed my ideas of what is nice and what is supernice. The dresses at O'Dell's are nice. I'd wear one. But they are not what people like Carolina wear.

As I slip the first dress over Carolina's perfect hips, I notice my bride looks bored or sorry that she lied—or both. It occurs to me that she was protecting her aunt but sabotaging her own wedding. Does that mean she does not want to get married Saturday?

"How are we doing, Macie?" Maurice claps his hands from outside the dressing-room door. Carolina's mother waits nearby on the chaise lounge.

I nod to Carolina and open the dressing-room door. She moves languidly, like the models at the bridal show we attended last winter. This dress is a pretty A-line with a seventy-two-inch train. But Carolina seems completely unimpressed. She drags herself and the dress over toward her mother, reaches for a scone, and nibbles delicately.

"If you'll notice the caviar beading here and here," Maurice says. "Very fashionable over on the Continent."

"Next," Carolina's mother calls.

Dresses two, three, and four rouse Carolina's interest just a tad.

"Makes my rear end look huge," she says about dress number two.

"It minimizes my waist," she complains of dress three.

"I look poofy," is her verdict on number four.

Donna helps us pull on the next dress. I think she smells a big sale because she has ignored every other customer in the store to attend to us. As she arranges the silk taffeta over Carolina's hips and closes up the back with the zipper hidden under a row of dainty, satin-covered buttons, I have a feeling this is the one. The narrow, strapless bodice is adorned with little clusters of tiny gold and glass beads. The ball gown skirt extends to a chapel-length train that can be bustled up neatly. It is really lovely. I could get married in this dress. I call to Maurice over the dressing-room door. He knows what this means.

Maurice hands a veil over the door. He follows that with a tiara he's been carting around for months. It was from a wedding that didn't happen last year—the bride bailed days before the big day—and Maurice was stuck with the delicate rhinestone-and-crystal piece. It's really elegant, but I know he would like to unload it on one of our brides. It cost nearly a thousand bucks.

I nestle the tiara into Carolina's hair, which I've twisted into a passable French knot. Then, with Donna's eager hands, we lift the illusion veil up and over Carolina's head, allowing the satin grosgrain ribbon edges to flutter down over her back and shoulders. Donna gives me a nervous smile. It's not every day that someone like Maurice comes into her store. She'll probably talk about this for weeks.

Donna pushes the dressing-room door open and Carolina walks out slowly. Carolina's mother looks up from her date book and smiles. Even Carolina seems fairly interested in her reflection. Maurice gazes at me with a certain amount of pride or maybe just disbelief. We have made Carolina look like a bride.

All of the images a woman is hit with over the course of her life make this moment different from any other. Sure, I've seen hundreds of dresses before, but this one is special. Maybe it's because the dress fits Carolina just perfectly. Maybe it is because we are desperate for a dress—any dress—for this wedding. Or maybe it is because I want to wear one of these myself.

I wonder what has happened to me. I used to care more about getting a good tan or reading the latest women's magazine. Being with Avery started out as a lark. He was funny, sweet, and caring. We talk about all kinds of things, and I feel like I can tell Avery anything. Well, almost anything. The one thing that's starting to matter most he just doesn't seem to understand. I shake my head slowly as Maurice frowns. I should be beaming, not thinking.

"Sweetie, this is a very nice dress," Carolina's mother says, crossing her legs and letting one leather mule flop off her foot. "What do you think?"

"I guess it will do." Carolina has a pouty face. I decide not to care.

Maurice takes this as a yes. "Donna, please wrap this up. We'll use the same veil and the tiara I brought in."

"We have several nice tiaras—" Donna offers helpfully.

"This will do, thanks." Maurice is on to other tasks. Donna backs away, chastened.

Our hope was to find five bridesmaids dresses at O'Dell's, but Carolina refused them all. "Tacky" was her judgment, so Maurice and I put our heads together. We need to find five dresses of varying sizes to match the wedding party. No bridal shop will have that many dresses on hand. Usually, they have only a sample size from which you order the real dress.

Carolina is exhausted, so we stop at a little coffee shop for a pick-me-up. While Carolina's mother chastises her for the fifth time that I've heard for being so silly about the dresses, Maurice and I huddle at a corner table. I suggest one of the better department stores at Phipps Plaza. This gets Maurice thinking, and I know he is on to an answer.

"We'll go to Rent-A-Gown. Perfect!" Maurice almost cackles.

I gasp. He cannot mean it. There is no way Carolina and her mother will follow us in their sleek foreign sedan out to the strip mall–ringed bargain highway where Rent-A-Gown is sandwiched between Hot Tub Heaven and a warehouse that sells unfinished furniture.

"They'll never go for it."

"That's where our natural genius comes in," Maurice says. "Here's what you do. Call that French café off Juniper. You know, the one with the vines and the murals. Get Elise to reserve the small room in back."

"Where we had Darby's shower?" I sigh. Dealing with the French owner was such a big pain.

Maurice nods. Then he tells me to invite Carolina there in two hours. "Send them out on errands. Make something up. I don't care."

There isn't time to drink our lattes, so we leave the two women and jump in Maurice's sports car. Maurice drives fast, talking on his cell all the way. He lets the Rent-A-Gown people know we have a sticky situation. He calls it a "bridal emergency." Meanwhile, I call Café Suite and speak with Elise. She breaks into French once or twice, saying she is *trés* happy to accommodate us. She says she'll even place a few vases of flowers in the room for us. I've always suspected she has a thing for Maurice, and this just confirms it.

When we get to Rent-A-Gown, I am speechless. I had heard of the store, of course. No one in Atlanta could miss their frequent commercials on late-night television: "Cinderella rented her dress here, and so should you!" followed by a close-up of a teenage beauty queen climbing into a carriage.

Nothing could have prepared me for what seems like acres of dresses in all colors, sizes, and really awful styles. Luckily, Marge, the special dresses manager, meets us at the door. "You must be the famous Maurice. Charmed," she says, offering her hand. I groan inwardly. Maurice's reputation has extended even to this dress barn.

But Maurice kills me. He takes her hand and kisses it. Right there inside the store as the automatic doors swish open and shut with a whoosh. Marge, all gray hair and bifocals, eats this up. I think she even blushes.

We start in Pageant and quickly make our way through the first few sections: Prom, Quinceañera, Funeral. This last section sounds like a joke to me, but I guess there are women who die without a good dress in the closet. When we get to Bridal, I feel stirrings of hope. Here is rack after rack of dresses, many of them in multiple sizes.

Maurice flings the dresses left and right. Poor Marge brings him gown after gown that he rejects. "Too polyester. Too horrible. Too 1987." She doesn't seem to mind, though. I guess with that many dresses under one roof, she knows people will eventually find what they need.

And we eventually do. The winning dress is a deep blue organza that Maurice likes because it "hides the Third-World stitching." One shoulder is bare, and it comes with a wrap Maurice regards as something nasty in a communicable kind of way.

After making polite conversation and posing for a picture with the Rent-A-Gown day managers, Maurice and I make a break for it. We stuff the dresses into his tiny trunk; our favorite dry cleaner will press them tomorrow. Then we careen over to Café Suite, arriving at the snotty little French café just in time. I really do not care for this place because I remember having Darby's shower here, and every memory about that woman stings like an ice-cream headache.

Elise meets us at the hostess stand and kisses Maurice on both cheeks. I am toting a bridesmaid dress in my size, a tiara, a veil, and a box of shoes, so I just smile nicely. Elise ignores me. They carry on in French, which I find rude.

In the bathroom, I tear off the rental agreement pinned to the blue dress and slip the garment over my head. I apply some deep red lipstick and try twisting my hair up quickly. Unfortunately, the humidity is making every hair on my head act a little nutty. I cram the loaner pair of heels from Rent-A-Gown onto my feet and take a deep breath. This had better work, or Maurice and I are going to be in big trouble. Sure, it's Carolina's fault that there are no dresses, but it will make us look bad. I think of snoozing old Aunt Gretchen and wonder if she's dreaming about being a seamstress to the stars.

Maurice lurks outside the women's room holding a bouquet of lilies. I don't even ask him where he got it, because I've learned that things just work out for Maurice. Some people are just like that. Everything works out for them, and mere mortals like me have to stand back and watch.

You could say Avery is like that, too. Thinking of him while Maurice hooks some kind of pearl necklace around my throat gives me pause. I miss him, I really do. I check my watch reflexively. I haven't missed any calls and there's no voice mail. After this little fashion show, I will give him a call.

When I enter the private room in the back of Café Suite, Carolina and her mother are nibbling on little fruit tartlets and sipping chamomile tea. They look refreshed and content, like there isn't anything more important in the world than this moment in time. I, on the other hand, wear a rented dress, carry over-perfumed hothouse flowers, and list a bit to one side in the loaner shoes.

"This is a sample dress I was lucky to steal away from one of our designers," Maurice says in a secretive voice. He motions for me to walk along the edge of the room. "Note the empire bust, how it flatters, and the sheer cap sleeves. I like the hint of whimsy in the satin cording, here and here."

I stop walking and stand beside my boss. He twirls his finger in the air. I turn again and again. Carolina has not uttered a word.

"What I adore about this frock is how it will complement the bride but not take away from her glamour. All in all, Margaret did a wonderful job with this one. I am sure it will be quite the rage next season."

I almost choke when I think of Marge—or Margaret—from Rent-A-Gown actually designing a dress. The closest she got to making this gown was stuffing it into a plastic bag and handing it across the counter.

Then Carolina is smiling and giving Maurice a peck on the cheek. Her fat diamond solitaire sparkles in the sunlight coming in through the cafe windows. The mother rises and gives the dress an appraising scowl but goes along with it. Then there are appointments to be made with the five bridesmaids and discussions about matching shoes. I slink away to change and call Avery. Maybe we can meet for an early dinner. I am starving.

After trying his cell and hearing his voice-mail recording, I hang up and call Avery's house.

"Well, hello, Macie. We haven't seen you much this week," Avery's mother says.

"I know. I've been really busy with a wedding," I reply.

"Of course, dear. You should drop by. I'm having a cocktail on the veranda."

"That sounds nice. Maybe I will. Is Avery around so that I can speak with him?" My voice sounds a little high. I am suddenly worried. Avery's mother is usually not this chatty.

"Oh, Macie. Avery's not here, didn't you know? I thought you'd know. Of all people."

My dumb voice betrays me and I waver, "Where did he go?"

"Italy, darling. He left the other day. I'm surprised he didn't tell you." Mrs. Leland's voice is flat through my phone. I hear the clink of glasses and the mumbled words of Mr. Leland. And then the phone is silent.

6

The Vegan Bride

It is only six o'clock in the morning, but I have been up with the seagulls much longer. The scruffy gray-and-white birds dart this way and that, wheeling over the almost deserted sands of the beach before landing and immediately engaging in a dedicated show of preening. As I shake out another tablecloth over a rented round table, it occurs to me that our bride is probably inside her beach house preening like the seagulls. It is her wedding day, after all.

Hilton Head Island at daybreak is beautiful. The rich and cloistered people are all parked inside their rich and cloistered houses, leaving the beach a place for the serious jogger or shell collector. The sun creeps over the horizon in a well-behaved manner, leaving me to think the day will be perfect for a sun-splashed outdoor wedding. I am working side by side with Taylor, the caterer's assistant. It really is not my job to help set up tables, but I've learned from Maurice that the more we are involved, the better.

Travel pains Maurice, but the fee for this wedding was apparently too good to pass up. Tallie St. Claire is old money, and her family is sparing no expense for her wedding to a prominent attorney. Of course, all the brides spare no expense, but Tallie is different. She simply has no clue as to how much cash it takes to buy something. And she never carries a dime on her willowy, five-foot-nine frame. I've probably shelled out about thirty bucks in smoothies downed by a woman who says, "I left my purse at home."

I don't mind bailing Tallie out; I've sort of become used to it, like she's my little sister. Last week, before we left Atlanta, Tallie made a final stop at the exclusive gift shop where she selected the wedding-party gifts. Tallie and her fiancé had picked out top-of-the-line putters for the guys and delicate gold-and-diamond bangles for the women.

"Macie! I need help," Tallie breathed into the phone.

"What's up?"

"Well, I'm at the gift shop and they won't let me take the putters or the bangles."

My heart quickened. Was something wrong with the order? We were getting close to the wedding date. "Why?"

"They want me to pay for them before I take them," Tallie said, lowering her voice.

I swallowed a giggle. I like Tallie, but I have to remember that she grew up with the St. Claire name behind her. Down in Hilton Head, that detail would have been enough for the gift-store owner to hand over the merchandise. Up in Atlanta, though, things were a little different.

"Well, let's get this straightened out, Tallie," I said. "Do you have any credit cards on you?"

Tallie inhaled so sharply, I could hear it over the phone. "Oh, Macie, I didn't even think to bring one. What am I going to do?"

"Don't worry another minute over it. Give the phone to the sales-clerk and I will take care of it." Luckily, I had a platinum card just for occasions like this. Maurice would reimburse me.

In the past few days, I have explored Tallie's Hilton Head. The island boasts huge "plantations" behind carefully guarded gates. Each plantation is nicer than the next, and, of course, Tallie's plantation is the best of the best. The family's oceanfront mansion sprawls over several acres of pricey real estate. It was designed to look like the Long Island estates of the early 1900s and it passes the test with startling authenticity. When I saw it for the first time the other day, I expected to witness Victorian carriages pulling up in the majestic front drive. The mansion's huge, squat pillars give a boost to painted cedar shakes that support grand cupolas, where white flags shimmy in the ocean breeze. Each flag is embroidered with a bold "S.C." Horses are stabled nearby, and an assortment of pools and tennis courts waits to be used. I began to see why Tallie was Tallie.

Luckily for me, Iris has traveled to Hilton Head as well. She needed a serious vacation and decided a few days on the beach would be the best way to go about it. She's helping keep my mind off of Avery's sudden departure for Italy. When I think about how he left without telling me, without saying good-bye, I feel sick. No doubt he is having fun, going to restaurants, and traipsing all over Italy. It seems like the things I had said about us planning a future didn't matter at all.

Iris is staying with me in the St. Claire guest house, so the two of us are having a blast, talking each night until an insane hour. I cleared her staying with me through Tallie, who was impressed because Iris is well known in Atlanta. Tallie, incidentally, ordered her cake from the island's best chef. Iris isn't taking it personally, although we both know who would have been the better choice.

Our guest house is more like a mini inn. There are six bedrooms, each with its own entrance and special theme. We live in the Egret Suite, so we have pillowcases, shower curtains, and rugs embroidered, patterned, and woven with the tall, white bird. Meals are served in the dining room of the main house if we want them. The common room of the guest house is stocked with enormous brownies, gourmet tea bags, and bottled water labeled with (what else?) S.C. I know I have found heaven. I may never leave.

"I think this is creepy," Iris said the night before the wedding. The rehearsal dinner party was finally over, and I was stretched out on one of the bird-covered beds. We had been at a trendy fish restaurant all evening. The toasts went on and on with each flushed face more verbose than the next, and the bridesmaids dancing more and more suggestively on an impromptu dance floor. I was glad when it was time to go back to the plantation. Tallie loved it, of course. The only snafu was a drunken ex-boyfriend showing up in the middle of dinner. He bellowed love poems to Tallie before swiping some shrimp off of the best man's plate. After he left crying, Tallie just smiled.

"What's creepy?" I asked sleepily. I had to get up early to meet Taylor and I was already dreading dawn.

"All of this excess. Doesn't it kind of make you feel, oh, I don't know," Iris said, waving her hand around the room, "kind of like under the St. Claire thumb?"

"You think too much. Let's just enjoy our free room on the ocean."

Iris laughed and pushed back her hair from her face. Away from Atlanta and without the worry of producing cakes, she was a lot more relaxed. "Yeah, I guess I should."

As I drifted off to sleep, I had to admit that Iris had a point. This was not the real world. I was reminded a little too much of Avery's family. They had nowhere near the wealth of the St. Claires', but they were very well off. Avery was using that money to finance his lark in Italy right now, I thought to myself. A heavy feeling fell over me. I had not received any word from him since he'd left. No call, e-mail, or airmail. The distance between us was literally an ocean, but it felt like more than just water and time.

Taylor and I worked quickly the next morning, snapping tablecloths and setting out the just-arrived vases of freesia and delphinium. The wedding ceremony would take place on the beach, and the sunset supper would be on the main lawn under an enormous white tent that was special-ordered from California. Two other workers unpacked hotel pans and portable burners in the outdoor makeshift kitchen designed to crank out about four hundred hot meals later tonight. On the food end, Tallie was very bossy and specific. Where some brides care about the dresses or the flowers, Tallie was all about the nibbles. I was sweating this one a little because Maurice had given me more rope than usual. I helped Tallie pick out her menu, researched selections, and interviewed the caterer by phone. I knew Maurice was handing off more responsibility as a sort of test. I felt up to it, but I lack his natural confidence. This will be no ordinary stuffed chicken breast and imported cheese spread type of wedding reception.

Tallie is a strict vegan. No dairy products, including milk and cheese. No honey or eggs, and, of course, no meat. She believes so strongly in this diet that all of her wedding guests are going to have to go along with her as well. "Just imagine, Macie," Tallie had gushed to me about two months ago, "We may win some converts to our cause!" Upon hearing that, I hastily tossed my double-chocolate milk shake into a trash can. No matter what, stay on the good side of the bride.

The rehearsal dinner, however, was a different story. It turns out Tallie's father-in-law-to-be is very passionate about meat, so the menu was completely his doing for Friday night. Saturday, on the other hand, was all Tallie's tempeh, tofu, and faux salmon.

As Taylor and I step back to take stock of the tables, I see the caterer's truck pull onto the lawn and carefully roll toward the tent. I exhale with relief. I often dream of my job, and when I do, I have nightmares of caterers who forget the date of a wedding or show up a week early, stocked to the gills with salmon croquets and chicken almondine.

I walk over to the truck. Two workers in blue coveralls unload countless pans and boxes from the back. Before I can introduce myself, I notice what is hooked to the trailer hitch on the back of the truck. I feel an ice-cold stab of panic in my chest. My palms instantly water as I clench my hands.

The truck is towing a pork smoker.

The heat-battered black metal smoker gives off a tangy aroma, not altogether unpleasing to me, a meat eater, but absolutely terrifying to a bride determined to love animals, not slaughter them a few yards from her bridal party. To make matters worse, the catering crew, now joined by a white van full of more coverall-clad workers, unloads a very dead pig strung up on a stick. Its little hooves tap together as it passes by. I feel the entire wedding slipping away. My mouth is dry. I turn to my right. Maurice is strolling down the landscaped path from the guest house. His usually handsome face is pained. He can see the pig from a mile away, I am sure.

To my left, Tallie skips over the main lawn, her veil flowing behind her, although the rest of her clothes are casual. Her hair and makeup are already in place, so she will wear the veil for the rest of the day and evening. As she moves closer to the tent, I start to babble a little to myself. Just little whimpers only I can hear. This cannot get worse.

And of course, that's when it does. I watch as the caterers unload a very roasted boar's head. I've never fainted in my life, but I start to swoon when Maurice reaches my side. Luckily, Tallie's view of the meat parade is blocked by the caterer's van and truck.

"Macie! Macie!" Maurice says.

"I know! I know!" I snap back, trying not to stare as another boar's head is unloaded, followed by a tray of trussed-up pheasants. Tallie stops, momentarily delayed by an aunt wanting a picture. She tells Tallie to pause, twirl, and turn.

"Well, what do they say? What are you doing about it?" Maurice gestures toward the caterers.

I feel as if I am standing at the bottom of a very deep well. The colors and sounds of the workers move slowly past me. Out of the corner of my eye, I see Tallie, all white tulle, satin, and pink lipstick.

"Where do ya want the carving station?" one worker calls to another.

"I think it's over here," bellows the worker. "Next to the baby back ribs."

Ignoring the sick feeling in my stomach, I lunge at the nearest foil-covered pan and yell in a loud voice, "Oh, here you are. The tofu-and-lentil salad! What a fabulous vegetarian meal!"

"Are you okay, Macie?" Maurice asks, with a quick look at my sweaty face.

The picture-taking aunt moves on to another subject. I have to do something. "Maurice, stop Tallie. She's over there." I fling my arm past his face. "Show her the water plants the florist put in the main pool. She'll love that."

Without a word, Maurice turns to greet his cash cow, who wears a funny look on her face. "Is that a pig?" I hear her say before Maurice shushes her with low, syrupy tones and puts one arm around her waist to guide her back toward the main house.

Whirling around, I stalk over to the head meat man who is marking up a clipboard. I clear my throat and announce there must be some mistake. My hands are shaking. If this man doesn't have four hundred slices of mushroom-and-millet casserole in the back of his truck, I will fall over and start whimpering. Maybe it is a major flaw, but I do not deal well with conflict. I'd rather things just work out on their own. I want the meat to fly away. I want Avery to call.

"Excuse me?" Mr. Meat looks like the surly catering type rather than the helpful variety.

"You have the wrong food here. This is the St. Claire wedding. We didn't order this menu."

Meat checks his clipboard and then squints toward the main

tent, where his minions are setting up roasting racks. A huge block of cleavers and other scary-looking knives graces one table.

"Nope, says right here that I'm to deliver to the St. Claire estate, One St. Claire Way. This is the right place, unless I miss my guess." The man starts to walk away on the lush lawn.

When I am stressed or worried, my voice takes on a wavering quality. I know that is not what is needed, so I try for a lower register. "Stop! Right there!" Way to go, I think. My cops-'n'-robbers dialogue will definitely scare the pants off of him.

Mr. Meat turns and delivers a look bordering on concern and contempt. "Look, sugar," he says. "I've got men to supervise before the chef gets here."

My hands shake. "Let's save each other a lot of work. Call Edward, the event manager. He will straighten this whole thing out. By the way, do you have grape leaves in that truck?" I'm hopeful we can find our food somewhere.

"Grape what?"

All around us, the wedding preparations ensue. As Meat dials Edward, I watch the band haul in speakers and what appears to be a healthy collection of cymbals. The bug man sprays the perimeter of the lawn one more time. No self-respecting insect would dare step foot on the estate today.

After talking with Edward, Meat snaps his phone closed. "There's been some mistake, all right. We're supposed to have this food out in Beaufort for an event that starts in four hours." He looks disgusted and I feel some pity for him. But then it hits me like my worst nightmare: Flesh is better than no food at all. I picture the well-heeled wedding guests tonight snacking on air.

"Wait! Where's my food?" I ask, my voice rising to an unacceptably girlish pitch. "What about the St. Claire wedding?"

"Edward sends his apologies. It's on the way."

As Meat Man gets his pigs, boars, and men packed up, I ring Edward and confirm that my food is indeed on a truck that has been turned around on its route to Beaufort. Apparently, the Low Country Association of Deer Hunters was about to nosh on tofu kabobs and kale crudités. The underarms of my blue V-necked shirt are soaked with nervous sweat, and I know that I should relax, but I won't until I see said kabobs and crudités. The wedding is still hours away, but I've learned from Maurice that as soon as one fire is put out, someone will invariably light a match to your best-laid plans.

I find Maurice alone on the back veranda of the main house. He is relieved to hear I solved the crisis, but just like me, he wants to see the food trucks arrive. Meanwhile, he says, Tallie is having her bridal-party brunch in the beach gazebo. At the mention of food, my stomach reminds me that it would like a little attention, too. I decide to head to the Egret Room to see if Iris can join me for something to eat.

I stroll briskly past the lush tropical plants guarding the entrance to the suite and turn my key in the door. But when I walk into the room, something strikes me as not quite right. Directly inside the door, beside the delicate Oriental writing desk, sit two dark leather suitcases with Alitalia airline tags. My mind knows these bags—they are Avery's, of course—but I cannot think fast enough to cobble together an explanation.

And then I see him sitting in the corner armchair. Avery does not move, but instead regards me as one might an egret in the wild. Carefully, cautiously.

"Hey," I say.

"Hey, yourself."

"What in the world are you doing here? And where have you been? Don't answer that. I know where you've been. Italy," I spit out as if the country is personally responsible for Avery's trip.

"Welcome home, dear," Avery says with a small grin.

"And your phone, was it broken? Or don't they have them over there in Europe?"

Avery shifts in the chair. "You could have called me, too."

I am angry. With the near-meat disaster, hunger, and the surprise of seeing Avery, I don't need this fight. "What? You wanted me to call you? You've got to be kidding. You take off for Italy and I'm supposed to track you down and ask why?"

Standing, Avery says, "Hold on, Mace. That was a stupid thing for me to say. I came back early because I missed you. I know it was wrong to go and even more wrong not to call you. At first I was mad because you wouldn't travel with me—"

"But I told you why and you said you understood!"

Avery puts up his hands. "I know, I know, but I've got feelings, okay? And when my little trip became this big deal, I wanted to split. I might not have let it show, but talking about marriage was, well, sort of scary."

I cross my arms over my chest. "Other people get mad and then they talk about it. Your type jets to another country. That's not playing fair."

"I know, I know. I'm sorry. And once I got to the resort, I just kept putting off calling you because I knew how mad and hurt you would be." Avery moves a step closer and tries to hold my hands. I pull away and sit on the soft, striped armchair.

He follows me. "Even though I left confused and mad and all of that, can I tell you what I thought about when I was gone? Here's a hint. You were a main character."

I refuse to look at him. "You should have called. I can't believe you didn't call."

"How did Carolina's wedding turn out? Did you get the dresses in time?"

I glare at Avery, ignoring his questions. "How did you find me? How did you get on the St. Claire compound?"

"Iris filled me in." Avery sits on the ottoman in front of my chair.

"Iris told you where I was?"

"Yup," Avery says. "She called my cell and gave me your exact address. I knew you were planning to be in Hilton Head this weekend, of course, but I wouldn't have known where to find you."

"I found out you left from your mother. I kind of think she enjoyed telling me."

Avery tries to hold my hands again. I cross my arms and lean back in the chair.

"I guess this is where we have our big, serious talk," he says.

My dislike of conflict surfaces here, but I try to stuff it back down. Avery matters to me, more than anyone else, and I know I have to try to make myself understood. And I have to understand him, even though I'm still furious.

"Wait—where's Iris?" I try to stall just a bit.

Avery smiles. "Don't think Iris will save you now. She's gone out to give us a little privacy. She said when we're done making up that you can find her beside the pool."

"Which one? There are, like, five," I say, craning my neck around the room. I am irritated and I need something to eat. My stomach is caving in on itself.

"Can we talk about Iris some other time, perhaps?"

I put my hands in my lap and duck my head. "Sure. Right."

Avery nods. "Okay, so there I was in Italy. Without you."

"Yeah, that must have been really terrible. That tan looks positively life threatening," I say. I still can't stand it that he went to Europe without letting me know.

"Macie, if you don't want to talk, I can get out of here. Really."

I shut up and listen. The least I can do is let him try to charm his way out of this one. But what if he says something awful, as in *I went to Italy and you were a distant memory.* Or: *It's time we saw other people because your small-town ways have worn thin.* What would I do then? I love Avery. I really do, with all of my angry, stupid, scared heart.

"Please, go on." My voice is quiet, bracing for whatever he has to say to me.

"So there I was." Avery continues, grabbing nervously at his collar. He is wearing a watch, something he rarely does unless he is traveling. I notice he has not reset the hour hand to eastern standard time. I want to reach out and take the chrome disc from his arm and roll the hours back, just to do something nice.

"And at first, I was like, 'Look what she's missing because she's hung up on us moving things to the next level. We could be here, having fun together.' The resort was nice, the beaches were nice. Everything was just"—Avery shrugs and looks at me from the ottoman—"nice."

"That's a long way to go for just nice," I say helpfully.

"Yeah, it sure was. But here was the thing: Everywhere I went, to the bistro or to the shore, I thought less about being right and more about what you said. I thought about how I wanted you there—after all, I had picked the resort with you in mind. I thought about what you would think of this or that, what you might order. I pictured you walking next to me almost everywhere." Avery stops and looks a little lost in thought.

This is going better than I thought it would. But I will my tart tongue to take a break. I need to let him have a say.

Avery's kind green eyes smile at me. "Before, I never minded that we didn't travel together. You had your weddings and I did my thing. This time, though, I noticed other couples our age. On the beach, in the tourist stores, at the hotel. They were together, and not just for the weekend or the summer. I noticed the fat gold bands on the men's hands. They weren't afraid to take it one step further, like you want me to."

"Now wait a second, I've never pressured you to marry me," I protest, heat filling my cheeks.

" 'Pressure' might be the wrong word. How about 'strongly suggested'?" Avery laughs, squeezing my knees. He ducks his head down to look into my eyes.

"Okay, I guess you can say it's a hazard of the job. I want to get married one day. Is that so terrible?"

"Nope, it's not. It's just that you never actually said that you wanted to get married to me. You were always so closemouthed about it. It's only been recently that you have hinted, and well, just sort of talked about us being more permanent."

I take a deep breath. "Avery, why haven't you wanted to get married to me?"

He pulls his head back a bit as if I had slapped him. "What do you mean? I want to marry you. Of course I do."

When I am very surprised or shocked, I feel like the whole world is dancing right at the end of my nose. All the tears, cries of joy, and groans of millions of people dash past in a frantic parade while I try to sort out my feelings. Are they good? Bad?

This feeling is good. It is very, very good. A tiny tear plops onto my eyelashes. "Well, then, why haven't you asked?"

Avery runs one finger along my leg. The motion gives me goose bumps. "I've wanted to, believe me. I've even thought of perfect places to ask you, ways I might surprise you. But something always keeps me from going forward."

I wait, eyebrows raised. Is it my small-town upbringing? Do I not fit in enough? Is my high school French too creaky, my knowledge of wine lacking?

He continues. I hear the ocean for the first time in what seems like hours. Somewhere, a woman named Tallie waits to be married. I honestly do not care a flip.

"I wonder how you will respect me when I don't have a job," Avery says. "Or an occupation of any kind. How will you feel when you head out the door to work and I don't go anywhere or do anything meaningful? How long will it be before you lose respect for me?"

"I don't know what you are talking about. I have plenty of respect for you. I love you, Avery."

He smiles sadly. "Well, maybe you do now, but over time, that might change if I'm always dipping into Mr. Trust Fund and not earning my own money."

I rub my palms along the arms of the chair. "Okay, I didn't go to college. One day, are you going to wake up and lose respect for me about that?"

Avery laughs. "No, of course not! You started working right after high school and have taken care of yourself ever since. I admire you. So what if you didn't go to school? It's overrated anyway."

Leaning forward, I take one of his hands in mine. "So, it's kind of the same thing. These are details about our lives that we've accepted in each other already."

Tilting his head to the side, Avery looks at me. "It's fuzzy logic, but I'll accept it because it makes me feel better."

"Problem solved."

"I've actually been thinking about pursuing some type of career recently," Avery says, a small smile appearing on his face. "Any openings in the bridal biz?"

"You wouldn't last two days." I laugh. "The first time a bride pulled some stunt, you'd tell her to get lost and that would be the end of your wedding-planning career."

Avery rolls off the ottoman and onto the floor. "I'm glad you think so highly of me."

"It takes a special breed of crazy person to put up with these girls."

"Well, I don't think you're crazy, but you are good at what you do. You know that."

I am quiet for a moment. "It's funny, I complain all of the time about Maurice and my job, but it really does give me a sense of accomplishment when we get a bride married off. I like closing the file on her, knowing her special day went perfectly. Or almost perfectly in most cases."

"I wish I had that," Avery says.

I can tell that a lot of things have gone through Avery's mind while he was away. Talking about getting a job or some sort of career is a new thing for him. As much as I want to keep talking to him, I know it's just a matter of time before Maurice tracks me down. I stand and check my watch. I need to head back out to see if the caterer has arrived with my veggies.

"Hey! Where's our romantic reunion? Is talking all that I'm going to get for flying across the ocean to see you?"

"So, now you want to talk after ignoring me for a week?" I offer Avery a hand getting off the floor. "Let me get this bride married off and then I'm all yours."

"I said I was sorry for being stubborn," Avery says as he slips his hand around my waist. "I never finished telling you about those European guys with their wives. They looked so content, you know, really self-assured. Like they had made the right decision. I want to look like that. I know I can. I've already got the hard part out of the way."

I lean my head against Avery's chest. "And what's that?"

Avery pulls me toward him, kissing my neck and my chin. "I've found the bride. I can check that one off the list."

7

The Evil Bride

I have never thought much about the Middle Ages. I'm not even sure if they came before the Dark Ages or not, or what even makes it a "middle" age rather than, say, the First Age or the Ice Age or something like that. My closest experience with this entire time period comes down to a day at the Medieval Fair south of Atlanta last summer. A dusty man selling homemade mead stumbled over to me and my cousin Melissa, who was visiting from Cutter, and tried to buy one of us to be his wife. We thought it was funny until we realized he was not kidding.

Devin, the bride who follows Tallie, has definitely done her research. She adores the medieval times and has decided to plan her wedding around a theme of mutton, velvet, and braided hair seasoned with a bit of bowing and curtsying. That's what brings us to this morning's appointment. She has actually found a history weirdo who is showing her how royalty would greet other royalty and other such fun facts.

"Milady, that's right, and turn and turn. Nod the head just so. Very nice." Professor Edwin Lance sits in a director's chair and nods as Devin practices. We are in his house, a fussily neat Queen Anne near Emory. The professor is a theater director, so he has access to all sorts of velvety robes and gold-looking crowns. When no one was looking, I sat one on my head, but I'm really not supposed to do things like that.

"What do you think, maidservant?"

I snap to attention. My mind was idly pushing Devin off of a cliff. Not necessarily a high cliff. More like one with a bunch of foam balls down below so she wouldn't be too hurt by the fall.

"Milady, you are looking pretty cool," I say, waving a yawn away.

Devin shoots me an angry look because I am not playing along with her fantasy. She told me this over dinner last night at Ye Olde Thymes Restaurant. We went there for "research," but I secretly think Devin just likes to be called "wench" over and over. The waiters are endlessly offensive, all in the name of history: "Would you like some more mead, wench?" "Wench, sit on my lap, 'tis the law of the land!" By our dessert of apple crisp, I was a wench ready to retch. That was when Devin leaned over and gave me a job evaluation.

"I don't know, Macie. It seems to me like you're not a team player. What say you?"

I crumpled my napkin in my lap. Even though Devin is ridiculous, she is still the client. I hope she hasn't blabbed to Maurice.

"Well, I am sorry if I gave that impression, Devin."

"Please, Macie. Let's go over this one more time. I am your employer, so you must call me milady or madame. This is not the time for informality."

"Ah, yes. Right. Madame," I said. I desperately searched the room for the restaurant's court jester, who has a habit of popping up at our table at awkward times like this. Devin believed he liked her span of historical knowledge, but I suspected his real reason for stopping by was the low-cut empire-waist dress she wore. Maybe he would interrupt us with a juggling show.

"Well, just so you know your place. If this was the tenth century, we wouldn't even be at the same table. You're lucky, you know." Devin tossed back the last of her fermented grape drink.

The evening went on and on like that. And now, today, I am play-acting through the curtsy practice with the professor as best I can. When I get home, I call Avery. My voice gives away my mood.

"Hey, you're whining. Bad day with the Queen of the Round Table?"

"The worst. I had to open her car door and curtsy when she drove away," I wail.

"Macie, that is a bit much. She's paying you how much to go through this?"

I sigh and sniffle into the phone. "Maurice is giving me double time for days like this. I told him he owes me more."

"Well, it will be over soon," Avery says. "She gets married next week, right?"

"Yup. It will not be soon enough. I think I dislike her more than any of the others."

Avery laughs over the phone line. "You say that about all of them."

"Wanna come over? I've got the rest of the day and night off. Maurice could see that I was going to snap."

Avery says that he will leave for my place right away. I hang up and smile into the mirror over my dresser. Devin may be in love with the Middle Ages, but I am happy to be right here, in this place in time.

"So, here's my list. You have to tell me what you think," Avery says, holding up a rumpled piece of paper.

I sit at the kitchen table, looking over the movie section of the newspaper. "What list?"

"Well, ever since we had our talk in Hilton Head about my career choices, or lack thereof, I decided to take on a little project."

I reach for the list, but Avery snatches it back. "Not so fast. Let me tell you what I've done."

Pulling out a chair, Avery sits down and tries to straighten his list. Bits of salsa stick to one edge of the page.

"At first, I made a list of what I thought I wanted to be, like an architect or a doctor, you know, things like that," Avery says.

"You hate the sight of blood," I remind him.

"True. So I crossed that one off the list. Anyway, it hit me that maybe instead of me trying to fit into a career, I should try to fit a career to me." Avery stops, looking pleased with himself. "Voilà! My list of things I do well. Or, at least, sort of well."

Things I Do Well
by Avery Leland

Swim
Play tennis
Grill meat
Sail
Travel
Read magazines
Organize things
Help friends
Talk to people
Listen to people
Kiss Macie

Avery looks at me expectantly. Smiling, I hand the list back.

"Now, all I have to do is find a career that lets me use these things." He folds the list in half and taps his fingers on the table.

"That's great, honey. I especially like the last one."

Leaning over the table, Avery gives me a quick kiss. "Just so I stay in practice."

"What do you think the next step is?"

"Unfortunately, I can't exactly walk into my future boss's office and hand him this attractively rumpled piece of paper and say, 'Hire me!' "

"You know that I don't think you need to get a job to prove anything to me, Avery. But if you are doing this for you, then we just need to zero in on something you really, really want to do, and we'll be halfway there."

I think about Mr. Leland. He must have tons of contacts, even though he doesn't seem to have a job either. I'm sure one of his high-powered friends can land Avery a position somewhere. The question now is: doing what and where?

"Did you tell your parents what you are doing?"

Avery yawns. "I think my dad said something like, 'Splendid, son.' My mother overheard us and she cried for about five minutes, until cocktails. I think she just doesn't want me to move out."

I nod. His family seems strange to me sometimes. When I decided to try my luck in the big city, my mom and dad sat down at the kitchen table in Cutter and plotted out the driving routes, my budget, and rental-truck options. If they hadn't had to work the day I moved, they would have driven me and helped unpack. Avery's parents seem to have neglected a few Life 101 pointers.

I decide to call Iris. She has such a cool head and knows a lot of people. Perhaps she will have an idea.

I reach her on her cell. It's very noisy wherever she is right now.

"Macie! I'm so glad you called!" Iris's voice is almost drowned out by voices and what sounds like applause.

"Where are you?"

"I'm at Food Mart. It's the big food expo, remember?"

I wince. I'm such a rotten friend. I had forgotten. Iris baked for weeks for this opportunity. She rented a large booth for the three-day fair. Thousands of food representatives, caterers, and media reps will walk past her booth each day. Her goal is to get more media buzz about Cake Cake. Iris has been talking about expanding to the northern suburbs, and this expo could be an important step for her.

"Yeah, how is it going?"

"Not so good. You know how I hired those two models to hand out cake samples? They didn't show and I am swamped. I can't talk to clients and sling cake at the same time." A clanging bell sounds. "Man, I have to go. That's the bell signaling the end of the cooking class. We'll be overrun in a few minutes."

"Hey!" I raise my voice. "We'll come down and help you out. Give us half an hour."

Iris's relief comes across loud and clear over the noisy crowd. "Park off Spring, I'm booth number 745. I'll leave two passes at the security desk."

Avery and I hop up. I change shirts and slick on some lipstick. Avery tucks his shirt in, and we jump into his car. We roar downtown to the Food Mart, the cavernous building that is host to a different food-related trade show each month. After paying way too much to park, we dash inside to find Iris.

Inside the main exhibition area, we both pause, momentarily stunned. The room is a few football fields long and is crammed with booths, chefs, appetizer-laden trays, and thousands of people. Almost everyone is eating something or leaning over a booth to grab something to stuff in their mouths. Servers pass by carrying cheese trays, petit fours, and arugula wraps.

"I think I've never seen anything so beautiful," Avery says in a shaky voice.

"We can eat later. We've got to find that booth."

Weaving in and out of people working their jaw muscles, we quickly decide that the booth numbers are based on a highly classified system not meant to be understood by nonfoodies. Luckily, I spot a familiar slice of polka-dot cake being carried by a portly man who also is devouring a plate of hot wings.

"That cake. Where did you get it?" I ask, pointing.

"Over there, about halfway down the aisle," the man replies without stopping his chewing. "These wings are good. Want to try them?"

We politely decline and race toward the Cake Cake booth. Within seconds, we are outfitted with white aprons emblazoned with Cake Cake's name and logo. Iris straps little cake hats to our heads, shoves trays of samples in our hands, and we're off.

It takes a while to get used to strangers lunging at me with outstretched hands, but after a while, I go with the flow. Free cake is free cake. I start to feel extremely popular. I chatter, "Cake Cake, Atlanta's Best" and circulate fairly close to the booth. I send several interested people to Iris, who always appears to be chatty and friendly. I am proud of her.

I lose track of Avery. Only when he comes back to load up with more samples do I catch his eye. He rubs a speck of frosting off my chin and dashes back into the crowd. I have a warm feeling inside. Loving someone else has to be the best thing a person can do. I take a deep breath and return to the samples before I think too much about Avery and his job situation. Somewhere out there is a solution to his problem. We just have to find it or make up something brilliant.

After the final bell, Iris, Avery, and I sit on the rented tables in the Cake Cake booth. To either side of us, workers pick up used napkins and empty plates of food. It all starts over again tomorrow. I am exhausted, so I can't imagine how tired Iris must be. I chide her for not asking for help.

"Right. Like you need anyone else telling you what to do after spending your days and nights with Miss Medieval?" Iris drops her black cooking clogs to the floor and rubs her feet. "I have a heart, you know."

"Please call me milady if you don't mind, wench," I say.

Iris reaches for a water bottle. "You know, Mace, I don't know why I haven't thought of this before, but 'Devin' is one letter away from what word?"

I drop my mouth open in mock horror. "Could she be? Might this wedding be an elaborate disguise for the forces of darkness?"

Iris takes a sip and nods gravely. "We need to face the facts. Devin is in league with Satan."

"'Tis true, saucy harlot," Avery says. "Aye, I've always suspected such."

We laugh at Avery's bad English accent. "Hey, maybe we've found your calling. You can work at Ye Olde Thymes and toss pheasants to people."

Avery says, "They really do that?"

"Yup," Iris nods. "When you sit down, your waiter stands at the end of the table and throws food at you. There's no silverware, so your hands just get dirty."

"It's pretty gross," I say, "but you would look cute in those tunics the guys wear."

Rubbing her neck, Iris asks, "What's this about Avery working? I thought Rich Boy was above that."

"Very funny, Cake Lady, but I've been searching for a job. A real career," Avery says. He sits up straight and tightens an invisible tie.

Iris gives me a look only a best friend can and then flashes Avery a bright smile. "I think that's great. What are you thinking of doing?"

I start to launch into a quick speech about his many prospects, but Avery says something quietly I cannot hear.

"What was that?" I ask.

"I said, I have a job. It starts tomorrow."

"How can you? I mean, that's great." I sputter like a broken faucet. "But why didn't you say anything before—at my apartment—when we were talking—"

"Macie, why don't you let him tell you about it?" Iris gives me the look again.

"Thanks, Iris." Avery stands up from the table and puts his hands in his pockets. "It's nothing, really, but I met a man tonight who makes those gourmet Chattahoochee Chocolates. You know, the ones with bits of peaches in them and everything?"

We both nod. Chattahoochee Chocolates are really tasty. Named after the river that runs north of Atlanta, the candy bars fall into the luxury chocolate category. I had a bride once who gave each guest one as a party favor.

"Anyway, Chattahoochee Chocolates just lost their number-one candy-bar tester. He burned his mouth and had surgery, and well, it's a really sad story."

"Avery, you are going to taste candy bars? For a living?" I wave my hands in the air. This is not part of the plan: Boyfriend ingests loads of sugar, gains fifty pounds, and becomes too consumed with eating to marry his long-suffering true love.

"Well, that's not all it is. I have to help brainstorm new flavors, develop marketing strategies, and do consumer research. The company's going national next year."

I am still speechless. Almost. "I still don't understand how a chance meeting with a candy-bar maker could lead to a job offer. That's not how it's supposed to work." Iris gives me a withering look. I know I'm not going to win Supportive Girlfriend of the Year for acting like this, but Avery needs to get serious.

"Right, right. I know that, but Ted and I really hit it off. Turns out he's a fraternity brother from the Clemson chapter and we're about the same age. I gave him some cake and we started talking. I told him the last few Chattahoochee Chocolates I ate were a little dry or something. So he gets all interested and asks me lots of questions. Apparently, they had switched cocoa-liquor suppliers, so I said, 'Man, you gotta switch back.' And now I'm going in tomorrow to taste test the production line."

"Won't you get sick? That's a lot of candy," I say.

"You chew and think about the flavors on your tongue, and then you spit it out. After that, I enter my comments into a laptop that transmits to the floor supervisor. If at any time I don't think the product is up to snuff, I can shut down production," Avery says with a flourish.

It is beginning to dawn on me that Avery is excited about this new job. Although I had thought he would find something more traditional, I decide to let it go. The cleanup crews move in to get everything ready for the next morning. A floor sweeper walks by pushing a broom, capturing used Popsicle sticks and discarded business cards. I feel a heaviness watching the trash pile move slowly past us.

"So, this is legitimate, right? Candyland's not a scam or anything?" I ask. So much for letting things go.

"That is ridiculous, Macie, and you know it. Give me some credit," Avery says and looks away from me.

"Ah, I think I've got to get a thing over there, down that hall," Iris says, quickly grabbing her purse and keys. She gives me a hug and disappears toward the front doors.

I sit on the table, angry and hurt. Part of me is mad because things come easy to Avery. But candy-bar tasting? Give me a break. It sounds like something only an eight-year-old would dream about late at night. I thought Avery wanted a real job; one with an employee manual and a confusing menu of health plans. I don't care how much money he makes or what his title is, but his new job should be something where he can grow, learn new things, and be promoted—in short, a real job like everyone else. What does the head candy-bar taster shoot for? More chocolate sprinkles?

"So, are you going to let me in on your sulk or do I have to guess what is wrong with you?" Avery walks over to the table.

I lift my head and look over at him. "You just don't get it."

Avery's mouth is set in an unhappy line. "No, I suppose not."

My mind whirls. I think of Avery in Italy, watching the married couples. I see us playing tennis or walking down Peachtree Street in Midtown. I picture our hike last year in the mountains of north Georgia. These are all good memories. Why doesn't he want to make them permanent by finding something more mature, something with a future? I thought Avery wanted to get ready for marriage by starting a career. This seems like a backward way to go about it.

"Well, if you aren't going to talk, I gotta get going. I have to be at the Chattahoochee factory at eight in the morning."

I slide off the table and glumly follow Avery down the almost deserted aisles of the expo center. The smell of fried grease and sugar sticks to everything. I want to gag. I am tired of food. I'm even tired of cake.

We are halfway back to my apartment when I try to say something, anything, to break the silence between us. "I hope you have a good day tomorrow, I really do. But I guess I was thinking that you were looking for a more, um, grown-up job. You seemed so serious about finding a career—something that you could really sink your teeth into. No pun intended."

Avery laughs. There is a loosening of anger between us and it feels good. I just hope we can get through this new stage in his life without always snapping at each other. I vow silently to be more supportive of Avery. If needed, I will eat Chattahoochee Chocolates by the case.

Devin's day in the Middle Ages finally comes. Before the first stein of mead is even poured and every guest is given a leg of mutton to tote around, I can no longer bear the sight of our fair bride without breaking into tiny hives. The final straw comes right before the ceremony when she demands I announce to the guests that they should bow when she enters the quaint outdoor chapel we've rented about two hours north of the city.

"Devin—" I start to say before she cuts me off with an imperious wave.

"Mistress—" she hisses, the gold crown taped onto her cruel head bobbing slightly. I hope fervently that it will tumble off during her low curtsy to her intended at the end of the aisle. We hide at the back of the chapel, waiting for our cue from the lute player.

"Whatever. Mistress Devin, I don't think that would be a very good idea. Americans don't really know how to bow. It might look awkward on the video."

The bride taps her red fingernails on her chin and thinks about it. I know Maurice is minutes away from calling for her to enter the chapel, so my stalling has a slim chance of working. I do not relish the thought of asking a chapel full of people who were forced to wear costumes for the wedding to go the extra mile and bow to this maniac.

"You know, Maidservant Macie, you have a point there. We colonialists have forgotten the ways of the motherland. Let us go forthwith unto my man."

I help turn the bride and her heavy, embroidered dress as we leave our little spot. Rather than a veil, she wears a piece of fabric that connects to her crown. It drapes down her back, where one long fake braid sticks out. The dress, an empire waist with gold-flecked ruching, is finished at the sleeves in gold-braid frogging. Devin's breasts are pushed up so high that a costume accident is bound to happen sooner or later.

During the ceremony, I sit in the back of the chapel. Once I've adjusted my velvet-and-brocade dress and the fake braids are safely thrown over my shoulder, I reflect that there has probably never been a worse bride with whom we've worked. More selfish, probably. More vain, most likely. But all in all, people like Devin give weddings a bad name. I don't think she ever talked about her fiancé. It was all about the wedding trip to—where else?—England and Scotland. It was all about the clothes and the horse-drawn carriages, the mead, and the famous lutenist. To Devin, marriage seemed like a stage play complete with costumes, directions, and grand entrances.

I lean back in the worn pew and close my eyes. The couple repeats their handwritten vows in loud, practiced voices. I think of Avery, into his second week at Chattahoochee Chocolates, testing chocolate and helping write marketing copy. He likes the job, and he and Ted get on like brothers. I have calmed down about the whole thing. There may be a future there for him after all.

Maybe one day, we'll repeat vows to each other. But when that day comes to me in my mind, I never think about the wedding. It is always the next day that I imagine. Day number two as husband and wife. It is that day I think about now, amid the fakery, rented costumes, and forced historical accuracy. When I marry Avery, it will not be for vain show. It will be for life.

8

The Rogue Bride

Maurice is always telling me that we do the impossible. We marry off Atlanta's rich and beautiful, no matter what their strange fascinations or weird passions. And we do it with a smile on our faces, the correct fork in our hands, and our heads tilted just so. In short, we make the bride's wedding day seem like a dream when they come to us, checkbooks and date books in hand. Then, we work like mad for months to make the nightmare happen.

When Eliza got engaged on a trip to Milan last week, her first call was to her mother and then to Maurice. All was well in bridal land until Maurice asked Eliza her preferred dates. Did she want a year from now? Nine months? Six was, well, you know, pushing it but he could *try* to nudge things around.

Eliza's reply was two weeks.

Maurice told me he sputtered into his cell phone and coughed a bit. Then he asked her if she was serious. Apparently, Eliza was incredibly serious and mentioned a signing bonus that made Maurice's heart sing. If he pulls this off, he walks away with a handsome six-figure check. All for a little sweat and panic. When he calls me, I offer a silent guess as to who is going to sweat and panic the most.

Without a doubt, Eliza will be one of the "rogue" brides who really throws us for a loop. Rogue brides do things differently; they buck our careful system. It's not that I can't handle a challenge. Like all jobs, this one has its dull points. One can only hear so many renditions of "Trumpet Voluntary" and see so many bouquet tosses. So, a different kind of wedding with a different timetable could be something new. And new is good, almost all of the time.

But this wedding challenge is falling on the heels of Avery's transition to worker bee, which has already given me a wee bit of stress. I know I encouraged him in his pursuit of a job, but I didn't know how it would all unfold. What has happened is much more perplexing.

It turns out that Avery likes to work. He really, really likes to work. I should have figured it out, I suppose. He pursues tennis with a single-minded determination. And he certainly pursued me when we met at my apartment building two years ago. It could stand to reason that he would attack a paying job with similar gusto.

Avery gets to the Chattahoochee Chocolates plant around seven in the morning. Some days, he will not leave until seven o'clock in the evening. Ever since he started, he has been given more and more responsibility at the company. Not only does he test candy bars, work on marketing strategy, and develop consumer focus groups, but he's also been dabbling in something called "presscake production schedules" and is pulling together a competitive analysis for the new candy-bar rollout. He also goes on and on about something called "conching," which I gather is a type of chocolate kneading.

I'm not sure what's really bugging me, but I do know one thing: Avery has not brought up our future since he took the job at Chattahoochee Chocolates. Since it was his idea to find a career, I am decidedly not mentioning it, but I wonder where his passion has flown for moving things forward with us. Have I been replaced by a chocolate confection?

"It's addictive, Macie," Avery tells me over a late supper. I have just had my first meeting with Eliza and I'm exhausted. We set up flowcharts, "to do" lists, and wrote her wedding plan for the next fourteen days.

"What is?" I ask idly, playing with my napkin. We are on his parents' veranda, where the menu is pork tenderloin and a green salad. It's too hot for me to eat something warm. I play with my salad and gulp down ginger iced tea.

"The candy industry. Haven't you been listening, Mace?"

I smile guiltily. "Sorry. You were saying?"

Avery reaches over for my hand. "I was just going to bore you with how much sugar the average American consumes, but I can see that you won't be impressed because you are off in wedding world. Am I right?"

"Wedding world it is. You would not believe the latest," I say.

"Try me."

I take a sip of tea and then press the cold glass to my forehead. "Okay, sit-down dinner for two hundred, imported Belgian dress, and twelve-piece orchestra."

Avery drops my hand and helps himself to another piece of tenderloin. "So? You could do that with your eyes closed."

"Did I mention she wants it in two weeks?"

Avery's laughs and then looks thoughtful. "That would be like rolling out the new Chattahoochee chocolate bar and getting it on the shelves in fourteen days. Can't be done."

"Well, Maurice says we can. And he's willing to share his bonus with me if we do." I frown slightly. "I mean, when we do."

"It seems to me like there are less stressful jobs you could have," Avery says. "Like maybe air-traffic controller? Brain surgeon? Just some ideas."

"Yeah, I know what you mean. But Maurice has been giving me more and more responsibility lately. He seems to trust me. And I haven't let him down. Yet."

"Speaking of responsibility, did I tell you that Ted wants me to go on some sales calls to big distributors next month? We need to build momentum for the new bar."

"That's great! They really like you, Avery."

He sits back in his chair and crosses his legs under the table. "Well, Ted's a really smart guy. I've learned a lot from watching him. Did you know he started his first business in high school? He had a lawn service and bought his first truck and trailer the month before he could legally drive."

"Wow, I was working at Happy Hams at his age."

Avery looks glum. "I think I was at tennis camp then. Or vacationing with my folks."

I try to cheer him up. I reach for the tea pitcher and pour both of us another glass. "What's important is that you are doing something now. You have a job that you're good at." I lift my glass in the air, faking a bit of lightheartedness. "To the future."

Looking only slightly less depressed, Avery raises his glass as well. "To us, and to the future."

Eliza and I meet the next morning at Lily's Finer Dresses in Buckhead. Normally, I would not even walk through the door of a haughty dress store like Lily's and ask for the impossible, but they owe us one. About six months ago, we brought in a bride who was a tad indecisive. She ended up purchasing three wedding dresses, each costing several thousand dollars apiece. When she was done with that, she bought all ten bridesmaids' dresses from Lily, along with shoes, undergarments, and her veil. Maurice has been on Lily's happy list ever since.

Lily's shop is in an old mansion that has been covered with numerous coats of paint, making every surface rather bumpy. I grasp the knob of the old front door and pull once or twice until it opens with a groan. A simple bell chime announces our arrival. Lily emerges from one of the various rooms to meet us, walking spryly across the uneven floors.

"Ah, Macie, so good to see you again. It's been a while, no?" Lily is a woman of indeterminate age and the owner of an indeterminate accent. She kisses me on both cheeks.

"And this must be the bride? Ah, let me take a look at you, dearest."

Eliza shyly turns in a circle and self-consciously pats her short brown hair. "Nice to meet you, ma'am."

"The pleasure is all mine. Now, let's have a seat, shall we? I understand from Maurice that we have a delicate timing issue."

While we settle into the flowered love seat in Lily's office, I look at the black-and-white bride photos displayed on the light blue plaster walls. Many of the brides are ours. Their gleaming teeth and perfectly sculpted hair reach out from the wall and seem to mock me. It's like a most-wanted list of bad brides. Shuddering slightly, I look away. Darby's on there, and so is Francie.

Lily's reference to the "delicate timing issue" catches me off guard. It has not occurred to me to ask why this wedding has to take place in two weeks. I am so used to brides demanding this flower shipped from Louisiana and that tartlet flown in from San Francisco, it completely escaped my attention to wonder why Eliza wanted this wedding to take place in fourteen days.

Now it all makes sense. I look discreetly at Eliza's waist, but that tells me nothing. She's as thin as a brunch crepe. They all are. I tend to gain a little poundage in my hips when I've had too many sweets, but my brides are more disciplined. Well, if Eliza is rushing a wedding to cover up a little oopsie, then maybe she's not so disciplined.

I try to imagine her fiancé. Does he want to get married? Were they planning on it and the baby speeded things up? Or did he enter this flurry of wedding planning reluctantly? Little Eliza was getting more interesting by the minute. We did not know each other very well yet. After all, she'd hired us two days ago. It would be just a matter of time before she spilled the beans. She was probably dying to tell someone about her premarital indiscretion. It might as well be—

"And I understand that she will be healthy enough to attend the ceremony?" Lily is patting Eliza's hand and offering a tissue. I snap to attention and away from my soap-opera dreams.

"Yes, his mother only ever wanted to see us married. We've been together since we were fourteen. And this might be her last chance." Eliza sobs into her hands. "They say she could go at any time during the surgery. She's been so sick this year. We don't know how long she will be with us."

I feel like such a jerk. I lean over to my bride and rub her back. "I'm so sorry, Eliza. I didn't know."

She looks up and wipes her eyes with the tissue. "And the worst thing is, everyone thinks we're having the wedding so quickly because I'm pregnant."

I shake my head sympathetically, sensing I have sunk to a new low. "People are so tacky."

Lily puts on a bright face. "Well, let's solve at least one problem. The dress." She stands and walks toward an antique armoire, where shoes and veils spill out in a creamy pageant of satin and tulle. A sagging rack holds five or six dresses crowded together, each one encased in a thick, plastic carrying case. I know these are dresses Lily has ordered over the years that were never picked up or paid for—a sort of gown graveyard.

We start trying on the dresses. Lily is very hands-on, unzipping and tying, fluffing and pulling in fabric, so there's not much for me to do. I sit in another flowered chair and daydream lightly. I imagine the type of dress I would select if I were getting married. Perhaps I would go for a 1920s kind of look with a Nottingham lace veil. Or I might go modern, selecting a thin, organza silhouette gown. There's always traditional, too, a strapless, silk A-line or something more sweet like the ballet-skirt look. The choices are deliciously endless.

But in Eliza's case, poor Eliza with the dying mother-in-law, she does not have choices. Since the wedding is in twelve days, she has to go with what she can get. And that might be the peau de soie dress with a rear inverted pleat she pulls on now.

"Oh, Eliza, what a beautiful dress," I say, sitting up.

And it is. The bodice fits her tiny frame nicely, while the chapel-length train touches the floor in a dramatic arch. Lily adds a scalloped-edge tulle veil with pearl details. The entire effect is lovely. I quickly stand and grab a bouquet of fake flowers from Lily's armoire. Thrusting them into Eliza's hands, I grab my digital camera. Maybe we can get a few shots for her future mother-in-law.

When I am finished, Lily takes up the hem with straight pins so that her seamstress can make the final touches to the dress. This will be rushed, too, and will cost a little, but that's what we have to do. The dress itself is offered to us at a discount since it is a season or two old. Lily seems pleased to have the garment taken off of her hands and kisses us both as we leave.

As we drive to our next appointment at the caterer's, I try to figure out where Eliza gets her money. She seems nice enough, not insufferable like many of our brides-to-be. I sneak glances over at her as she flips through a bridal-planning book. Her clothes are well made, her nails tastefully manicured, and her shoes look expensive, but not in a flashy way. I decide it must be old money.

I ask Eliza about her fiancé. "It sounds like you have been together for a long time."

"That's right. We met the first day of freshman year. It's always been just Ben and me. Ever since he asked me in geometry class if I needed a ride home and then admitted he couldn't drive yet."

"That's cute." I had about ten boyfriends freshman year, each one lasting no more than a week or two.

"People ask me if I ever get curious about dating other people, but it always just made sense, you know?"

"I actually do understand what you mean. Now, anyway," I reply. "But a few years ago, I wouldn't have gotten it."

Eliza closes her wedding planner and turns to me with a grin on her face. "Macie, are you married?"

"Um, no. Not yet, anyway. I have a boyfriend. His name is Avery."

"Are ya'll serious?"

"We're getting there," I answer, slowing to turn onto Northside Drive. "He's just started a new job, so when that settles down, we're supposed to, you know, move things forward." I groan to myself. What a dorky thing to say. Why not just tattoo the word "insecure" on my forehead?

"So, this Avery is it? He's the one?"

I glance out of the car window to the posh homes lining the street. Each yard is green and perfectly trimmed and mulched. Avery's house looks much the same. My gardening efforts extend to the pair of nearly dead geraniums that have been cast out onto my tiny balcony due to their insistence in dropping leaves.

"I think so."

We drive in silence for a minute or two, and then I decide to throw a question back to Eliza. "What do you do when you're not planning a wedding in less than two weeks?"

Eliza laughs, a surprisingly throaty, deep kind of laugh. "Well, when I'm not torturing wedding planners, I work for a nonprofit foundation."

I am impressed. It sounds really important. "That's great. What do you do for them?"

"We have a recreation angle to our mission, so we look for ways to engage inner-city children and those without access to parks or sports. We run camps all over the country. It's a really great job."

"What kind of camps?"

"Well, soccer, tennis, basketball—you name it. Whatever the community tells us they need. My job is to meet with community leaders and talk about what they want for their area."

I am glad that Eliza found us. I enjoy working with her, even though she is a rogue bride. I ask her the name of the foundation.

"The Seller Foundation."

It is only later, when I drop Eliza off at her home, that I realize her name and the foundation's name are the same. Of course, I knew her last name, but it didn't hit me until I was driving back toward home. The concern for her fiancé's mother, the ease with which she accepted the graveyard dress, the philanthropy job—it all made sense. Eliza was a rogue bride in more ways than one. Rogue does not always mean bad; sometimes it just means nice.

Before I head home with an early dinner of Thai takeout, I decide to drop by the Chattahoochee Chocolates plant and visit Avery. He gave me the grand tour the week he started, so I sort of know my way around. The plant is near West End in a once down-and-out industrial area newly populated with lofts and shiny new cars. I pull into the employee lot and head inside. The air-conditioning feels perfectly chilled against my hot skin. Just the walk from the cool car to the cool building is a stretch. Outside, the sun is shining like a blowtorch, and for the first time, I look forward to fall and the changing season.

The receptionist calls Avery and then returns to stuffing envelopes. I wait, walking around the small lobby and reading the press clippings framed on the wood-paneled walls. I learn Chattahoochee Chocolates has won the Confectionary Newcomer Award and the Food Traders New Start medal, and has been voted "Best Candy Bar in Atlanta" by the alternative weekly newspaper four years in a row. I look around, hoping for a free-sample tray of something chocolaty. It is hard to read about candy for more than a few minutes without wanting to taste it.

I hear a noise and look up, expecting Avery. Instead, it is Ted, whom I've met just once. I already like him, though. He talks superfast and uses his hands constantly to illustrate his point. He also seems to really care for Avery, and that makes me happy.

"Hey Macie, how's it going?" Ted asks cheerily.

"Good. Just finished up with a bride for the day."

"Cool. Avery's around back. He wants to show you something."

"It's not candy tasting, is it? Because I have to warn you, you don't want to turn me loose back there in the lab. I could be dangerous."

Ted laughs and opens the front door of the lobby leading back to the parking lot. "Don't worry. I won't let you near the stuff."

I follow him back outside, into the heat and the sun. Ted leads me around the back of the building, where three loading docks stand ready for shipping. Wads of newspaper have blown against the chain-link fence and weathered to a dull beige. As we climb the stained stairs to the first loading dock, I catch sight of Avery inside the bay. It looks like he's playing tennis. I give Ted a wry smile. "You pay him for this?"

"Just wait," Ted says.

When we get closer, I can see that Avery is gripping a racket head in one hand and extending the grip toward a boy. Two boys, actually. They look about nine or ten years old, and they watch Avery with wide eyes. A man in a white T-shirt stands nearby, his arms crossed over his chest.

"Now, see, what you do here is shake hands with the racket," Avery says to the smaller boy.

The boy giggles. "Why I wanna do that?"

"Because you have to hold the racket the right way or you can't hit the ball."

"Let me try," the taller boy says.

"Let's give Antwon a try first," Avery says with a calm voice.

I watch the two boys and Avery for a few minutes before I am able to catch his eye and smile. The boys each get a chance to hit a few balls Avery gently tosses their way. The man, their father, chases down stray balls. When Antwon thumps a ball solidly out of the bay doors and into the parking lot, Avery calls it a day.

"If your dad lets you, we can practice tomorrow," Avery says. He shakes hands with the two boys solemnly. "Remember, tennis is your friend."

The boys nod, and repeat after him with seriousness, "Tennis is our friend."

"That's enough, boys. Let Avery get back to work now," the boys' father says. The boys scamper off to their bikes propped up against a chain-link fence nearby. "Bye, Daddy!" they call, spinning around the parking lot and popping wheelies as they pedal away.

"Get on home to Mama. Go straight there."

With a last giggle, the boys leave the parking lot, looking both ways before they roll across the street. A tractor trailer lumbers by and turns into the next lot.

The smell of exhaust lingers over the loading dock. A stray dog lopes by on the sidewalk, head down and ears back.

"Macie, this is Louis, Antwon and Damon's father," Avery says.

I nod hello. "They seemed like they were getting the hang of it."

"Antwon, he'll do whatever Damon does. And he'll try to do it better," Louis says.

Ted reaches for the tennis racket and takes a couple of air serves. "That's me and my brother. Always competing." He tosses the racket to Avery and walks back inside with Louis.

Thinking idly about children and their pluckiness—the boys' determination to learn tennis even in the punishing heat of a summer afternoon—made me think. Somewhere in life we lose that determination. Or do we? Avery was starting anew with his job at Chattahoochee Chocolates. Iris dreamed up Cake Cake from her first tiny, cramped kitchen. Maurice practically willed himself to please every bride and nearly always did.

I walk over to pick up a stray tennis ball that had rolled under a beat-up dolly. As I squeeze the ball in my hand, my thoughts tumble over and over in my head. Avery wants to please me by having a job, by bringing home a paycheck. He thinks unless he walks out the door to work just like I do that I will not respect him. Will he admire me if all I do is work for Maurice, grumpily tossing brides for a living? It is possible that he will eventually lose interest in me for being just kind of average. A trickle of sweat snakes down my spine. The heat out here is making me crabby.

"I gotta go, Avery." I place the ball in his hand.

"Not so fast," he says and grabs for my waist. "We're all alone out here. Don't you find loading docks incredibly sexy?"

I kiss him and smell the sweet saltiness that is Avery after a few ground strokes. I start to feel lost in our own secret moment and then I remember Eliza. She is at home waiting for me to confirm a few last-minute appointments for tomorrow. I have to get on the phone. "I need a lip rain check."

Avery presses the side of his face against my neck. "I'll give you a Chattahoochee chocolate bar not to go to whichever bride is freaking out."

"Oh, so my affection is worth just a few ounces of chocolate?"

Avery lets me go. He picks up his racket and points it toward me. "That's *premium* chocolate, honey bun."

Before I go, I pause on the dock stairs. "That was pretty neat, you teaching those kids the basics."

"I walked outside earlier to meet some of the guys on the line, and Damon and Antwon were here. They live up the street," Avery says. "They were just playing around and I thought about my racket in the car. You know how I never go anywhere without it."

I nod. This is true. Avery is incredibly prepared when it comes to playing his sport.

"So, I asked them if they wanted to hit a couple of balls and that was it." Avery looks down at his racket. "I really think I could teach them the game, get them started."

"That's sweet. But don't get too disappointed if they don't like it. Kids that age change their minds a lot."

"I know, I know," Avery says. He looks thoughtful. "Maybe I could have been a gym teacher, you know? Or a tennis coach."

"My bride Eliza works for a foundation that brings sports to inner-city kids. They host camps all over the country." I am proud to have a bride who does more than wear an extremely heavy engagement ring.

"Really? That's great. I never thought of that. I guess some kids just don't have parks and tennis courts and—"

"Their own swimming pool? Yes, it's true, Avery. Not everyone had a barn filled with ponies, either."

"You're such a jerk. We only had two ponies. One for me and one for a friend," Avery says, menacing me with the racket.

"I'm out of here. You'd better get back to work or they'll dock your pay, college boy." I walk down the steps.

"What, you mean I'm supposed to be getting paid?" Avery calls out after me.

I stick my tongue out at him and yell back, "I'd take my wages in chocolate if I were you."

I stretch out on the couch, the cordless phone in my hand. It's Saturday evening and I have yet to remove my sensible wedding-planner suit. I kick off my pinchy little pumps and scrunch up my toes. I could use a neck massage, but Avery is across town. He answers on the first ring.

"I was hoping it was you. How did it go?"

"Oh, Avery, it was beautiful. It was one of our best."

"That's great. Was Eliza happy?"

I unhook the top button of my silk shirt, cradling the phone to my shoulder. "She cried, the groom cried, his mother cried. It was wonderful. His mom made it down the aisle. Really slowly, but she did it. And the preacher had this great talk about blessings and I just about lost it. That never happens to me."

"See? I told you that you could do it."

"And the best part was that Maurice was barely involved. He was there, of course, to make sure the caterer did his thing and that the champagne was chilled to a pleasant forty-five degrees. But he really didn't need to because I had everything under control. Even when the cellist was late and the prelude had to start without her, I just bumped Bach for Mozart and it looked like we meant to do it." Take that, wedding fiends, I say to myself and settle into the couch cushions.

"Before long, you'll be the sought-after wedding planner in town. Maurice who?" Avery says over the line.

"Nah, I still don't have his presence. Brides just feel better when they're around him. I'm too loosey-goosey."

Avery yawns. "Well, Damon and Antwon each brought a friend to the lesson today. We had enough for the most unruly doubles game ever played."

I laugh, picturing the two brothers jockeying for position on the court. After Avery's impromptu lesson, they came back the next day and the day after that. Avery made them a deal that he would give them a lesson each Saturday if they would find something else to do besides hang around the loading dock on summer afternoons. They met for the first time last Saturday at the public courts a mile from Chattahoochee Chocolates.

"I really think Damon has what it takes," Avery says. "He's got this something in his eyes. Like he really gets it. Louis says Damon walks around the house bouncing a ball on the strings of his racket. I taught him that."

"I know," I say, stifling a laugh. Avery sounds so proud of the boys.

"Well, you just never know where life is going to take you. If you had told me a year ago I would be working for a candy-bar company and teaching tennis to boys on the side, I would have said you were crazy."

Turning on my side, I reflect that just as Avery is doing something he's never done before, I have been venturing into unknown turf as well. Planning a two-week wedding stretched my organizational skills past their breaking point. I had sticky notes on top of sticky notes. Voice mails to myself. Three different alarm settings on my watch to remind me of appointments. And through it all, I tried to be tender toward Avery and not so grumpy. He is really trying to build a life for himself. And maybe one for us. I say good night and close my tired eyes, just for a moment. If I dream this night of weddings or brides or towering cakes, I do not remember. My last thought is of Eliza's bouquet. I picture catching it after the toss, the wide-eyed daisies tumbling end over end until they are safe in my outstretched hands. When I know all is well, it is then that I fall asleep.

9

The Greedy Bride

Before I became a wedding director's assistant, I did not know a thing about the fabled sweet-tea spoon. Silly girl that I was, I was not aware that a regular teaspoon, adequately stirred around a glass full of the sugary brew known as sweet tea, would fail to produce desirable results.

But it does, and the brides all want them: sweet-tea spoons. It's a long-handled version of the normal item every person probably uses a least once a day. Sweet-tea spoons are an addition to a flatware set and are given out when serving sweet tea or laid ahead when setting the table. They can be plain or fancy or monogrammed along with the rest of the set, and are always easy to pick out because of the long, narrow neck. The spoons almost never fit into traditional silver serving trays, and must be stored separately in a soft, fabric bag.

The sweet-tea spoon is an elusive beast. Not all flatware companies make them. After the traditional five-piece place setting—salad fork, dinner fork, teaspoon, large spoon, knife—a flatware company might make a special dessert fork or espresso spoon. They do not always bow to the whims of southern girls who demand their sweet-tea spoons.

My latest bride, Tika, must have her spoons. And they had better match her set or a certain overworked wedding-planner assistant will hear about it and a certain famed wedding planner will grouch and grumble. I am dispatched to research all available patterns containing the aforementioned spoon.

On an overcast Monday morning, I glide around one of Atlanta's better department stores, hoping to find something I have not seen before. Perhaps a new line or a new pattern will emerge that has been blessed with the golden spoon. I stake out my territory in the china department, every footfall landing in lush, scarlet carpeting. The overhead lighting is bright but not garish. The dozens of china patterns sit in recessed cabinets with soft accent lights. Crystal wineglasses and goblets sparkle nearby in tall, stand-alone display cases. Every detail pushes tradition and consumption. My brides usually love this department above all others.

Tika is no exception. She has spent weeks combing through the department stores and crafting her gift registries with intense concentration. She seems to take the prospect of receiving many, many gifts very seriously. I frequently field phone calls like the one I received this morning before breakfast.

"Macie!"

"Hey, Tika. What's up?"

"I'm on-line going over the registries. I'm thinking that maybe I should add dessert dishes and ice-cream bowls to my registry at Homespun. Maybe some crepe plates, too."

"Don't you have something similar at another store?" I held back a yawn. I needed some orange juice to wake up.

The sound of typing came over the line. "Of course I have. I have those cute clear dishes at Allen and Berring, and I registered for fruit bowls—the little footed ones—at Pantry. Why?"

"Um, that's a lot of dessert dishes if you add more to the registry." I did some quick math. "If you receive them all, you'd have somewhere around sixty dessert plates and bowls, not counting your everyday dishes and formal china."

"Macie, Macie, Macie," Tika sighed into the phone. "I know you are, like, single and everything, but just try to follow me, okay? Sometimes a hostess wants a variety of dishes to choose from. I might want the footed bowls for a summer party and then the clear bowls for later in the year. Can't you just see a cloud of angel food cake and strawberries in the Pantry bowls? Or maybe something chocolate in the Allen and Berring dishes?"

"I guess I hadn't thought of it like that," I said.

"That's kind of obvious." Tika sounded distracted. "So, are you and Maurice still going to be sticklers about not including my registries in the wedding invitations?"

I sat up straight. We had been through this before. "Absolutely. That just isn't done, Tika. It looks, um, like you're asking for presents."

She inhaled quickly, "But I was thinking, what if we print out the stores where I'm registered on pretty little magnets that match the invitations?"

"Magnets?"

"So the guests can stick it on their refrigerator or something. It will remind them they need to shop for my present."

"Tika, no. We're not going to do that. People find out your registries the old-fashioned way—they call your mother or sister or your best friend."

Tika pouted silently for a beat or two and then said, "Well, we can always revisit this discussion a little later on. I gotta go."

Tika grew up in a nowhere town somewhere outside of Atlanta. When she was fifteen, her mother had a hunch and played a combination of her and Tika's birthday dates in a huge lottery drawing.

The resulting payday set the family up for several lifetimes. The funny thing is, Tika is gunning for every present she can get her hands on—it's starting to wear on Maurice, and that almost never happens.

Without turning to the folders under my arm, I would venture a guess that there are ten showers planned for Tika (two couples' showers, eight women-only showers), two brunches, and one girls' beach weekend. By almost all standards, this number is excessive. It would be different if Tika had recently moved from one state to another and had two sets of friends. Or if her family was extremely close-knit but spread all over the country. Neither of those situations applies. Tika just wants it all. I can't figure it out.

Running my hand along the first china shelf, I read the label: Fox Manor. The plain gray china is etched with delicate dark gray scallops. We had a bride last year—Maria? Shontelle?—register for this pattern. To the left of this cabinet stand the flatware cases. Each wooden case holds four large drawers that slide out with a soft whoosh.

I start with the first drawer. From across the room, I smile and wave to Jasmine, the floor manager. She knows if I need something, I will call her. I grasp the handle and pull, revealing shiny, just-polished flatware with 18/8 stainless steel handles. The real silver is in a locked cabinet near Jasmine's elegant little Chippendale-style desk that sits in the center of the crystal display.

The first pattern is another favorite with our brides: Tangelle. There are no sweet-tea spoons in this one. The next four patterns, Regale, Trotter Lane, Buffington, and Laura are by a British company. They all cost an arm and a leg. No spoons. I move faster now. Drake, Butterfly, Hampton Cove, Sundown. Raised rosebuds blur, fleur-de-lis edging speeds by, brushed stainless accents whirl past my eyes. A person can look at only so much flatware.

Tika wants stainless for every day. Her fancier dinner parties will be served with real silver in a pattern we picked out last week. Of course, Tika giving dinner parties assumes that she will still have friends after soaking all of them for multiple shower presents and wedding gifts.

Maurice does not give our brides nicknames. I do, of course, as a way to keep them straight. It becomes difficult to remember all of the Ansleys, Ambers, and Allisons, but I can always recall the Evil Bride or the Horse Bride. Maurice thinks this is petty of me, but he does not spend the time with them that I do. He's always on the phone, charming this shop owner or that caterer. I am in the trenches, helping the brides pick out Crème Peach or Elegant Apricot for their wedding-day lipstick. I assist the Tikas of the wedding world with registering for enough pots, pans, tablecloths, linen napkins, and ice-cream dishes to open a small café.

Tika, of course, is the Greedy Bride.

I do not know why she wants so many parties, so many presents. It's not like she can't just call up Lotto Mom and order anything she wants. I have been to Tika's house, I've seen her little appetizer dishes and her milk-glass vase collection. Tika has nice things already. Not that a bride wants to keep her old baking pans when she marries. I understand wanting new household items when beginning life with your love, but it's not like Tika lives in a hovel and she has to surround herself with nice, new things immediately.

All of our efforts to convince Tika to tactfully limit her number of showers have been met with silence or worse. She even accused me of being jealous that she was going to have so many parties. We were shopping at La Pantelle, one of those useless home stores that carries about two things and they both cost four hundred dollars.

"I don't know, Macie, it seems like your status as an unmarried female is clouding your judgment."

"My what?" I put down a silver salt mill, but not before gawking at the price tag: $136.

"You know, how you're single and all. Waiting for Mr. Right to save you. Well, maybe you think I'm having too many parties because you are so far away from being married yourself."

Tika carries herself with confidence and flashes a frequent smile when speaking. Then, with a flip of her glossy, dark brown hair, Tika will spew some awful statement that makes you feel as if you've been slapped. I've seen her do it to salesclerks, her hairdresser, and the owner of the car-repair shop where she takes her little German coupe. I guess it was only a matter of time before she turned on me.

"Tika," I said, my voice squeaky. "What did you just say?"

By this time, she had already moved on to the forty-dollar tea towels imported from Switzerland. "Hmmm?" she said, not looking at me.

"You know what you said, and it's untrue. And mean," I said, trying not to cry. Tika does not know a thing about Avery—she doesn't even know I am dating someone—but what she said stung anyway.

"Well, I am sorry if it hurt your feelings, but I just have to wonder why you are so eager to ruin my happiness." Tika walked past me toward the exit. "Let's go. You can register me here later."

I followed the hateful, spiteful bride because she had the car keys, and also because I knew her venom was not directed at me. Rather, it was most likely a result of Tika's equally hateful and spiteful fiancé, Chet. On the three occasions I had the displeasure to meet Chet, I have seen him critique Tika's hair and weight, ridicule her choice of a reception location (she later changed it), and make fun of her mother's side of the family. He's a real prince.

We do not often see the fiancé, but sometimes, when we do, it makes me feel sorry for the bride, no matter how awful she is on her own. Our little excursion to La Pantelle was not one of those times, but it did make me think about money and its effect on people. Avery's mother did not look very happy, but she was not ugly to strangers. Tika crossed the line somewhere, sometime, a long time ago.

As I wander through the department store, picking up piece after piece of stainless out of the cushioned drawers, I remember how Tika demanded that I find just the right sweet-tea spoon. What would someone like her do if she did not get her way? I really did not want to find out, so I call Jasmine over.

"Macie, dear. Finding everything to your liking?" Jasmine asks.

"Ah, no, unfortunately. I am on a mission to find a pattern with sweet-tea spoons."

Jasmine shifts into sales mode. "What about Currant? Bethel-waite?"

I nod. "This bride has seen it all. She wants something different. I was thinking that we might have to special-order."

"Okay," Jasmine says and rubs her forehead. "Tell me about her."

"She's about twenty-three. Dark hair. Little tiny lips. Big eyes. Likes old things. Lives in a bungalow."

"Rich?"

"You have to ask?" I laugh and Jasmine joins me.

"Is her mama involved?"

"Yep."

Jasmine reaches into her pocket for a small walkie-talkie. "Juan, please bring me Casey Kane's new line. It's not display-ready yet. Just send up the box."

A few minutes later, one of the stock boys brings a narrow silver-colored cardboard box to Jasmine. I eye it greedily. This could be the solution to my problem.

Jasmine opens the box with one practiced flip of her fingernail. She slides the five-piece set into her hand. Each piece is individually wrapped in plastic to protect the stainless steel from scratching. As Jasmine pokes a hole in the knife bag, I exhale quietly. This could be the set.

The knife is weighty but delicate, with an elegant curve. A thin line forms a bit of drama in the design, but other than that, it is very functional, almost sparse. There is a historical feel to the pattern. I can immediately see Tika, Chet, and their mean friends using this knife to stab fresh kill.

"And there's a sweet-tea spoon?" I ask, daring to breathe.

"You got it. I'll place an order for twelve." Jasmine smiles and slides the knife back into its wrapper. "The pattern is called Anderson."

"I'll take that one, if you have it in the system already."

"Macie, for you girl, I'll fudge the rules a tad. Show it to Her Highness and get it back to me by Saturday. That's when it goes on the floor. If I'm not here when you come in, just give it to one of my staff."

I practically yelp and give Jasmine a hug. This is one more task checked off the list of Ms. Gimme. I call Maurice on the way out to the parking lot.

"I've got the pattern!"

"Well, what took you so long? It's just a teaspoon, Macie." Maurice's voice sounds flat.

"What's up, Maurice?"

My boss pauses. "Tika just rang. She wants to schedule two more parties—a luncheon for her coworkers and a shower at her great aunt's nursing home out in Snellville."

"But the coworkers are already invited to, like, four or five other showers."

"Exactly."

I reach my car, check the backseat for bad men, and unlock the door. "So, what did you say?"

"I told her sternly that her behavior was unbecoming. And that this was bordering on vulgar."

I crank on the air-conditioning. "Wow, you said all of that?"

Maurice's voice softens slightly. "Well, I may have used more gentle language."

"I thought so."

Maurice inhales. "Anyway, I think we may be getting fired."

"You're kidding! Just for trying to save her embarrassment? And from being inducted into the Greed Hall of Fame?"

"I think she likes the attention, Mace. That's all it is. She sees herself as the center of everything, flowers blooming—you know, all of that wedding drivel—and all eyes focused on her. It's more than she's going to get from Shet."

"His name is Chet."

"I know," Maurice says.

Leaning back against the seat, I sigh. The triumphant flatware pattern moment is a distant memory. "So, what are you going to do?"

"Well, part of me says to forget the whole thing. Who needs this headache? But the other part of me says this is a big challenge, and that intrigues me."

All that intrigues me is how and why I find myself in wedding craziness over and over. One minute I'm happy about a spoon, the next minute I'm fretting about maybe getting fired by a gift-loving bride. Are there any happy brides? Any at all? Surely somewhere, a bride-to-be sits quietly, dreaming of her day. I drive away from the department store where, no doubt, several bridal types are heading right now, each looking for the perfect teaspoon.

The next day, after I finish early with wedding errands for a few of our upcoming brides, I call Iris and discover she is just wrapping up her monthly pantry ordering for Cake Cake. Tired of thinking about mounds of butter, flour, and sugar, Iris is ripe for a trip to Mr. Smoothie. I tell her I will swing by the studio.

I find Iris hunched over a calculator and her laptop. Since it is a Monday, the studio lacks the smell of fresh-baked cake. Even though we are heading out in a few minutes for sweet smoothies, I am disappointed. Iris notices my furtive glances and nods her head toward the stainless-steel refrigerator.

"There's some pound cake I'm experimenting with if you want it."

With no further invitation needed, I pounce. Iris is trying out all sorts of recipes in anticipation of opening up a satellite Cake Cake north of town. She will continue to churn out her fabulous wedding cakes in town. The new store will have bakery items to go, specialty orders, and other tasty treats.

"Have you thought of a name for the new place?" I ask with my mouth full. The pound cake is light and lemony. Our smoothies are looking like a thing of the past.

"How about 'Cake Cake to Go Go'?" Iris looks up from her laptop. "What do you think?"

"I love it!"

"Now, all I have to do is find the right location, hire a pastry chef and staff, train everyone, and still find time to keep my real business afloat. Remind me why I am doing this again?" Iris drops her head onto her hands.

"Because you are a risk-taker and a talented woman. And because you like a challenge."

Sitting up, Iris says, "Yeah, yeah. What would you know? You just work with sweet little brides who listen to every word you say."

I snort, thinking of the Greedy Bride. "I forgot to tell you. Tika might fire us."

"Tika, the give-me-presents bride?"

"The very same. Apparently, she does not like being told she's just a little bit selfish."

"You can get fired for advising a bride? I thought that's what you are supposed to do," Iris says.

"One would think so. But not this bride-to-be. I don't care what happens. She's unbearable, just like the rest of them." I flip through Iris's display book, pausing at cakes I remember. If I were to make a scrapbook of my life over the past year, it would include about fifty slices of cake.

"Now, now. Is Miss Macie getting cynical on me again? What's wrong? Are you and Avery having trouble?" Iris asks, concern in her eyes.

I slide onto a high silver stool near the pastry island. There are so many things I want to tell Iris. I want to let her know I've barely seen Avery since he took his new job. Sure, I'm happy he likes it. It is what he wanted to do to prove to me he could keep a job and work like the rest of the world. But I didn't know he would like it so much or get sucked so completely into candybarville. He's hardly mentioned our future plans at all, and I've been determined not to bring it up.

"It's a long story," I say with a sigh.

"I can do a long story. And while you're at it, pass some of that pound cake. We can do smoothies another day."

I swipe a piece as I hand the cake plate over to my friend. "This stuff is good, by the way."

"Nice try. Spill the beans," Iris says, taking a delicate bite of the dense cake.

"Well, ever since Avery started working for Chattahoochee Chocolates, he has been all wrapped up in sales reports, texture ratings, and sugar pricing. We haven't been to the park or to Tang since he began working."

"Do you think it's just the new job? Some people are like that, you know. They burn the candle at both ends when starting a new project."

"Maybe. But I think it's more. Something bothers me, and I can't figure it out."

Tilting her head to the side, Iris studies me for a moment. "Could it be that Avery doesn't depend on you as much anymore?"

I ask her what she means.

"Well, it used to be that Avery waited for you to get off work. He waited in the parking lots of countless stores while you stopped to pick up something for a bride. He's even set up chairs for outdoor receptions when you were short-staffed."

"So?"

"So, perhaps Avery having his own gig means he doesn't hang around waiting for you anymore. And that stings."

I start to protest. Avery does not wait for anyone. He is his own person. But then I think about it a little bit more. There have been times when Avery cooled his heels while I worked. I always figured it was just the way things were: Rich Avery did not have to be bothered by a pesky work schedule. He would wait for me and then we could go wherever we wanted.

"Maybe you have a point there," I say. We have gone through a pretty big change, the two of us. Avery has transformed from a man of leisure to a man with a time card.

"The question is, can you get used to this new way of doing things? Can you get used to the new Avery?" Iris pushes the plate toward me.

Suddenly, the taste of cake is not what I need. I want to see Avery. "Thanks, friend. I needed that."

"No problem. I'll call you the next time I need to unload my latest recipe."

I give Iris a hug and walk outside into the warm air. I know where to find Avery. I take a deep breath to settle my cake-stuffed stomach.

As I drive over to the west side of the city, I think of the first week I met Avery. Before our first real date, we spent several lunches and dinners just talking and figuring each other out. Looking back, I remember how my heart pounded when he would pick me up for each friendly date. I always felt a little off-kilter, as if I had a splotch of ketchup on my T-shirt or my shoes were on the wrong feet. Like learning a new dance step, I had to strain to keep up with the turns in our relationship.

It was not until our fifth date that I knew Avery liked me as more than just a new pal with whom to see movies or to walk around the park at dusk. We were sitting in a crowded coffeehouse, crammed into the corner near the bathrooms. The waitress gave us repeated dirty looks to clear out after we took the last sips of our lattes, but we ignored her. As a busboy stopped to clean off the table, Avery looked over at me and blurted, "You have a beautiful nose."

And just like that, I knew he liked me in that crazy, new-love way I liked him. I figured a person who was only interested in friendship would not bother to notice my nose. There are more obvious choices: hair, eyes, lips. But someone's nose? My heart did a skippy little dance. That night, we kissed for the first time outside my apartment. It was instantly comfortable, like we belonged in a small space, just two-by-two, each with room to breathe.

I drive toward Chattahoochee Chocolates, absentmindedly tapping my fingers on the stick shift. I have the entire week ahead of me crammed floor to ceiling with endless wedding details. If Tika does not fire Maurice and me, I will have her to deal with as well. I zip down Juniper Street, heading into Midtown. If I time it just right, I can catch Avery right after the line shuts down for the day, usually about two o'clock. He will be more inclined to go out for lunch if his tasting is done. Lately, he has been so wrapped up with the new candy-bar line that he has forgotten to eat, a concept I have a hard time understanding.

As I drive past the trendy eateries on Juniper, I notice Elise's café at the corner of Fifth. Since it is between the lunch and dinner shifts, the parking lot is empty, but it will be packed later in the evening. Out of the corner of my eye, I catch a glimpse of Maurice's car in the deserted parking lot. That man never stops schmoozing.

I think about Maurice as I cross over Ponce de Leon Avenue, braking to miss a street person walking against the light. Over the past year, I've grown to like and admire him, although I often struggle to keep up with his vision of how things ought to be done.

When I first started working for my boss, I knew next to nothing about getting married or choosing a wine. I could not tell the difference between a mousse and a flan. But I have observed Maurice, kept my mouth shut (mostly), and learned how to suggest Casablanca lilies over birds of paradise. I am grateful for Maurice. It does not take away from the nastiness of some brides, such as Tika, but it helps that on most days I like my boss. As I drive, I wonder idly if Maurice is happy. He has been grumpy lately and seems to take our various bridal challenges more seriously.

I turn into the parking lot of Chattahoochee Chocolates, searching for Avery's car. I do not see it, but turn once around the lot to be sure. I pause near the trash bins beside the loading docks. They are deserted; the line staff has gone home for the day. I think of places he could have gone and ring his cell phone. Avery rarely turns it on, so that's no help. I decide to go home. While I would have liked to scoop Avery up and take him to Tang for a late lunch, it looks like a bowl of cereal will have to do.

After parking in the lopsided lot beside my apartment building—the very same building where Avery and I met when I moved to Atlanta—I dig out my key and unlock the front door. The front hall is deserted, since most of my neighbors are still at work. Something on the floor catches my eye. It is the familiar silver-and-red packaging of a Chattahoochee bar. I stop and pick up the bar, thinking that it is strange to find gourmet chocolate on the ground downstairs from my apartment. They are not exactly cheap. Someone will be missing this later. I decide to put it in the building's mailbox niche, where the owner might be reunited with his lost treat.

Then I see another candy bar on the first step of the tilting front staircase. Is this someone's idea of a joke? I cannot see Avery doing this. He is probably across town, overnighting chocolate bars to food writers or scoping out cheaper shipping boxes.

Climbing the stairs, I pick up three more bars. They trail down the hallway, moving closer together near my apartment door. When

I finally stand in front of no. 124, hands full of Chattahoochee Chocolates, I stare at my door with a stupid expression.

Hanging from an ancient nail on the old door is a large flower wreath with a sash across the front. Glittery gold letters read "Bon voyage." I step back, as if I expect the flowers to reach out and touch me. What is this wreath doing on my door? By now I suspect Avery, of course, but I have no idea what he is doing.

I swing my head around, but the other three apartment doors are closed. The hall fan whirs to life, stirring Ms. Cotton's fake potted plant down the hall. I turn again to my door and put the key in the lock. Pushing the door open, I lean into the apartment. "Hello?"

In the middle of my tiny living room are three packages, each wrapped with pink-and-purple polka-dotted paper. Propped up against the largest package is a handwritten sign. It reads: "Come into the apartment. This is from Avery."

I smile and release my hold on the door handle. He knows me well. After relocking the door from the inside, I settle onto the futon couch and examine the packages. The largest is the size of a picnic cooler or chest. The second looks like a book, and the third is sized about as big as an envelope. I pick up this third package, which has another handwritten message on it: Open me first.

My hands tremble just a bit. This is a fairly elaborate setup, even for Avery, and I feel as if I am walking down an unfamiliar path. My fingers finally pry off the paper to find one plane ticket to Abigail Island, Georgia. The traveler is Macie Fuller, and she will be flying first-class. A small sticky note tells me "Don't freak out. Open the medium-size present."

I place the package on my lap, feeling the heavy wrapping paper with shaking hands. A plane ticket from a man who knows I do not want to jet around without plans. A trip planned to the Georgia coast that I have never even seen, even though I live in the same state. I allow a deep, quivery breath to escape.

The wrapping paper falls off to reveal an elegant hardback book with a picture of a wedding cake on the front. "The Smart Woman's Guide to Planning Her Wedding," I read aloud.

The smart woman. Me. I look up and catch my reflection in the wall mirror across from the futon. Clutching the book, I see the girl in the mirror do the same. She even wipes her eyes of a few happy tears. Pieces of purple paper surround her as the afternoon sun colors the apartment a perfect warm yellow. I lean back, grasping the book to my chest. There is one more present to unwrap.

I carefully place the book on the futon and sit beside the large gift. I tear off the paper like a child, giggling with excitement and wishing Avery were here to see it. I wonder where he is right now. He has obviously put a lot of thought into surprising me. I laugh out loud, just because I am happy.

The third gift turns out to be a lovely leather suitcase and matching carry-on bag. A curlicue *M* is embroidered onto a leather nameplate on each piece. I trace the letter with my index finger. It is such an Avery gift: needed, thoughtful, and elegant. A small card is taped onto the side of the suitcase. I rip it open and recognize Avery's personal stationery. He has written a note.

Dear Macie,

I hope you like the presents. I can't wait to see you. Take these suitcases and fill them. Meet me at the airport at 7 P.M., gate B3. Bring your left hand.

I love you,
Avery

P.S. Don't forget your ticket!
P.P.S. Yes, I cleared this with Maurice. Now get crackin'!

I jump up. What time is it? I knock over the suitcase and stumble back onto the futon. My foot twists under me and I groan. Great, that's what I need to do: break my leg before getting engaged.

That will make a nice story, Mace. I glance at my watch: 3:00 P.M. That gives me an hour to pack, an hour to get ready. I wonder if I have time to get a pedicure at one of those nail places over on Ponce. Do I have a good sundress? I own a few, but none that say "Engagement Trip."

I pick up the suitcase and carry it back to my bedroom. I pause at the threshold. Suddenly, everything looks different. My stuffed giraffe from childhood seems old, just like the folding screen with the flamingo print. All of these things were pre-Avery. Now, there is a whole new world of post-Avery. I will have to fill that world up as well.

Unzipping the suitcase, I discover more surprises: three sundresses and two pairs of sandals, their tags still attached. A beach towel, sunglasses, and a pretty pair of earrings complete the goodies. I will try on the dresses and wear one to the airport, but first, I have to talk to Iris. I ring her at home.

"Oh, so that's what was going on. He asked me for your dress size last week. I couldn't figure out why," Iris says.

"And you should see this cute wedding-planner book he got for me. Get it? I'm a wedding planner and now I get to plan my own wedding!" My words tumble out of my mouth. I am babbling, but I do not care.

Iris sounds amused. "Yes, I get it. I have to hand it to him. I did not see this coming. I mean, not now."

"I guess all of his work has made him get a little more serious," I say, glancing down at my left hand. I have "sweet-tea spoon" scribbled on the skin with black marker. That will have to go.

"Have you called your parents?"

"Not yet," I say. "I want to be officially engaged when I call them. Mom will start asking me all sorts of questions about wedding dresses and flowers, and I want a chance to be really engaged first."

"That makes sense. Oh, Mace. I am so happy for you. I know you have been wanting this for a while," Iris says.

"I have. Maybe more than I even admitted to myself." I stare out of the window. A cardinal flits from branch to branch of the old pecan tree outside. Ordinarily, the sight of a bird would not move me to tears, but this day has changed everything.

"Oh, Iris, I want to sing, like in a musical? I want to run down the halls belting out show tunes about love and weddings and flowers. What's happened to me since you saw me last?"

My best friend laughs. "Silly, you are in love. And about to get engaged. It's okay to be like this. I would keep the singing to inside your apartment, though."

"Good point. Can you take me to the airport tonight?"

"It would be my pleasure to squire the almost bride-to-be to her almost fiancé-to-be."

And it is then the word "bride," dropped so innocently from Iris's lips, makes me pause. I look around the apartment, at the wrapping-paper piles and the brand-new sundresses, the plane ticket, and the candy bars, and I take a deep breath. I am almost one of *them*. Shaking it off, I run into the bathroom and dive underneath the counter for the hot rollers I use about once a year. I will curl my hair, pack cute beach clothes, tuck the wedding planner into my new luggage, and head to the airport. With Avery and the Georgian coast, there is nothing that can stop me now.

10

The Beach Bride

I lean over the stainless-steel sink, willing the electronic sensor to catch and release warm water. After waving my hands back and forth a few times, I give up and stare at the reflection in the mirror.

Wide, startled eyes look back. My skin is flushed, and my lips are parted a bit. Other travelers rush past, bumping into the new carry-on bag slung over my shoulder. I hope to be on my way to becoming engaged and the rest of the world whirls by, casually living normal lives.

It is hard to believe I am in the airport rest room, mere steps from the gate. My heart thuds in my chest, a reminder that Avery is somewhere in the airport. Perhaps he is walking down the concourse right now. I dig around in my bag for some lip gloss and then think better of it. When I see Avery, I want to kiss him for a long time, not smear gloss all over his face. I cannot wait to tell him about finding the presents in my apartment and twirl around in the sundress he picked out.

Women come and go at the bank of sinks, and the intercom keeps up a steady stream of departing flight announcements. Our plane boards in about thirty minutes. I wonder if Avery is as nervous as I am. Getting the surprise ticket, wedding-planning book, and luggage tells me he has been thinking a lot about this trip and his hopes for it.

My ears catch the sound of someone crying. I look around, half expecting to see an upset child. The crying continues, although it's more like sobbing at this point. Two or three women exit the stalls, but none looks upset. I walk closer to the stalls, feeling a little funny.

"Ma'am? Are you all right?" I say to a stall with feet under it.

"I'm—I'm okay," a voice says.

"Are you sure? Is there anything I can do?"

"No."

Something won't let me walk away. There is a note in the woman's voice that makes me feel as if I know her. And then I see what has drawn me to the stall like a homing beacon. Hooked over the door is a wooden hanger quilted in pink satin and topped with a tiny, pink bow. I know that hanger. It's the signature of Rudolph Dutch Bridal Gowns of Peachtree City.

"Are you getting married?" I ask.

The woman catches her breath and then sobs quietly. I hear the rustle of tissue. "Well, I was. How did you know?"

"I can see the top of your hanger. That's a Rudolph Dutch, I believe."

Two or three toilets flush at the same time, and I don't hear her response.

"What did you say?" I ask.

"I said, I've got one of his dresses in here. You want it?"

There is a sadness in the woman's voice. I decide to let her know that I'm on her side. "Do you want to talk about it? I'm a wedding planner."

From the other side of the stainless-steel door, I hear a click and then the hanger is lifted and the door swings open. A woman, younger than me, stands inside, clutching a garment bag to her chest. Her face is red and tear-streaked. I open my arms up—it just seems the natural thing to do—and she embraces me, one arm holding the garment bag.

"I know you don't even know me, but I don't care," she cries into my sundress. "An hour ago, I was supposed to walk down the aisle, but the place we rented—a really quaint old house—burned down today just before we arrived, and there was all this smoke and fire trucks everywhere. It was a small wedding anyway, so we said 'Let's just call the minister and move the ceremony to another place.' But when we called his cell phone—get this—we find out he double-booked us! He's somewhere on the other side of Atlanta, getting ready to marry another couple."

This is one of the worst wedding stories I've heard. "I can't believe your day—how awful. But why are you at the airport?"

"Our flight for our honeymoon leaves tonight, and Kevin figured we could just get on the plane and leave this nightmare behind us. He doesn't care when we get married, but I do! This is supposed to be my wedding day." The poor bride tries to hold back another round of tears.

I help the woman over to the sink, where we hang the dress up on a nearby hook. I trip the water sensor and encourage her to splash her face. She does and pats her skin dry with some paper towels.

"I look like a mess," she says, glancing at the mirror.

"No, you're fine. You're just upset."

"I'm Jessica, by the way. Sorry you had to see that."

"My name is Macie, and don't worry about it. Weddings are stressful on their own, and anyone would crack if their dream day turns out like yours did."

Jessica shakes her head. "The worst part about it was, we didn't have very much money. This was kind of our shot at something nice. We put a deposit on the minister and the historic house, and I bought this dress at a sample sale. We put the rest of our savings toward a condo at Abigail Island for the honeymoon."

My ears perk up. "Abigail Island?"

Jessica pushes her hair off of her forehead. Her brown eyes are red and swollen. "Yes, it's this little island near Savannah, but I don't feel like having a beach vacation. I want it to be my honeymoon. Kevin says we can get married down there, and I know our folks will be fine with that, but how am I supposed to plan a wedding in a strange place?"

My mind starts to whirl. I think I can do this. We would need a few days, of course, a place for the ceremony, food, maybe a nice string quartet. And then there would be flowers, if they wanted flowers. Perhaps a nice daisy bouquet? Jessica has a simple beauty that shouldn't be overwhelmed.

"Jessica, I want to help plan your wedding."

She looks confused and shoves her hands into the pockets of her capri pants. "But I just told you, it's over. We're getting on a plane to Abigail Island."

"So am I! I'm meeting my boyfriend in a few minutes—" I pause and take a deep breath. Avery! I can't believe I have forgotten why I am even standing in an airport bathroom. "Avery, my boyfriend, is waiting for me out there. We're going to Abigail, too. It's kind of a surprise trip."

"I think our plane is boarding soon. We should get out there," Jessica says with a glance at her watch. "Kevin is probably wondering where I am."

I reach over and give Jessica a hug. "I know it's weird to meet like this, but I plan weddings for a living. Well, I'm a wedding planner's assistant, but you get the idea. I'd be happy to work with you once we get to the island. It would be my gift."

"Oh, Macie, I couldn't accept that. I know wedding planners are expensive. It wouldn't be right to take your help. And you're on vacation!"

"It would be an honor to help you get married. I would hate to think of you and Kevin being miserable all week."

Tears well up in Jessica's eyes. "I'm a complete stranger! I can't believe anyone could be so nice."

We collect the dress and walk out to meet our guys. A man in a dark blue T-shirt and khaki pants rushes over and pulls Jessica into his arms. "I was getting ready to head in there myself. You really had me worried, honey."

"I made a new friend in the ladies' room! This is Macie," Jessica says.

"Ah, nice to meet you," Kevin says.

But I am turning around in a circle, trying to find Avery. Our plane is about to board; a short line of travelers stands expectantly, boarding passes in hand. I don't see him—could he have gotten stuck in traffic? I don't want to try his cell and spoil the romantic-getaway mood he's created. Still, I am concerned. People pass by quickly, moving to gates and connecting flights. The smells of coffee and hot cinnamon rolls are in the air.

And then, before I can say another word to Jessica and Kevin, I feel Avery's arms around me, and we are laughing and hugging. This huge, anxious bubble leaves me and everything is all right. We are together, in the airport, and we are going somewhere—perhaps a journey that will last for a long, long time.

"You made it," Avery says, oblivious to Kevin and Jessica, who have watched us with small smiles.

"You did, too," I laugh. "Avery, I'd like you to meet some new friends."

Avery stops kissing the tips of my fingers and looks up. "Avery Leland, nice to meet you." He shakes both of their hands. "How do you know each other?"

Jessica and I laugh. "Well, it's kind of a long story," Jessica says. "But Kevin and I were supposed to be married today and on to our honeymoon on Abigail Island. But everything went wrong, and then I met Macie. She wants to help us get married on Abigail, Kevin."

Kevin's mouth drops open. "That's nice and everything, really. But I think we just need to regroup and try again—"

"Macie's a professional wedding planner, Kevin." Jessica shifts her garment bag from one hand to the other.

I dig around in my bag for my card. "Here, just so it's official."

Kevin takes the card. "Maurice de Trammel? Sounds fancy."

"Well, Maurice is a bit of a celebrity, but I'm his ordinary assistant. I told Jessica I would be glad to help you get married down on the island, and it would be my treat."

The line starts to move and we join it, digging out boarding passes. Jessica and I promise to exchange numbers on the plane and make further plans.

Avery holds my hand as we walk down the jet way toward the waiting plane. "You are unbelievable," he says, shaking his head.

"What?"

"Only you would find the one bride in this airport who needs saving. How do you do it?"

"Oh, Avery, it was so sad. She was crying and I asked if she needed help, of course, I could only see her feet, but I just knew something was wrong. Her wedding location burned down and the minister stood them up, and well, no one should have memories of their wedding day like that."

Avery laughs and puts his arm around my shoulder. "Okay, I accept that my girl is an emergency wedding planner. Anyone else around here need saving?"

I snuggle closer to him as we wait to walk on the plane. "I can think of one person—he needs a loving and fun travel companion. I might decide to take him up on an offer to fly to the coast."

"I'm shocked you showed up," Avery says with a straight face.

"How could I say no when presented with such an appealing offer?"

Once we get on the plane, there is some initial awkwardness. We have never flown together before, so we kind of dance around the bag stowing and the seat belt buckling, bumping heads and fumbling with who wants to sit where. I end up in the window seat.

During the forty-five-minute flight to the coast, I feel a shyness I have never known around Avery. It's as if there is a large, unfinished event that has to take place. He teases me a few times, asking if there is anything I want to do once we get to Abigail, anything at all? I just punch him in the arm and look out of the plane window. We are approaching the island.

"Careful," Avery says. "I think punching a passenger is a federal offense."

"So is torturing your girlfriend," I retort.

Avery leans over and kisses me gently. "Thanks for coming."

My stomach flip-flops at eight thousand feet. "Thanks for inviting me. The presents you left were interesting."

"Well, I had to lure you down here somehow. My evil plan worked." Avery strokes an imaginary goatee and tries to look menacing.

I grab his hand and lean back in the seat. "Well, you've got me now."

Our condo is just steps from the beach, over a sand dune or two. Since we arrived at night, I couldn't see the view, but in the morning, I am amazed at the waves, the sun, and the strip of undeveloped beach right outside our window. I sit up, blinking and listening to the ocean through the open balcony door.

"There you are, sleepy head," Avery says, poking his head around the bedroom door. "Ready to rise and shine?"

"I can't believe I'm here. I would be knee-deep in bride stuff by now back home." I rub my eyes and yawn.

"That's why we needed to get away from Weddingland. You work so hard. But even my best-laid plans didn't matter because you found a bride in the airport bathroom."

"That's an overstatement," I say. "Sort of. And while we're down here, I won't take any calls from old brides. Now Jessica, that's a different story. Hers is just a little wedding."

Rolling his eyes, Avery motions to me. "Come on and get breakfast. I have orange juice, too."

I scramble out of bed, my stomach doing those flip-flops again. I know that sometime soon there is the possibility I will be asked the most important question of my life. It does not matter how much you have waited for it to happen, when it does, a person can still feel unprepared. I have test-taking hands. They are sweaty and altogether unfeminine. Asking for my hand would be like embracing a bowl of wet noodles.

We eat breakfast on the balcony. We watch kids play in the surf, the early-morning sun lighting up the sea oats on the sand dunes. They rustle in the constant breeze. I know I will love their rattle-rattle sound forever, just like I will always love Abigail Island.

"I adore this," I say, leaning back in my canvas chair.

"Let's go for a walk," Avery says. His face looks anxious, and my stomach takes a dip.

I slip out of cotton pajama pants into shorts and quickly choose a yellow T-shirt. Is yellow romantic? Does it say "love me forever"? I wonder how far we will walk before—or if—he pops the question. I hope it will not be in front of anyone else. I want a little privacy. Our options run through my head. The sand dunes are nice. So is the space a little to the left of the condo building. But farther down the beach, well, that is too crowded. I leave my shoes in the bedroom and walk out into the living room.

Avery waits by the couch. As I cross the room, I notice he looks a little funny. I guess I do, too. If this is the day, we are getting ready to take a huge step.

"Macie," Avery says, his voice a little stringy, "Before we leave this condo, I want it to be as an engaged couple. I want to walk outside knowing we will spend the rest of our lives together."

All thoughts leave my head. The beach, sandals, walking—it all floats away in an instant. I reach for his hands. They shake.

"Macie, from the first minute I saw you and slyly wormed my way into helping you move into your first Atlanta apartment, I have been captive to your charm, your independence, and your good humor. You are lovely, funny, and so loyal. I am a better person because of loving you. I taste candy bars for a living because I want you to be proud of me. I can only think of growing older with you," Avery says, his eyes wet.

I reach up to dab an escaped tear at the corner of his eye. "Oh, Avery, honey."

And then he is sinking down onto the condo floor and pulling out a ring from his pants pocket. "Will you be my wife?" he asks, looking up at me. I do not like being so far away from him, so I sit on the floor, too, laughing and kissing him.

"Yes, yes, yes!" is my answer. I say it again, just to be sure. "Yes! I will marry you!"

The end of a lopsided pier is not my idea of the best place for a wedding, but it was available on short notice, as was the minister, a man who goes by the professional name of the Reverend Love. He is waiting for us at the end of the pier, floral-print surfer shorts and a week's beard included. I get that familiar rat-tat-tat in my chest that usually signals an hour to show time. An additional tightness reminds me I am also worried because I have no idea where Avery is, no idea at all.

The beach crowd thins as children splash out of the surf reluctantly and couples stroll off the sand toward waiting villas and dinner reservations. It is probably about 7:00 P.M. By the time the string quartet I've hired at the last minute plays the final song, the burnt orange sun will be slowly melting into the horizon, coloring the waves a shadowy red and yellow. It will be perfect.

As if on cue, a car pulls into the public parking lot and parks in the first space closest to the pier. Immediately, deep, thumping bass notes and the whine of an electric guitar float out of the car. Two teenage boys jump out and open up the doors to allow the music a little more freedom. Mission accomplished, they each take a side of the hood and lean back, arms folded in almost the exact same pose.

I groan inwardly. This would have never happened on a private beach, the kind with which I am used to working. Although I usually ridicule those beaches for their snotty barred gates and gangsterlike security personnel, I was starting to see certain advantages to the finer things, namely a well-secured entrance and a guard named Slake. Maybe when Avery shows up, I could have him chat with the loud music boys. Or maybe they would leave on their own before the ceremony.

From another end of the parking lot, a group walks slowly toward the pier. Right on time, it is the string quartet with each member toting an instrument case across the sandy lot. A wind whips up the dresses of the two women in the quartet. I glance up to see a cloud tumble overhead in the sky. I silently will any raindrops far away from the beach. No rain can fall on this event. It has to be perfect.

There will be few witnesses at the wedding ceremony, but I still do a practiced check over the weathered boards of the pier, looking for trash and anything out of order. I greet the Reverend Love and assure him that yes, he will be paid once the groom arrives.

I wonder if Avery will ever get here. He is bringing the flowers and a garland of sea grasses to string along the railing at the pier's end. Without the flora and fauna, I am afraid the ceremony will be little more than a few words rushed into the sinking of the sun. Bending down to pick up a spent gum wrapper, I see the new flash of the diamond on my left hand. My impatience washes away in an instant. The details do not matter, only that one bride and one groom show up and make vows they mean to keep for a lifetime.

Avery arrives a few minutes later and he kisses me gently, his arms full of two large boxes from the only florist on the island. He mentions that I still have a dazed look on my face. I know it is funny, but I haven't stopped smiling since he put the ring on my finger.

And it was that easy, I reflect as Avery and I string garland on the pier. We have now been engaged for four full days. I love it. I love thinking about living with Avery as husband and wife. I love looking at my ring and letting the light catch the four points of the princess-cut stone. I love the two dark blue sapphires on either side of the diamond. It is corny, but I love being in love.

When we finish setting up the pier and arranging the musicians, I look at Avery and take a deep breath. The loud car in the parking lot pulled away a few minutes ago. Everything is in place. "Are you ready?"

He reaches for his cell phone. "Ready."

Within a few minutes, Jessica and Kevin walk toward the pier holding hands. She wears a flowing, white, layered chiffon dress and no shoes. A wispy veil falls to the middle of her back. Kevin looks over at her with almost every step and nervously adjusts the collar of his white dress shirt. He looks scared, but confident at the same time. Their intertwined hands rock back and forth as they walk. When they approach the end of the pier, they turn away from each other and face Avery and me.

"Jessica, you are a beautiful bride," I say and give her a hug. A seagull lands on the pier and regards the garland suspiciously from a tall post.

"Thanks to you, Macie. I don't know what we would have done without you," Jessica said.

I hand her a pretty bouquet of wildflowers. Avery pins a simple boutonniere to the lapel of the groom's suit coat. The Reverend Love glances at his watch. It is time to get this couple married.

"Lucky for you, Jessica and Kevin, my fiancée has a soft spot for weddings and a habit of talking to strangers," Avery says.

Jessica laughs and rejoins her hand with Kevin's. "I hope she never stops. If I hadn't run into her at the airport, we would be down here without knowing what to do. In four days, Macie called all the right people and now, we're getting married!"

"It's not my dime, but we're losing the light," calls the Reverend Love, clapping his hands together.

I take my place beside Jessica, and Avery stands up for Kevin. I nod to the musicians, who begin a spirited movement from Handel's "Water Music." When the last note is played, the reverend says a few words about love and harmony and peace, and just when I think he is about to wax poetic on the environment, he asks if the bride and groom have any special vows.

Kevin looks to Jessica. "I have something I want to say. It's not written out or anything."

The Reverend Love glances to the sun that is starting its descent to the water. "That's cool."

Kevin turns and faces his bride. Gripping her hands tightly, he says, "Jess, I am standing here because I love you, and everything that happens to you matters to me. I knew how upset you were when our original wedding plans didn't work out, but I just figured we would get married later. It was only after our plane flight down here that I saw how much you wanted to be married. And that's what I want to say to you. For the rest of our lives, I want to always look through your eyes and see what matters to you, what you care about."

Jessica starts crying, but her eyes do not stop looking at Kevin. A soft, sunset light falls across our little party as we listen. Even the reverend looks interested.

"I stand here now, asking you to share my life. I don't have much, but I promise to honor, love, and cherish you all the days of my life." Kevin pauses, unable to speak another word.

Jessica stands up straight and in a soft voice says, "And I will honor, love, and cherish you, knowing that when I fell in love with you, I found a love for the rest of my life."

The reverend has the couple exchange rings and promise to forsake all others. As the sun drops by gentle segments into the sea, the quartet plays an arrangement of Saint-Saëns's "The Swan." I cry, something I never do when I am working. But this feels different, like I am doing this for a friend. Even though I have only known Jessica five days, it seems as if we have been friends for a long time.

"Do you want to come with us to dinner to celebrate?" Kevin asks as we walk toward the parking lot. A brisk wind whips at our clothes. Jessica's veil twirls behind her.

Avery and I look at each other. "That's sweet," I say, "But you should be alone. This is your honeymoon, after all."

Kissing Kevin, Jessica tosses her bouquet in my direction. "You're next. I don't need this anymore!"

I clutch the bunch of fresh flowers. They smell sweet and clean. I am suddenly happy with every small thing about life. Avery catches my eye and offers his hand to Kevin. I hug Jessica again and whisper, "Be happy."

"We will."

Avery and I walk back toward our rental car. The lot is deserted, our only company a stray cat hopping in and out of the trash cans in the corner.

He puts the car in gear and we head for the condo a few miles away. "Well, it certainly was awesome that Jessica ran into you," Avery says. "You will be in all of their stories from now on: 'And there we were, depressed and unmarried, when Jessica struck up a conversation in the ladies' room at the Atlanta airport with a pretty wedding coordinator who ended up saving the day.' Yep, I can hear the dinner table conversation now.

"You were great with them, Macie," Avery continues, turning his face toward me in the car. "I was really proud of you."

I am quiet, the flowers in my lap. I think about the last four days. First, there was the engagement and all of the excitement surrounding the trip. After Avery proposed, we walked on the beach for two hours until we were exhausted. We dropped into a little seafood shack off the beach and discovered the world's best she-crab soup. When our waitress found out about our engagement, she brought us slices of key lime pie on the house.

I called my parents, and Avery called his. No one was very surprised. That was when I found out Avery had driven down to Cutter to ask my parents for my hand. His own folks knew what he was up to this weekend, and they seemed genuinely happy for us. I immediately wondered what I should call his parents once we were married. Dad? Mom? Mr. L.? Babs? The whole thing gave me a headache, so I decided to worry about it later. Maybe when I got home I could find a book about being a daughter-in-law at the library. I also called Iris, of course, and Maurice. He did not pick up his cell phone, so I left a message.

"What are you thinking about?" Avery asks, pulling me back to the present. We're getting pretty close to the condo.

"Oh, just how wonderful it is to have an entire life stretched out in front of you. And to be in love at the same time."

"You haven't mentioned any of the planning or when you want to have the wedding, Mace. That surprises me," Avery says.

We reach the condo and head up the wooden steps. I am suddenly tired and long to fall asleep to the sound of the rambunctious waves outside the window. I stifle a yawn. "Can we talk about this some other time?"

Avery gives me a funny look. "Okay, whatever you want to do. I just figured you would be hopping on that right away. You know, get Maurice all involved. Although, honestly, I don't know if my parents can afford him."

"What's that supposed to mean? Don't you think my parents can pay for my wedding?" I put my hands on my hips as Avery fumbles with the key.

He turns, surprised, and holds out his hands. "Whoa, easy, tiger. I just meant, well, Maurice is expensive. You know, he's the all-star wedding planner. I know your parents can pay for your wedding, but if my parents have their way, I'm sure we'll need everyone's pennies."

"Have their way? So, this is your mother's wedding now?"

"No! I mean, I'm sure she will have input. Everyone will. But it's our wedding. You and me." Avery tries to nudge me inside the condo, but I pull away.

The ocean rolls close by in the darkness. Our condo neighbors have their windows open, the sounds of a television game show tinny in the air. I wonder if the neighbors are a married couple, bored of the beach and its distractions. Or they could be a young, newly engaged couple like us, enjoying a few brainless moments in front of the tube.

"Mace, what's wrong? What did I say?"

"It's nothing. I guess I was just cross for a minute." We walk inside, something between us in the air. I go into the bedroom and kick off my sandals. My sundress is wrinkled and needs ironing if I want to wear it again this week. I notice for the first time how Avery's suitcase takes up half of the floor space near the bathroom door. Is this how rich kids grow up, with all of their stuff spread out everywhere?

Avery walks into the room, unbuttoning the cuffs on his dress shirt. "You want to order dinner in or go out?"

I turn to face him. "You know, other people need the floor, too. You can't just hog every bit of carpet."

"Macie, what is wrong with you? You aren't acting like yourself."

For an answer, I collapse on the edge of the bed, cramming my face into the white pillows. Adding a few more wrinkles to my dress, I scrunch up my legs and try to scoot under the covers. I feel Avery sit down on the narrow slice of bed beside me. Unable to stop myself, I roll toward him on the soft mattress until my hip touches his leg.

"Don't try to make me feel better," I say.

"If I knew what was wrong, I would try. But you're not telling me anything," Avery says with a tight voice. "You always do this. You make me guess what is bothering you. It's not fair."

"No one asked you to save the day." I roll over on my back. My feet are gritty from the sand drifts on the pier.

Avery stands up, pitching me back toward the middle of the bed. "Fine. Pout if you want to. When you're done, I'll be ready to go for dinner. I'm starving."

Food is the last thing on my mind. The television in the living room starts up, and the sounds of a newscast float down the hallway. I sigh loudly, just in case Avery is interested in what I am doing. Then I sigh again for effect. A few moments later, the balcony door opens to the sound of wind and ocean. I hear a gentle click as the door closes again.

Curious, I crawl over the bed to peer out of the bedroom window, but the balcony is dark and in shadow. I quickly pull off my sundress and tug on a T-shirt and yoga pants. My ring flashes in the mirror as I run a brush through my hair. I feel a pang of angst. We have only been engaged for four days and this is our first fight. And to be honest, I do not know what we are fighting about, really. Sure, I am being mean, but why?

This night feels like another time when I played the part of a first-class jerk. It was the day of Girl Power Club sign-ups in the fifth grade. I had been a part of Girl Power since the first grade, and knew all the campfire songs, had earned my GP pins, and even gone to sleep-away camp one summer. But as the sign-up day approached that September, I dragged my feet. I wanted to try the singing club or the camping club, but Girl Power took up a lot of time. If I did GP, I would not have any free time after school to try something else. The problem was I did not know how to tell my best friend, Madalyn.

She loved GP and had warned me not to be late for sign-ups because the last girl on the list had to lead the Girl Power motivation song. I dawdled at my locker, applied clear lip gloss—the only makeup I was allowed to wear—and retied my purple tennis shoes seven or eight times. Finally, Madalyn spotted me in the deserted hallway. She wore her Girl Power headband and clutched the GP handbook.

"You're not coming, are you?" Madalyn cried, wiping her nose on her hand. "You don't like me anymore!"

"No, no, that's not it," I said, glancing down the hall. The singing club was warming up, treble voices running through the scale.

"Yes, yes it is. And I checked, your name isn't on the sign-up list. You know how much I love GP, and how much it matters to me. I talked about it all summer. You should have said you weren't going to do it."

I tried to think of a way to tell Madalyn that I was bored with GP and wanted to try something different. I was tired of chanting the GP motto: "Girl Power, Girl Power, all that I can be. Girl Power, Girl Power, watch me fly so free!" If I joined the singing club, I had a chance at the Florida beach trip they took each year. But I didn't know how to tell Madalyn all of this. So I leaned against my locker and heard awful words coming from my mouth.

"The truth is that Girl Power is for babies. I hate it, and I hate everyone in it," I said, wondering who was making me say these things. Poor Madalyn stood there, her GP headband stretched crookedly across her face, trying to stop crying. But I wasn't finished.

"You are embarrassing. Why do you want to sit around and do service projects when everyone else who matters is having fun? Girl Power sucks," I said.

That day and the mean things I said to Avery wash over me in a shameful rush. I had lost Madalyn's friendship. I am not going to lose any part of Avery. I walk outside to the balcony. He sits in the hammock, one foot stretched down to the floor. The air is warm outside, and the nearby ocean rages in front of us like a nature sound track.

"Hey," I say.

"Come out here to beat up on me?"

I reach out to tap his bare foot with mine. "Nope. Just wanted to apologize. I was nasty, and I am sorry."

"Apology accepted. But you still owe me something." Avery moves over in the hammock, making room for me.

"What's that?" I ask, leaning against his shoulder.

"You have to right now, right here in this hammock, tell me what it is that is bothering you."

"I don't know, I just got cranky," I offer.

Avery rubs my hand, and kisses the tips of my fingers. "I think there is more to it than that. When I asked you about planning the wedding, you turned into this other person. Why?"

I think of all of the things I could say: I was tired, grumpy, and overly emotional from the last few days. But I do not buy those reasons, and neither would Avery. I suddenly remember Jessica's wedding. While I was busy with her, I did not have time to think much about my own upcoming day of marital bliss. But then Avery brought it up and I got upset. Bingo! Problem solved.

I explain it to Avery. "I guess I am overwhelmed by thinking about being a bride. You know, planning the whole shindig and everything. I know I do it for a living, but making a wedding your own, really planning it, well, that's something else."

If Avery is unconvinced, he doesn't let on. "Just don't take everything on at once. Let me and Maurice and Iris help you out. Give us lots of things to do."

We snuggle in the hammock, my arm draped across Avery's chest. "Speaking of Maurice, he never called me back. I left a voice mail telling him we were officially engaged. I expected him to call by now."

"Maybe he's just busy with the bride du jour."

I lean back into the taut cotton of the hammock. "I guess so. You'd think he'd ring, though. Maybe I'll give him another call."

"How about we eat dinner first? Just a suggestion."

"So, we're okay now?" I stand up and offer Avery a hand out of the hammock.

"Yep."

We stroll that night to a small bistro near our condo. It is the kind of place open only during the season, which gives me a wistful feeling. The owner, a large woman in her fifties with curly red hair, walks from table to table chatting with guests. When she discovers we are newly engaged, she dramatically clasps her hands, saying, "Young love! Is anything more beautiful?"

Avery chatters on, talking about the yummy fish and the frozen drinks. I listen as attentively as I can, but part of me is still stuck in our little fight. There will be more to come in our years together, of course. What nags at me is that part of my mind knows I did not tell Avery the entire truth.

I do not feel like a radiant, content bride-to-be standing on the edge of a new life. Instead, I am still that fifth-grader, slouching against the locker, saying hurtful things to a friend. I will soon be a bride, and after that, a wife. Even though it scares me, I must learn to move about in this new world, one where I do not know all of the rules. As the ocean rolls outside the bistro, I put those thoughts aside. Tonight is a time for happiness, seated with dinner and a fiancé, on a trip by the sea.

11

The Celebrity Bride

Getting fired was not as bad as I thought it would be. I had this idea that getting canned involved some sort of dressing down or screaming match. It was actually not that traumatic. There was simply a message on my machine when we returned home to Atlanta. Avery was downstairs, retrieving the mail when I pressed the red flashing button on my answering machine.

"Macie, this is Tika. Since I can't reach your sorry boss, Maurice, I will tell you I have chosen to go with another wedding planner. I really just never saw eye-to-eye with your style of planning a large event. You didn't seem to grasp the importance of my wedding. You have your deposit, of course. Good-bye."

And that was it. I stood there for a minute as the tape rewound. Maurice was fired? Brides stood in line to get a date in his book. How dare she? But then I remembered how snotty she was to both of us, and I clearly recalled her out-of-control greed. I knew I was better off without her, but I wondered how Maurice would take it.

From her message, it sounded like Tika was having no luck getting ahold of Maurice, either. That in itself was very strange. He was extremely punctual about returning phone calls.

The first week I worked for him, I forgot to call two brides who were waiting on dress appointments. When they tattled, he chewed me out for making them wait. "These women pay a lot of money to have us at their disposal any time of day!" Maurice blustered, throwing his hands into the air. "If you are out to dinner with your friends or playing a game of tennis, you are reachable. That's how I run my business. If you can't do that, then you need to think about finding another job."

I learned pretty quickly. To this day, I try to return phone calls within the hour if at all possible. It calms the brides and makes them feel like we are on top of things. Even if I am with another client who is trying on twenty pairs of white shoes, I make the bride on the phone feel as if I am only thinking about her blessed event. Even if I can't remember her wedding date or what she looks like. Believe me, attending about fifty weddings a year starts to look like one white blur.

"Tika fired us," I say to Avery, who has returned to the apartment.

Avery's face is blank. "Is she the bride who wants her golden retriever to be the best man?"

"No, this is the greediest bride ever. The one who wanted ten bridal showers?"

Avery nods. "Oh, her. Well, lucky for you, wouldn't you say?"

I pace back and forth across the living room. "Me, yes. Maurice, no. He depends on these girls to love him and recommend him to other brides. You know that."

"I don't see why anyone needs a wedding planner at all," Avery says, plopping down on the futon couch. "What's so hard about getting married? You pick out a dress, order up some sandwiches, find a church and there you go."

Rolling my eyes, I pick up my new suitcase and carry it to my bedroom. "It's a little more complicated than that, and you know it."

When I walk back into the living room, Avery is poring over the real-estate section of the newspaper he picked up at the airport.

"What are you looking at?" I ask.

"Houses," Avery says, his head down.

"Houses? Why?"

Avery lowers the paper and looks at me. "Why? Because I am about to acquire a wife. Something tells me we can't move in with my parents."

I stand still and breathe deeply. Of course, we will need somewhere to live. I had not thought about that yet. My cute and dumpy apartment would have to go. There was no way we could live here. And Avery was right, moving into Chez Leland was not an option.

"Isn't a house a kind of big step?" I fiddle with my necklace, a silver shell charm Avery gave me on Abigail Island.

"You would prefer a tent or wigwam?" Avery sighs, dropping the paper to the floor.

"No, I mean, what about an apartment? Bigger than this one, but still an apartment. Or we could rent a house."

Avery shakes his head. "Macie, renting is just throwing money away. If we buy a house, we will pay ourselves, not a landlord. Come on, this is basic stuff. What's wrong?"

"Nothing, nothing. It's just a big shock, I think," I say, ducking into the kitchen to pour a glass of water. I never thought about owning a house. It seemed years away to me last week, and now, I am practically looking at kitchen appliances. White? Stainless steel? We'll have to buy a lawn mower, look at paint chips, comparison shop toaster ovens. I know I love Avery, but there is so much stuff that comes with marrying him. Not to mention how much money we will need, which I don't want to even think about right now.

"Where are we supposed to get the down payment for a house? That's a lot of money." I cannot help myself.

Avery picks up the real-estate section again, a small smile on his lips. "I think I may have a little bit saved for something like this."

A surge of worry runs through me. If Avery's money is going to save the day, where does my little salary come in? I need to feel I contribute, too. I have always worked, ever since the Holiday Hams job I had when I was sixteen. Paying my way seems like the most natural thing.

"Do you want to stay in Virginia-Highlands or do you want to live in Midtown?" Avery asks, flipping a page.

"Do we have to figure this out now? Why can't we just be engaged for a while?"

Avery closes the real-estate section and puts it down. "If we narrow down the neighborhood choices, it will help our agent."

"Our agent?"

"I haven't called her yet, but I was thinking of Sandy, my parents' friend. She knows Atlanta really well."

I take a big gulp of water. "What about my agent?"

Avery looks surprised. "You have a real-estate agent?"

"I could." I look around the apartment and avoid Avery's eyes. "What if I did?"

Frowning, Avery says, "What's wrong, Macie? Is it Tika? Did her message upset you?"

"No. Yes. It's all this talk of moving and buying and selling. I just got engaged! I want to savor the moment, not talk about clauses and contracts and stuff. You have us practically moved into a new house."

Avery stands. "I am not doing that, and you know it. Come on, Mace, this is supposed to be fun—where we're going to live after the wedding. We can figure it out together."

"We're not doing this together. You've got the down payment, the agent, and the—the—newspaper already." I sound like an idiot. What is wrong with me?

Avery grabs his car keys off of the kitchen table. "You know what? You can have the newspaper. I'm going home until the real Macie returns. Give me a call when she does." He pulls the front door closed behind him.

"You are impossible!" I say to the empty room. Stomping out of the kitchen, I run back to my bedroom. I throw open the new suitcases and start pulling out clothes. The sundresses are rumpled and will have to be cleaned. A thin line of sand rests in the bottom of one bag. A sob catches in my throat. I am the one who is being impossible.

I had such a fuzzy idea of being engaged when I was on the other side of it only a few days ago. I thought the hard part was planning the wedding and making one hundred details line up in a row. Now I am seeing that the more important piece is joining one man and one woman's lives together.

Sweet, lovable Avery appears to have worked through his issues prior to offering me a ring. It pains me to think I am acting like such a confused, moody girl who says she wants one thing but really wants another. The truth is, I really, really want Avery. I decide to tell him that right now.

Calling his cell is no help. I just get his voice mail. I leave two sweet, desperate messages. Then, there's nothing to do but wait. I think about calling Iris, but she is looking at potential commercial spaces today. Her new loan was approved while I was at the beach, so she is ready to move forward with Cake Cake to Go Go.

I pace around the apartment, putting sunscreen lotion back in the bathroom wicker cabinet and sandals in the closet. I pick up the phone and then sit it down again to check if it was off the hook. Avery has not called back. It serves me right. I cannot act like there is something wrong with him because I am having fits. I need to figure out why I am going bonkers, but that's another honest moment I will have with myself later.

I grab the phone again and flip back through the caller ID numbers to see if maybe Avery called but somehow the phone did not ring. I scroll past Tika's name. I wonder if Maurice received a similar phone call from her. I do not want to be the one who breaks it to him that we were fired, but he should know sooner than later. And I still haven't talked to him about getting engaged. I try his cell, get voice mail again, and then hang up. I decide to call his home, something I rarely do since Maurice always answers his cell phone.

Evelyn picks up on the first ring. "Yes?"

"Hi Evelyn, it's Macie. How are you?"

"Just peachy, thank you." Her voice is brittle. It must be a bad time.

"Ah, I just got back in town and I wanted to touch base with Maurice, but I can't get him on his cell. Is he there?"

There is silence on the other end of the phone. I think I hear Evelyn take a drag on a cigarette, which is odd because she does not smoke. "No, Macie, Maurice is not here because he doesn't live here anymore."

"What?" I am stunned. The woman I am talking to sounds nothing like smooth, polished Evelyn, who is an echo of smooth, polished Maurice.

"Yes, that's right, dear Macie. Maurice has decided he wants a little fling with a Parisian barmaid named Elise, and there's not a whole lot I can do about that, now can I?"

Evelyn begins crying. I would bet there is a liquor bottle on the other end of the line. "I am so sorry, Evelyn. I had no idea." I rewound the last few weeks in my head. Maurice's car at Elise's café. Their coziness at Carolina's fitting. All in all, not a lot of damning evidence. I did not see this coming. I feel a rush of anger toward Maurice.

"And the worst part about it? He wasn't planning to leave me. No, no, he was having his fun and then coming home. I was the one who found him out."

"Evelyn, you don't have to tell me this," I say.

"No, Macie, you need to know how piggish men can be since you are getting married yourself. Maurice told me you were at the beach, picking up your little sparkly. Well, how nice. Young love; it must be sweet," Evelyn says with a bit of a slur.

"Well, if there's anything I can do—"

"So, there I was, minding my own business on Monday night. That's my book club, once a month, like clockwork. Sherry D.—we call her that to distinguish her from Sherry K.—insisted we stop for a drink after our discussion. I tried to beg off because I have little tolerance for wine late at night, but there was no stopping Sherry D., let me tell you." Evelyn pauses to catch her breath.

"And we end up at this little café in Midtown. I had never been there. That area has changed so drastically, I hardly recognized any of the streets. Anyway, I excused myself to go to the bathroom and when I did, I nearly ran into a couple necking like barbarians in the hallway."

My heart sinks. What a way to find out your husband is cheating. Shivering, I think of Avery. Could he be capable of something like this?

"Well, I kicked him out right away, even after he begged me to understand, asked me to forgive him. Ha! I think not."

Evelyn continues on for some time. After I hang up, my mind spins with this new information. Maurice, of all people. He is awash in the world of weddings every day. New love, new beginnings, new vows. One would think he would have a more romantic view of things. And having an affair with Elise? She was too, too something. Oily? Practiced? Creepy?

I am now faced with a delicate situation. I need to get back to work, but my boss is unreachable. Maybe he checked into a downtown hotel on Peachtree Street. Perhaps he was shacking up with his lover. Whatever the case, Maurice has brides coming out of his ears. Anywhere from ten to twenty women could be mad at him right now. It was only a matter of time before they took it out on me. I reflexively check my cell. No voice mails or text messages so far. Good.

I pace around the apartment, unpacking less from necessity and more to give my hands something to do. I pile T-shirts, shorts, underwear, and socks into the laundry basket. As I work, my mind keeps slinking back to Avery. I have acted like such an emotional boomerang. This should be a time of excitement and wonder before our upcoming wedding, but so far, my contributions are fairly pathetic.

Emptying out my traveling cosmetics bag, I dump my brush, comb, and hand lotion into a basket beside the sink. I unpack my razor, hair mousse, lemon-scented body lotion, and pink nail polish, thinking about poor, loyal Evelyn. Maurice's betrayal seems too unbelievable to me, although I have no reason not to trust her story. Evelyn has always been Maurice's rock, available for brainstorming ideas and helping plan five-star weddings. It was Evelyn's idea to marry a bride named Bernice at the High Museum of Art and give guests smocks and acrylic paints. With the help of a team of professional artists, the guests created a huge mural that the couple later installed in their vacation home. Evelyn dreamed up simpler themes, too, for couples like Cole and Emma who were dedicated organic gardeners. Each guest at their wedding entered a quaint, outdoor chapel bearing gifts such as an eggplant and cantaloupe they then deposited near the altar. The minister blessed the couple, the fruits of their labor, and their future pursuits.

I wonder where Evelyn and Maurice had gone wrong. Obviously, he made a horrible decision, and it destroyed their careful life together. They had married a little later in life, had no children, and seemed devoted to each other. A chilly finger of fear tickles the back of my neck. If a stable, seemingly happy couple could run headlong into ruin, it could happen to Avery and me.

Sitting at the hand-me-down kitchen table, I try to gauge Avery's cheating chances. He is loyal, attentive, and honest. To my knowledge, he has never lied to me or dated other girls after we started seeing each other. He is not like those guys who check out other women in front of their girlfriends. Avery acts proud to hold my hand and starts sentences like, "Macie thinks . . ." or "My girlfriend, Macie, is really good at . . ."

I draw an imaginary heart on the kitchen table with my index finger. Avery clearly is not like some of the fiancés I have seen in my time with Maurice. We know of men who cheated on their brides right up to and during the wedding week. We have seen with our own eyes the roving eyes and wandering hands of some—not all—men who were weeks away from slipping a wedding band onto their bride's manicured hand. It was disgusting, of course, but ultimately none of our business. We had a job to do and it did not involve marital counseling.

What was it that made some women blind to the obvious shortcomings of their men? Evelyn obviously did not see Maurice's affair on the horizon. I feel like I can honestly judge Avery's weaker points, and I am reasonably sure he can judge mine. The wonderful thing is, with all of our faults and imperfections, we have still managed to make things work, and to plan a future.

On second thought, planning a future has hit a bit of a snag. I want to marry Avery, but I feel this huge weight tied to my feet. If I jump into setting things in motion, I am afraid I will get sucked down into something powerful, something huge. If we buy a house, we have to buy furniture. When we buy furniture, along come sheets and towels. After that, you might as well pop out a couple of babies to fill the spare bedroom. It's all too much. I plop my head down on my arms.

The phone rings. I glance at my handset and see it is Iris. I grab for the phone, happy to chat with her after being away a week.

"Hello!" Iris says. Something metal bangs in the background. I hear men shouting.

"Where are you?"

"Oh, this new strip mall up in Sandy Springs. I'm getting the royal tour, but we had a break and I wanted to see if you could get together later. I have to hear all about your week of romance."

To my horror, I start to cry. "Iris, I screwed everything up and now Avery is mad at me, Maurice is cheating on Evelyn, and I think I don't want to get married."

With alarm in her voice, Iris says. "Okay, hold on right there. I am coming over. It will take me about thirty minutes, but you hang tight."

Although embarrassed, I am grateful. Sometimes, the only way to see things clearly is with a best friend.

Iris hears the entire story, both mine and the Maurice saga, without uttering much more than a sympathetic murmur now and again. Luckily, we have some goodies on hand since she swung by her studio to pick up a dozen chocolate-cinnamon cookies. In between a few tears and sighs, I munch a little.

"And that, pretty much, is the disaster that is going on right now in my life. I have pushed Avery away after he did the one thing I really wanted—ask me to marry him—and my boss is missing while cheating on his wife, which makes me ask the question: Are all men like this? Will Avery cheat on me?" I sink back against the futon cushions. Iris, sitting beside me, reaches for a cookie and takes a bite.

"Needs a little more butter, I think," she says.

"What?"

"Oh, sorry," Iris says, taking another nibble. "I'm self-editing. These need a little more oomph, maybe a touch more fat."

"Got it," I say. "So, what do you think?"

Iris tilts her head to the side and pauses for a moment. I glance at my cell for the hundredth time to see if I somehow missed a call from Avery. I have not. I wonder where he is right now. Maybe he has gone in to Chattahoochee Chocolates. I haven't called his house because I do not want to talk to my future in-laws. Just thinking of the word *in-law* makes me squeamish. How do I become this new person? A person who has parents who are not really hers, but belong to someone else. I will have to memorize two more birthdays and think of additional witty things to say around the dinner table.

"Macie, are you spazzing inside your head, because from where I sit, your mouth just started working and your face got all scrunchy. What is going on with you?"

"I've just told you. Avery expects me to buy a house tomorrow—"

"You're exaggerating."

I blow a lock of hair out of my eyes. "You're right. But what about Maurice? Avery could end up like him and I will be alone and heartbroken."

"That is not going to happen. Maurice is all flash and Avery is very down-to-earth, even with all his parents' dough. There's something else going on here, and you need to figure it out. I don't think it's the house or the money or the in-laws. Or even Maurice. You have some serious fears that are not going to be resolved by a well-meaning best friend and a plate of cookies." Iris stands up.

"Where are you going?" I wail.

"To get back to my real-estate agent. I'm signing a lease on the Sandy Springs property."

Suddenly reminded that the world does not revolve around my problems, I put on a brave smile. "That's great, Iris. How long until you open?"

Rolling her eyes, Iris says, "I'd like to think two months, but it will probably be longer."

"I'll be there to help you every step of the way, you know."

"I'll be counting on it. And if you know of any crack pastry chefs, send 'em to me."

I walk Iris to the door and follow her out to the hallway. "Thanks for listening. I really needed that."

"Oh, I almost forgot. You have homework," Iris says. "I want you to write down every detail of what is scaring you."

"Well, I know that. I told you what was bothering me,"

Iris puts her hands on her hips. "No, you told me the *symptoms* of what is bothering you. Moving from this dump to a nice house. Planning your wedding instead of talking about it. Having in-laws after you are married. I want to know why those things are striking a nerve. Get it down on paper."

Giving Iris a hug, I promise to write my list. We agree to meet for lunch later in the week. I walk back into my apartment and lock the door. It is time for dinner, but I am holding out hope that Avery will call and we can eat together. I don't feel like going to Tang. Pancakes or waffles would fit my mood better. If I know Avery like I think I do, comfort food will top his list as well.

The summer light is waning in the apartment and I think of the same light slipping away from Abigail Island a few hundred miles away. A sob bubbles up in my throat. The short week at the beach meant so much to Avery and me. We became engaged, helped another couple marry, and started talking about the future. Of course, then I had to go blow everything.

The phone rings and it is a number and name I do not know. I pick it up anyway. You never know if one of our brides is calling from a shop or a friend's phone.

"Hello? May I speak with Macie Fuller?"

"This is she speaking." It has to be a bride, I think. Her voice is full of hope, as if she wants us to like her and book her wedding. Ah, the power of my job.

"Macie, this is Baker Land. Maurice gave me your number. He said he was tied up at the moment and I could speak to you about planning my wedding."

It takes me a second to think these two thoughts: *Maurice is found again* and *Baker Land! The movie star!*

Baker Land is one of the biggest actresses in Hollywood. Her romantic comedies and dramas rake in zillions of dollars, although I recently read that she desired to do smaller, more meaningful films on the side. She is beautiful in an approachable way: big green eyes, long blondish-brown hair, and a cute but mysterious smile. I cannot believe she is on the phone with me.

"Are you really Baker Land?" I ask.

"That's what it says on my driver's license."

"Do you actually drive yourself places?" I know it is off the subject, but I think it is an appropriate question.

Baker Land laughs into the phone. "Yes, yes I do. Especially now that I have moved to Georgia. I live on a farm right outside of Atlanta."

I remember reading something about Baker Land relocating to the Peach State. She planned to marry here, as well, because her fiancé is from the South. "So, you are getting married," I say, striving for a little professionalism.

"That's right. And I hear Maurice is the best man in town to get a wedding together. We're thinking early October. Would that work for you?"

Work for us? Maurice would sell his vital organs to land this wedding. If that did not work, he would bump brides and rearrange receptions to get his hooks in a celebrity wedding like this. And not only a celebrity wedding, but *the* celebrity wedding. Baker Land's smiling face is on the cover of a magazine at least once a week. The exposure would make Maurice giddy for months.

That being said, it is awfully peculiar how he passed off the wedding planning to me. Maurice must be going through the wringer with Elise and Evelyn. Apparently he is out of commission, even for movie starlets. I shake my head. Life has become too confusing in the past six days.

"Let me get my book, Ms. Land. I'll check on our October dates."

"Please call me Baker."

"Of course," I say. Call me Baker! I'd be glad to. Maybe we will hit it off and become pals. It could happen. I am starting to feel a little delirious. Take it easy, Macie, I caution my inner child, this woman made ten million dollars off her last movie. I inhale sharply. Wait until I tell Iris who called today.

"We have openings on Saturday, the fourth; Sunday, the fifth; Friday, October tenth; and Saturday, the eleventh. I'm looking at weekends, of course. If you want a nontraditional day, we have plenty of those open, as well."

"I think Saturday, October fourth."

"It's a done deal. Did Maurice tell you about our policies?"

"For all of the details, I will have you speak with Kathleen, my assistant. She handles all of that stuff for me. But I wanted to talk with you personally about planning the wedding—all of the girlie odds and ends. Can we meet for lunch this week?"

"I have tomorrow free," I say. I am already searching my closet for an appropriate outfit to wear with a superstar. "I know a great place in Midtown."

Again, I hear Baker's laugh. "Oh, I can't go out to eat. We wouldn't get a thing done. Come down to the farm. It will be much quieter."

I feel so stupid. Of course, Baker Land can't just pull up a table at the local pizza joint. Reporters and photographers would flood the place, disturbing my new gal pal and begging to know my name. Baker interrupts my daydream of local stardom and says Kathleen will call with directions within the hour. We hang up, and I hit the speed dial to connect with Iris.

The next day, I call Avery again. He picks up and I start talking fast, hoping he is not too mad at me for being so flaky.

"Avery? I am really sorry for yesterday. We came back from such a wonderful week and I really flipped out. I don't know why, but I apologize."

Avery's voice is oddly flat. "I think you need to figure out what's going on in your head. Every time I bring up the future, you get a little weird."

"I was fine when we were on the island, you know."

"Sure. When you were in your element, helping Jessica and Kevin get married, or when you and I were having a romantic time strolling on the beach, you were happy."

"I'm happy!" I say a little too loudly.

Avery sighs into the phone. "Macie, do you not want this? Do you not want to get married to me?"

"Of course I do, honey. I just am having a hard time adjusting, I guess."

"And it's hard on me, always waiting for the next blow up," Avery says. "I think I should give you a few days to be alone and really figure out what's going on."

I think this over, glancing down at my ring. It might be the mature thing to do. The last thing I want to do is drive Avery away with my mood swings. We hang up after I promise to think about what's bothering me, and I sit down on the couch. My mind is going a million miles a second and I just can't sit still.

I decide to stroll down Highland and hit my favorite coffee shop for a latte. I have two hours before I need to get on the road to visit with Baker. I have selected one of the sundresses that Avery bought, and I will wear my dressiest sandals. With a leather briefcase and simple, silver jewelry, I should look professional but also stylish. At least, that's what I tell myself.

I pick a corner table and doodle on a piece of scrap paper. I know the wedding planning part by heart, but I want to think of things Maurice has probably never dealt with like paparazzi, helicopters, and security teams. We will need to hire out a firm that specializes in events for the rich and famous. My guess is that Baker wants a truly southern wedding, so she came to Maurice. The other details can be worked out with various vendors.

Without Maurice's guidance, I should be scared, but I'm not. I can't explain it. Even though I am meeting with one of the country's most famous people today, Baker Land is still a woman who wants a meaningful, pretty wedding. I understand that. A meaningful, pretty wedding is what I have wanted for the last year or so.

My mind rolls back to what Iris said yesterday. Sighing, I turn over my little piece of paper. If I can plan a celebrity wedding, I can make a dumb list for Iris. I cap and recap the pen, thinking.

This is what I write:

What Scares Me About Planning My Wedding
by Macie Fuller

Then I sit there, tapping my pen against the leg of the table. I sip some latte and then sip some more. I stir the contents of my paper cup. What is it that Iris said? I replay yesterday's conversation in my head. She said that my fears mask something deeper. What it is, I do not know. But I promised I would do this little exercise, and Avery's waiting on me to get my act together, so here goes:

Picking a date—Once I do that, everything gets set in motion
Buying a home—We have to work out where we live and how much money it will take. Also, once you buy a home, you have to fill it with things!
Planning a wedding—I do this for a living. Will it be special?
Having a new family like the Lelands—They are so different!

I stare at the list, trying to think of something else to write down that might magically explain all of my twisted-up feelings. Before I know it, the latte has turned cold and it is time to head back to my apartment, dress, and travel south to Baker's farm. I am eager to meet her, nervous, and excited. In the back of my mind, I think of Avery. I want to tell him all about this meeting, but I know he is more interested in what is going on in my head, not celebrity brides.

I drive south on I-85. The diamond on my left hand winks in the morning light, reflecting its own little patch of sparkle. I force myself to look squarely at the cars and trucks on either side of the car. Think of Baker's wedding, I tell myself. Plan her day and worry about yours later. Luckily, the traffic is heavy and I have to drive carefully. There is little time to think of anything else.

This morning I dialed up all the brides we have on the books. I made the calls under the guise of "checking the status of your special day," but in reality I was covering for Maurice. Just in case we had any mad brides out there, I wanted to go ahead and face the fire. Only two women told me they had left messages for Maurice that he did not return. I apologized, mentioned a summer flu, and everything was forgiven. After that little bit of playacting, I called Maurice's cell phone to tell him what I did. I also informed his voice-mail box that I was meeting with Baker Land and I would take care of everything until he was, um, back in the swing of things.

Using a tiny compass Avery gave me a while ago along with Kathleen's directions, I find the farm after only two wrong turns. I am delighted to be out of the city. The roads are only two lanes instead of six, and everywhere I look I see sheep, horses, and cattle. Baker's farm appears to have all three, plus four or five dogs that rush out to greet me once the main gate opens.

In every direction, pastures stretch almost to the horizon, offset by sturdy black fences. I pull to a stop before an old farmhouse that has been renovated and expanded. Huge pots of geraniums flank the front door. The dogs circle around, curious and friendly. Walking toward the front door, I breathe deeply. The air just smells better out here.

Kathleen turns out to be an efficient, superserious assistant who is in her late forties. I can tell that I will have to be on my best behavior around her. Trying to break the ice, I ask Kathleen how she came to work for Baker, but I get nowhere. "I'm from L.A." is her terse reply.

Kathleen holds court in a large office in a converted stable near the main house. I am surprised that Baker is nowhere to be seen in the well-lighted room decorated in soothing khaki and crisp white. When I mention this to Kathleen, a thin smile floats across her face. She closes a file drawer with an exact movement.

"Ms. Baker cannot be bothered with the myriad of details required for planning a wedding. You will work strictly with me."

"Oh, I thought Baker wanted to meet with me over lunch to go through the wedding design. You know, girl to girl."

"However nice that might sound to you, ah, Macie, a woman of Ms. Land's talent and demand cannot be bothered with having lunch with anyone who wants to."

"No, you have it wrong. Baker asked me to have lunch with her."

"That may be true, but we must always assume that Ms. Land does not know every last booking on her schedule. We must look out for her," Kathleen says. "Now, join me over here at the table. We must get going on these plans."

Perhaps it is because I have had a week off at the beach and I have gotten lazy, but I resent having to work under these conditions. My brides might be beastly, spoiled, or just plain misguided, but they are my brides. I work with *them*—not their assistants—and any combination of fiancés, sisters, and mothers. Kathleen is shaping up to give everyone a run for their money.

Within a short thirty minutes she informs me that the wedding will be at the farm, the tents and other privacy screens have already been ordered, the caterer will fly in three weeks early, and security measures are in the works. I am not to talk to the media. A stack of nondisclosure documents is shoved into my hands.

I start to feel very small, sitting there in my sundress. The list of wedding ideas for Baker sits unread in my bag. I really don't know how I can be of any use. I am about to tell Kathleen this when the door opens. Baker Land, movie star, strides in the door giving me her famous smile.

"I am so glad you are still here! I was forever with an appointment. I am so sorry. Have you eaten? 'Cause I am starving," Baker says. Instead of shaking my outstretched hand, she hugs me. Startled, I hug her right back, noticing that she is shorter than I would have guessed.

"Baker, dear, Macie and I were just finishing up. I know you have that one o'clock with Zip Henderson. We don't want to make him wait."

Baker gives Kathleen a look. "Zip will keep. If he really wants me for his next film, a few minutes won't hurt. I want to plan my wedding."

The squishy feeling in my stomach starts to leave. This is what I know: a girl who is excited about the day she walks down the aisle.

Kathleen's face softens just a bit. "I'll go and get something for you both to eat." She leaves us alone.

I look at Baker, who sits in the ladder-back chair next to me. Her famous face wears a touch of mascara. Her long hair is captured in a plain ponytail holder, and she sports a worn pair of jeans and a red T-shirt. A ring with the largest diamond I have ever seen rests on her left hand.

"Kathleen can be a little overwhelming," Baker says. "I hope she didn't run you over."

"Well, I was starting to wonder why you needed a wedding planner," I say, smiling. I like this movie star already. "All of the major details seem to be decided."

"That's exactly why you are needed, Macie. I want someone to shop with, someone to look at place settings with. I don't care about security and all of that. I want to do the girlie things." Baker jumps up and walks around the office. A large, erasable white board behind her is covered in writing. The words "Press Tour for 'Love Sunny-Side Up'" are scrawled across the top.

"If I leave it up to Kathleen, she'll have my dress ordered before I know it. My manager would rather I not get married because it takes me out of circulation for two weeks. The director of my next film wants me in Milan the day after I say 'I do.'" Baker trains her eyes on me. "I just need someone on my side who will let me enjoy the fun of getting married. I don't want a bloated Hollywood wedding. I want something simple and very elegant."

I tell Baker that I am the wedding planner for her. She looks so happy, I feet embarrassed. By the time Kathleen returns with vegetable sandwiches and yogurt smoothies, we have made plans to fly in a couture designer from New York who has promised to make Baker's wedding gown. After that task is crossed off, we'll select crystal and china. Apparently, movie stars want a china pattern just like the rest of us girls.

The familiar rhythms of wedding planning start to come back to me as I take notes in my folder labeled "Land, Baker." I still cannot believe I am helping this celebrity get married. It seems impossible, but here I am.

"So, when is your date, Macie?" Baker asks me. She takes a long sip of her smoothie and nods toward my left hand.

"Ah, well, I don't know."

"You don't know?"

Blushing, I think of how to change the subject. But Baker Land is used to getting her way and I don't think she will budge. "We just got engaged last week," I finally squeak out.

"Congratulations! That is so fabulous," Baker says. "I'll bet you will have the best wedding. You know all the secrets."

I think about that for a minute. Do I know all the wedding secrets? I can tape down errant breasts with duct tape, sober up a drunken groom with Mexican hot chocolate, arrange peonies like a pro, and pinch a size-twelve gown down to a four with the help of a few well-placed plastic clamps.

"Yeah, I guess I have learned a few things," I say, not mentioning my one tragic flaw: When it comes right down to it, I don't really seem to know how to pull off my own wedding. Iris's list haunts me like a bad horror movie. I see the words scrolling across my forehead. I am such a phony. Baker can probably see right through me.

Right after high school, when most of my classmates marched off to dorm rooms and undeclared majors, I took a job as a knife saleswoman. After about four days of classes about the product, I was set free to unleash the magic of Turbo Knives. It was supposed to be fairly easy: Call on those stay-at-home moms who had made the mistake of noting on a survey they were interested in possibly purchasing a new knife set.

I quickly found out that knives are something people forget about until they need to whip up a four-course meal for the boss and his wife, which for these housewives, consigned to sweat suits covered in jelly and Cheerios, was never. I had doors slammed in my face, lies told badly to get me off the porch, and just plain indifference delivered almost every day.

I think I was the most unsuccessful saleswoman in Turbo Knives's history. I left that job and never took a sales job again. Sitting in Baker Land's office, I finally piece it together. I was a lousy knife seller because people could see through me like I was plastic wrap. I did not believe in the product—I did not even like it. I never cooked, so I wasn't exactly a friend of knives. Besides, the Turbo Knives were kind of cheap and flimsy.

Maybe Baker sees through my false happiness. She has checked me over for honesty and found me lacking. *This wedding planner sure doesn't look like she's in love. In fact, I think she's going to barf on my crisp sisal rug. Her face is flushed and she has a clammy sheen to her skin. How sad. They sent someone who is a bad, bad fiancée. I should have never called Maurice.*

"Macie, are you listening?" Baker looks annoyed. "I was saying that we should get one of the big magazines to cover my wedding. But only one. They'll call it an 'exclusive,' like the mag is great friends with me or something. Let me tell you: They are not friends and don't ever think that they will be."

"Okay," I say, trying to snap out of my weird mood. "Magazines bad."

Baker looks thoughtful and reaches for a strawberry on her plate. "No, not always. That's where it gets confusing. When they put you on a list, you know, like the most famous or most handsome, then you adore them. Most of the time, though, I just deal with it. Publicity comes with the job."

I think, for ten million dollars a movie, I could put up with a lot. Shaking my head, I gather up my folders. I want to be gone before Kathleen comes back. If I play my cards right, I can be back on the highway in twenty minutes. Too late, the door opens and Kathleen walks into the room.

"Baker, you have a fitting for your charity-ball gown after your meeting with Zip, who is still waiting. If there are any things to tie up, I am sure Macie and I can take care of it." Kathleen's eyes rest on me as if I am an unsavory leftover.

Baker stands and stretches. "Macie, I'll see you later on this week. And I'll tell Kathleen about our plans so she cuts you some slack."

I smile weakly, knowing that people like Kathleen love power, even more than they love keeping their well-paid jobs baby-sitting celebrities. This is going to be a long journey to the altar. Baker may say she wants one thing, but I will have to get around Ms. K.

Sure enough, as soon as Baker leaves the office, Kathleen peers down at me. "Baker is to be managed like one would handle a rare, priceless piece of art glass. One bump too hard and there will be ir-reparable damage to her reputation and her value."

I nod, not knowing what else to do. Kathleen then gives me a crash course in Baker's box-office worth, and the difference between good press and bad press. I end up with more notes and a bad headache.

Finally, Kathleen tires of hearing her voice and I excuse myself. Luckily, I have Baker's private cell phone number, so I will contact her later about our plans. On the walk to the car, I think of every bride whom I have worked with and come to the conclusion that Kathleen is the perfect combination of them all. She is demanding, exacting, unreasonable, drunk with power, rude, unfriendly, and conniving. I could go on with the list, but something stops me. My mind switches tracks, back and forth from Kathleen to the list I made for Iris.

Kathleen is not the bride in this situation. If I really think about it, Baker is the bride. But Kathleen is taking on the role of the brides whom I am used to working with and so I have lumped her into the bride category. I like Baker. I don't want her to be the bad guy, to be one of my bad brides. Maybe she won't turn out like all the rest.

I have tossed more brides without knowing the answer to the eternal question: How does a ring turn certain women mean and spiteful? I have not figured out the answer, I just know that I des-perately do not want to wake up as one of them.

I start the car, turn on the air-conditioning and laugh out loud. The answer is almost too simple. I need to call Iris or Avery. It took me a visit with a celebrity and her guard-dog assistant to recognize what was staring me in the face. Behind the white lace of a wed-ding, around the corner from the flowers, and before musicians ever set up to play, I have discovered what scares me the most is becom-ing that which I have learned to despise and fear. I am afraid—of all things in this crazy world—of being a bride.

12

The Child Bride

When I was a little girl, I had a favorite doll with long, blond hair that poked up out of her head. A round wheel on the doll's back turned the blond hair in and out, making a dolly with short or long hair at the whim of her owner. I spent hours yanking her hair out, brushing it, and then turning the plastic wheel to roll the hair back up into her head. Had my parents given me more construction toys, I probably would have built bridges with Legos and engineered planes from balsa wood. Instead, I can imagine possible hairstyles from all sorts of angles, both long and short. Sometimes, with a sigh, I realize there was probably more I could have learned along life's path.

Kimmie sits in the hairdresser's chair, chirping like a happy, excited schoolgirl. Then I remember, Kimmie *is* a happy, excited schoolgirl. Today, I feel like I have zoomed into the future and found myself the owner of my very own real dolly. Kimmie's hair is the same color of my old plaything. The only detail missing is the plastic knob jutting from her back. I lean forward from my chair near Kimmie's to peer at the back of the girl's pink tank top. With the weird week I have been having, a knob might not be out of the question.

"So, up or down? What do you think?" Kimmie asks, dramatically lowering her hair with one hand and then scrunching it up and piling it on top of her head. "Macie, Macie, help me fix my hair," she sings in a whiny voice. For a fleeting moment I think of my old doll and how I could yank her hair out without fear of punishment.

"What I think is that we have taken far too much of Leif's time," I say sternly, nodding to the exhausted stylist. He shoots me a look of thanks, drops his brush, and hightails it into the back room.

"Where is he going?" Kimmie asks, clearly put out that Leif does not get the chance to try a tenth hairstyle on her shimmering blond locks. "I haven't selected my 'do yet."

"I think numbers three and seven were lovely," I say, collecting my files and Kimmie's veil. "Do you want to see the digital pictures again to help you decide?"

"Nope, I'll think about it later," the bride says, and swings out of her chair.

I hurry to keep up with her lanky frame. Kimmie has the body of the lacrosse champion that she is and the energy of a kindergartner. I have to work to keep pace with this eighteen-year-old. Our working hours are limited to afternoons, once she is dismissed from her private high school, but before homework begins.

Normally, I would be against tossing such a young bride. It seems odd, or worse, unseemly. Last time I checked, Maurice was not into marrying off the young chickies. But Kimmie's father is a family friend of Evelyn's, so Maurice is trying to make everyone happy in the hopes of scoring points with his estranged wife. He told me so a few days ago.

Maurice called me up—the first time I had heard from him in person since the Elise scandal—and asked for a meeting. For the past ten days, he has lain low, leaving voice mails with instructions or brides' phone numbers. For our meeting, he suggested the coffee shop near my apartment, a definite step down for Maurice. The only other time he went there, he informed me it was dirty (he used the word "squalid") and that the coffee beans were roasted far too long.

Upon entering the coffee shop, I spied Maurice in a rear booth, his back to the door. He was actually wearing sunglasses inside. Poor Maurice, I thought. He was hiding out in plain sight.

"Hey, Maurice."

"Macie." He stood and offered the bench seat in the booth as if it were a gilded armchair in a Buckhead mansion. That's Maurice—always loads of style.

"How are you doing? I mean, I'm not trying to pry, but I know things have been rough for you."

Maurice lowered his shades and looked down at his espresso. "They have, but it's my own fault. I'm trying to take responsibility for what I did. Evelyn says that's the first thing I have to do to win her back."

I try to picture tiny, composed Evelyn lecturing Maurice, maybe with a few self-help books by her side like *Loving When Hating Feels Good* and *Bad Husbands, Better Wives*. Everyone has a different relationship, of course, but taking back a cheating spouse? I don't think I could do it.

"Of course, it's still early and she could always change her mind," Maurice said. "I wouldn't blame her. And we'll have to find a top-notch counselor. But I want to save our marriage. Unfortunately, I think Evelyn could go either way."

I thought of Elise and wondered what she was doing. It was morning, so she was probably sleeping off a late night at the café. I pictured her in a very Parisian apartment, maybe with a few of those large theater posters framed on the plaster walls. Of course, maybe that was just how Americans thought the French decorated.

"Macie, are you drifting?"

I nodded. "Sorry. I've been working so much that my mind is pretty fried."

"Ah, about that. I regret that my personal problems have prevented me from taking an active role in my business. You will be paid well, I assure you."

"That's not what I want, Maurice. You and Evelyn should take all the time you need. I have been doing fine, really." I twist my engagement ring over and over on my finger.

Maurice looked a little stricken, like he was truly sorry for sticking me with all of the work over the past ten days. It had been a wild ride, too, with attending to Baker Land and a few other brides coming up on the calendar. When Maurice called and told me about Kimmie, the child bride, I knew I was close to cracking. To make matters worse, Avery and I were still having problems. Right after I had my big breakthrough, he left town for a Chattahoochee Chocolates business trip with Ted to the All-American Confection Convention in St. Louis. That was followed by a week with his father checking out some property they owned in the Virgin Islands.

"Sure, I'll miss you, Macie. But maybe this time will give you space to figure out why every time I bring up the future, you still get a little crazy," Avery said before he left for the airport with his father. As much as I missed him, I knew he was right.

That left me with Maurice, who was coming back onto the scene, battered and guilty, but still sort of functioning. We quickly got down to work at the coffeehouse and he handed me the child bride's folder.

"Good grief, Maurice. She's only eighteen."

"A hundred years ago, she would have had three kids on the farm by now. No one would have cared," Maurice said, waving his hand in the air.

"Well, that was a hundred years ago. This is today. What are her wacky parents thinking? And is this legal?"

"They are friends of Evelyn's, as I mentioned, and they are thinking that it is better to support her rather than lose her. An older daughter has already run off with some sort of guitar player."

I flipped through the file, noting that Kimmie had been educated in Europe until ninth grade and had traveled extensively in South and Central America. When she was thirteen, she started her own baby-sitting business. "Sounds like she's kind of mature for her age at least," I said.

"Yes and no. Anyway, let's toss her and move on to the next one. If we treat Kimmie nicely now, maybe she'll use us for her next wedding."

I frowned at Maurice. "That's rude, Maurice. Let's give her the benefit of the doubt."

Maurice placed his empty espresso cup off to the side of our pile of papers and sighed. "You're right. I am sorry. It's just that I've been so cynical lately about love."

"Things will get better, they will," I said weakly. A greeting card sentiment was not what my boss needed, but I did not know what else to say.

Maurice looked up, a tentative smile on his face for the first time. "Where are my manners? Congratulations on your engagement. I cannot believe I forgot to say something."

It felt weird to talk about marriage with Maurice's own union on the rocks, but I chatted with him for a few minutes about the beach trip and Avery's proposal. I dreaded the inevitable question, and it was not long before he delivered it.

"So, when's the big day?" Maurice asked, eyebrows raised.

Later in the week, when I am with Kimmie, I think about the unartful way I dodged the question with Maurice. I hemmed and hawed, eventually half-lying to get out of answering the truth. What was I supposed to say? "Well, Maurice, it's like this: I am afraid of turning into one of our freakishly selfish, inconsiderate, and mean brides."

But of course I said nothing, and my reward is that I get to drive Kimmie around town for another hour instead of facing my very real problems. When I am with the child bride, time seems to stop and every little thing becomes very important.

"Macie, do you think the salmon should be wrapped in the banana leaves or just left on the plate all by its little lonesome?"

Forcing myself to pay attention, I examine the two plates in front of me at Kimmie's parents' club. The salmon with the banana leaves is exotic, but the plate with the salmon solo looks pretty darn good, too. I run my finger along the gold-edged charger ringing the banana leaves salmon. "This one I think."

The club's food and beverage manager scribbles furiously on a clipboard. "And the starch?"

"Do you have a nice polenta?" I ask, my mind a million miles away from this stuffy club with its hobnailed leather chairs and hovering kitchen staff.

Kimmie wrinkles her nose. "What about french fries?"

We get through the rest of the tasting fairly quickly. I simply make most of the decisions, knowing Kimmie's mother and father will not mind. When I met them for our initial meeting, they just said to keep the whole affair "under a low six figures." Kimmie could buy a whole boatload of french fries with that budget.

I quickly discover that a younger bride is not as polished in the art of being nasty, but she is quickly learning her trade. At the department store linen counter, Kimmie sniffs to the poor clerk that her selection pales in comparison with the fine boutiques of London. When we stop in for a consultation at the stationery store for Kimmie's thank-you notes, the store manager is told that ecru, not cream white, is the card stock of choice for brides everywhere except Atlanta.

I do what I can to minimize my junior bride's warpath. Smiling brightly, I take her arm and steer her away from slack-jawed clerks. I try to model good behavior, much like Avery models good sports-

manship to the boys on the tennis court. Winning isn't about jump-
ing up and down, he tells them. Torturing store clerks is bad form,
I inform Kimmie.

By the end of our third afternoon together, I am worn out. I decide to take a break from my eighteen-year-old charge for a day to
help Iris wade through pastry chef résumés. I know she needs the
help, and it will keep my mind off of Avery.

Iris posted the job opening for her new store on several culinary
Web sites and she has been overwhelmed by the response. Apparently, there are a lot of talented and unemployed people out there
who make five-star goodies.

"Macie, the proper word is pastry or cake or brownie, not 'goody.'
I think hanging out with Miss Teen Bride has dumbed down your
vocabulary," Iris says crossly the next day at her studio. She sifts
through a dozen résumés and several brochures that lay on her
desk. A stack of unopened envelopes sits nearby.

"Get with it, graybeard," I say, imitating Kimmie's pert voice.
"Sometimes you are *so* twenty-seven!"

"Forgive me, oh wise one. I forgot that you have the world figured out." Iris pauses, distracted by one of the résumés. "Oh, look
at this goody. He's at Quelle Fromage right now, which is impressive
enough, but check out his picture."

I walk over to her desk and peer down at a catering brochure for
Quelle Fromage, one of the city's busiest bakery-restaurants in Midtown. One picture shows a handsome, tanned pastry chef standing
next to a tall wedding cake. Quelle Fromage makes an amazing
cheese muffin dotted with imported Gouda from Amsterdam. I
melt when I eat this treat.

"I don't know," I say to Iris. "Is hiring someone because he looks
tasty sound business practice? Just a thought."

Iris gives me a fake pout. "You mean I can't hire and fire on the
basis of looks? Come on."

I take a stack of the résumés rolling out of the printer and flip through the pages. Most everyone has studied somewhere impressive or interned under big-time head chefs. I try to picture the perfect person for Cake Cake to Go Go. He or she should be creative, a hard worker, and someone who is okay being left on their own since Iris will be across town. They should also be liberal with the free handouts, as I might be stopping in from time to time.

"What about him?" I ask, handing her a two-page résumé. "This guy attached some pictures of specialty cakes. He definitely has a sense of humor."

Iris scans the document and then puts it in the "keep" pile. "I like his use of color and space. See the way he pulls the eye into the top tier?"

We work like this for another hour or so. Some of the candidates Iris rejects without another glance. Reputations get around, she informs me. Others are not experienced enough. One woman mailed Iris a piece of cake, urging her to try it. "Ugh," she says, before dropping the squashed package into the trash can.

In the end, Iris selects four finalists and gives me the task of setting up the interviews. I pretend to be her assistant and call the four, telling them that Iris Glen would very much like to interview them, and when would they be free?

"I like having you make the first call," Iris says. "It seems more professional. If I called, I would start blabbing on and on about how scared I am to expand and how they would be crazy to give me a try but oh, you know, could you start tomorrow?" She kicks her feet up onto the desk and drops the pile of rejected résumés into the trash.

"You are so brave," I say, settling into a chair. "I can't imagine running my own business."

"Didn't you just do that very thing when Maurice flaked out on you?"

"Yes, but—"

"But nothing. From what you told me, you contacted all of your upcoming dopey brides, landed a movie star's wedding, and kept all of the current brides happy like nothing ever happened. That's running your own business, even if you don't think it is."

For once, I shut up and listen to Iris. There may be some truth to what she says. I did shoulder all of the day-in, day-out tasks that Maurice usually performed. I chatted with brides, consoled them, humored them, and when necessary, chastised them. I had been to see Baker Land three times since our first meeting, each time feeling more confident in my position. Although I was still uncomfortable wedged between the taskmaster Kathleen and the fairly nice Baker, I was beginning to stand up for myself.

"I never thought of it like that," I say.

"And speaking of men who go cuckoo, what is the latest with your absentee fiancé?"

"He is not absent, we're just taking things a little slowly. I need to get my head together, you know, really figure things out." I tuck my hair behind my ear and look up at Iris, daring her to question my position.

Of course, she does. Iris crosses her arms over her chest. "Macie, that is pure drivel, and you know it. You've figured out the problem—you don't want to turn into one of those Frankenbrides. Okay, we get it. Now what are you going to do about it?"

I know Iris is right. She usually is, much to my chagrin. I have spoken to Avery several times since I self-diagnosed my bride paranoia. He believes me, Avery being the loyal soul that he is, but I know the fixing part is up to me. Holding me close before he left for the Virgin Islands, Avery said he would marry me tomorrow if I wanted. When he said those words, my heart started to pound.

I feel close to tears when I ask Iris, "What if the problem I have is with Avery and not just being a bride?"

Iris smiles at me, a touch of sympathy in her eyes. "Then, you had better figure that out, don't you think?"

. . .

Leaving Iris's comfy studio, I feel a little lost. I do not want to go home or work on any weddings. Avery is not due back for a couple of days, but even if he were home, things are so strained that hanging out together would just be terrible.

Maybe a smoothie will help cheer me up. I drive over to Mr. Smoothie on Fifth Street and order a large cantaloupe blended with soy milk. Mr. Smoothie has no inside tables, just a tiny order window with the day's flavors written on a chalkboard and several painted benches outside.

I pick a bench in the shade and sip my drink, turning over my dilemma in my head. A few families walk up to the order window. I examine the couples to figure out if they look happy or bored or simply content. It is hard to say, of course, but I think they all might be a wee bit tired of life. It's no scientific study, but a slump of the shoulders here, an extra-large mocha fudge smoothie there, and the casual observer starts to see things.

One of the women catches me staring at her, and I look away, only slightly embarrassed. I know it is wrong to make sweeping generalizations about complete strangers, but I do not know what else to do. There are no titles in the bookstore that give me the advice I need. *Engaged but Crazy?* and *Got the Ring and Totally Chicken* have not been written. I am waiting.

I have considered calling my mother for some advice, but I do not want to pop her bubble. My parents are proud of their little girl for making it in the big city and for landing (Mom's word) a nice southern boy. They dream of grandchildren. There is no way I will call home to Cutter and tell them I am having a serious case of cold feet. Trouble is, I am running out of excuses for stalling my mother. She wants to crank up the ancient wedding machinery that rests in almost every female's breast. Mom has even asked me for Mrs. Leland's phone number. On my parents' next visit to Atlanta, they want to meet my future in-laws. That will be something to see, my parents and Avery's parents chatting over drinks on the veranda. It will give my folks something to talk about for months back home.

Growing up, I did not know a single rich person. Everyone was sort of just getting by, living in modest homes, and driving used cars. It was not until I moved to Atlanta that I witnessed displays of wealth on a daily basis. I also saw how stacks of cash affected people. From my perspective, it seems like the more money someone has, the more they want, and excessive wealth shelters people from reality.

I wonder how Avery and I will handle money issues when we are married. I have taken care of myself ever since I got out of high school, and the idea of pooling funds with someone else is strange. Even still, I know marriage is about sharing everything. I cannot do it alone anymore.

My cell rings and I am surprised to see the Lelands' number. I answer it and hear Mrs. Leland's breezy voice.

"Macie, dear, are you terribly busy? I was wondering if you could stop by the house. There are some wedding details that we should take care of today."

I am shocked to hear from Avery's mother. She's never called me before.

"I'm not too far from you. I can be there in thirty minutes."

"Excellent, dear. See you then."

After I hang up, I finish the rest of the smoothie and try to figure out what Mrs. Leland could possibly want from me. I did not even know she had my cell number. I immediately feel nervous, although I am willing to give her the benefit of the doubt. Maybe we can be friends, or I can be like a daughter to Mrs. Leland, even though she is not the easiest person to get along with. She floats from massage appointment to tennis game to dinner party with hardly a turn of her head. She does not seem to be affected by other people's hardships or their joys. I saw her the week after we became engaged, and she hardly mentioned her son's upcoming wedding. Of course, *I* hardly mention her son's upcoming wedding, but that's a different story.

It is midafternoon. Mrs. Leland has probably just awakened from her "beauty nap." She takes a little siesta almost every day. It is something she has done for years. Avery said that when he was young, he knew from three to four o'clock was the time to get away with mischief.

It is strange to approach the Lelands' front door without Avery leading the way. But I take a deep breath and ring the doorbell. Amina, the Lelands' housekeeper, opens the door and smiles at me. "Pleased to see you, Macie," she says, and gestures for me to come inside.

The house is cool and I blink for a moment, as my eyes become accustomed to less light. I ask Amina if Mrs. Leland is available, and she giggles.

"You to talk of wedding plans, yes?"

Not trusting my voice, I nod. Amina shows me to the casual den. It is a grand room, silk curtains spilling from tall rods and antique furniture reupholstered in eye-catching modern fabrics. Like a room out of a magazine, every fabric complements one another and each accessory has a story to tell.

Mrs. Leland enters the den, grabs my shoulders, and gives me a rough little hug, enveloping me in a cloud of her perfume. She wears a black velour tracksuit and gold jewelry. "Macie, it's so good to see you. I'm glad you could come over!"

I am surprised by this unexpected affection, but I hug her back. "Thanks for having me."

Mrs. Leland sits in an overstuffed chair with matching ottoman, inviting me to sit as well. "I was just waking up from my beauty nap. I take one each day if I can squeeze it in. Keeps the face young. You might want to try it once you turn thirty." She sizes up my complexion. "Or maybe a little sooner, dear."

"Thanks, Mrs. Leland."

"You should call me Babs, Macie. I'm almost your mother-in-law. Oh, I am so happy that Avery is going to settle down. I never liked him globe-trotting by himself. A young man should have a wife. 'Get a wife' I've said to him a thousand times. I guess he finally listened to his poor mother."

Amina walks silently into the room and hands Mrs. Leland a squat glass filled with brown liquid. Mrs. Leland's eyes light up. "Cocktail, Macie?" she asks.

"I'm driving. I'd better have a sweet tea, please." I resist the urge to look at my watch. Cocktail hour is coming early today.

"I remember my wedding. Jack and I were so much in love." Babs closes her eyes and smiles. "Oh, it was a magical time. We went on a three-week European honeymoon tour. I brought six suitcases, two of them filled with peignoirs. Of course, little Avery was our memento from that trip. My, was he a surprise later on in the year."

I cross and uncross my legs, unsure of how to respond.

Her eyes snap open again. "I've always felt Avery was a special child, Macie. We always took him everywhere—the club, Switzerland, Jack's investment trips. I always felt he was at his happiest with us. Now, I suppose he'll move out and make a home with you."

Babs seems lost in thought. I decide to take an interest in the oil painting over her head.

"Now, as I was thinking about the wedding plans," Babs says, her eyes narrowing, "I realized that you probably hadn't yet seen an important little piece of paper. Avery is so busy with his candy business, I don't think he has had the time." Mrs. Leland takes a large sip of her drink and stares at me, a tiny smile on her lips.

"I'm not sure what you're talking about, Babs."

Amina returns to the den and hands me a tall glass of sweet tea. "Thank you, Amina."

My future mother-in-law dips one pinky in her drink and wets the lip of her glass. "Well, dear, not to be too direct, but I am speaking of the prenuptial agreement."

"Prenup?" I squeak.

"Yes, dear. The one Avery will be asking you to sign. Don't give it another thought, Macie. Of course, turn out some adorable grandchildren and your settlement goes up per child. And each year your union lasts means a more generous severance for you should something happen. It's all very civilized."

Amina appears on the scene again with another drink for Babs. I want to scream, "She's had enough!" but I restrain myself. If someone fast-forwards my life, will I be Babs, informing a future daughter-in-law to push out some kidlets so that she gets more money when my son dumps her?

"When I married Jack, I signed something, too. I never gave it another thought. You may not know this, but I came from a little country family. My father ran a dairy operation in White County. Meeting Jack was marvelous and he gave me a life that I would have never dreamed of. I had to go along with certain understandings, Macie. You do the same."

I stand to excuse myself. "Babs, I need to get going. I have to see a bride and I can't be late." It is a lame excuse, but Babs is sufficiently lubricated by alcohol. She might not even notice I am gone.

"Macie, do you have the time?"

I check my watch. "Four forty-five."

As usual, Babs looks delighted that I know what time it is. "You're a smart girl, Macie. Avery is lucky to have you. When you quit that party-planning job of yours, you'll have even more time together."

I wait until I am past the security cameras on the Lelands' property before I start to cry. Prenuptial agreement? Quit my job? Have children to increase my value? Avery has not said a word about any of this. I loved Avery, not his trust fund. I fell in love with him, not what he inherited from some moneybags great-grandfather. In fact,

I never even knew Avery was rich until we had been dating for a while.

My phone rings. If this is Avery, he is going to get one heck of an earful. Instead, I see that Kimmie is calling.

"Macie?" a tearful voice wails. "I need your help. How do you know when you are in love?"

I try not to give off an audible sigh. How can I think about Kimmie's love life when my own is in such trouble? For the first time, I wish my job were anything other than manufacturing wedding bliss. But I know I need to try to help. Pulling off the road into a post office parking lot, I ask Kimmie what is wrong.

"Whitner is m-m-mad at me. He says I'm not serious enough about g-g-getting married. But I am, I am," Kimmie says, and then I hear what sounds like a nose being forcefully blown into a tissue.

"When did this come up?"

"Whitner asked me about the ceremony. He wants all these words and vows and other boring stuff. And I am more focused on me and what I will look like when I walk down the aisle, you know?"

I lean back, touching the fabric headrest. I have to give this Whitner some credit. For a man who wants to marry a high school student, he sounds like he has some brains. To be fair, he is twenty-one, not exactly a lecherous old man on the playground, but almost a kid himself.

"I don't mean to pry, Kimmie, but have you ever thought of pushing the wedding back a few months or until this time next year? It's just a thought."

"Why is everyone against me?" Kimmie starts crying again.

"Hush, there, Kimmie. I'm on your side. It's just sometimes, it takes a little while for everyone to get on the same page about a wedding. Maybe taking more than just four months to plan it would be the best thing. How about late spring? That's a lovely season," I add, going for Maurice's smooth confidence.

"Can't," Kimmie replies. "Too close to prom."

"I see. Perhaps we can address Whitner's concerns, then. What, exactly, does he want in the wedding ceremony?"

Kimmie pauses, and I picture her doll-like features concentrating very hard. "Um, well, he wants to have a poem and some songs, like from the church hymn book. I don't know any of them, but he says that's okay."

So far, so good. "What else?"

"And he wants me to write my own vows. Like I have time for that!"

"Anything else?"

Kimmie sighs. "Yeah, I'm supposed to find someone to sing a solo, like right before we are pronounced man and wife. I don't have to tell you that is not an option. I don't want everybody to focus on some singer while I am standing up there in my dress!"

A few cars zoom by on the side road beside the post office. I wish that I were in one of those vehicles, being taken somewhere, anywhere, but where I am. Just when I think I have seen the worst in bridedom, it just keeps getting better and better.

My conversation with Babs comes flooding back in my head. I want to scream at her, tell her off—something to make this awful feeling go away. My stomach feels sick, like I ate too much.

"Kimmie," I say, "I know you're upset right now. What I recommend is that you and Whitner sit down tomorrow morning—"

"I have a student council meeting at seven."

"Okay, then after school. Talk about what you both want in your wedding. There's still plenty of time before the ceremony has to be set in stone. Can you do that?"

"I guess," Kimmie says. I picture her trembling pouty lower lip and her china-doll skin flushed pink. Oh, to be eighteen and planning a wedding. I say good-bye and head for home.

13

The Golden Bride

The hot air balloon strains against the tether lines, heaving with all of its might for a takeoff into the rosy pink sunrise. Eight stories of ripstop nylon tower above the pilot and me, the liquid propane–fueled burner keeping the entire production upright. The pilot asks if I want to climb into the gondola, "just to see what it's like," but I decide to keep my feet firmly on the ground and out of the wicker basket. When my bride walks through the field to the waiting balloon, I want everything to be perfect.

"You know, I took *The Sun Cat* to Albuquerque last year and she was the belle of the ball," the pilot tells me from inside the gondola, nonchalantly firing the burner to keep the right mix of hot and cold air in the balloon's envelope. I'm getting a lesson on the yards and yards of yellow-and-pink ripstop nylon that will carry Annette and Lee up, up, and away. I've learned that unless the air temperatures are a happy mix, the balloon's envelope slowly sags and collapses. Too much air and it becomes aloft. So far, Tony and his crew seem to be doing a good job keeping things together.

Annette is in a lower part of the field, saying her vows to Lee, her sweetheart from nearly fifty years ago. For the past hour, I've been helping Tony and company spread out the envelope and then slowly fill it with cold air using a large fan. I am so happy to help this dear woman, whom I've dubbed The Golden Bride, marry her long-lost love. But first, there is the matter of getting this older woman into the gondola. With a stab of panic, I realize Tony's crew has forgotten the stepladder they said they would bring.

"Don't worry, Macie, we'll get her in here," Tony tries to reassure me.

I want everything to be perfect. Lee and Annette have already waited too long to be together. I don't want her to be heaved like a sack of potatoes over the wicker basket. Not with the couple's children and grandchildren watching. With a sigh, I realize there is nothing I can do. The wedding party is coming our way, stepping through the tall, green grass of this farmer's field south of the city.

Annette and Lee are first, of course. She wears a purple dress with a flowing silk scarf that promises to look quite dramatic as the couple ascends into the sky. Lee is dressed in a simple blue suit, his white hair shining in the early morning sunshine. The bridal couple is attended by a posse of running, shrieking grandchildren. The girls wear flower crowns with ribbons twirling down their backs. The boys carry sticks wrapped in blue ribbon. As they run, the boys joust at each other, annoying the ladylike girls. Behind them walk the adult children, arm in arm, laughing and pointing at the inflated hot air balloon. The pastor in his black suit brings up the rear.

I have learned so much from Annette, just by watching her and how she treats her family and those she loves. Hers was a relatively simple wedding that Maurice scheduled in the few weeks while everything was going crazy. I think he needed the money. "We don't have much time," Annette told me when we first met, "so make it snappy."

This got my attention. It was right around the week that Baker booked us, and I was stuck between battles with *Toot Magazine* and Zafir, Jeweler to the Stars. Meeting Annette was a refreshing change.

Over coffee one unusually crisp August day, Annette told me about her love affair with Lee. Before I heard the whole story, though, Annette confessed she felt a bit silly hiring a wedding planner.

"I know I am a good deal older than most of your brides, Macie," Annette said with a deep, southern accent. "But I want to move quickly. Maurice told me you do a fabulous job with his nontraditional weddings."

I paused, mouth dropped open. Maurice gave me a niche! This was big news. He trusted me enough to label me as someone who took on the tough brides.

"My fiancé and I want a nice wedding, and it has been about fifty years since I planned my last one. I need help, Macie. I won't lie to you. I don't know the first thing about putting on a wedding today, let alone in a big city."

I smiled at Annette over our cups of plain coffee. Maurice taught me a casual meeting in a good coffeehouse is the best way to close the deal. When we meet with the brides, produce pictures of past weddings and talk about their special day, most of them practically pant to sign us up immediately. Maurice calls it the "Dream Meeting."

"Lee and I met the second year of high school and dated for three years. We were madly in love at a time when people did things like that. If you found your fella, you made plans and got married."

"That sounds so romantic," I said, forgetting my problems with Avery for a moment.

"It was less dreamy and more the way things were done back then," Annette told me, her hand trembling slightly on the coffee cup. "Lee was headed off to engineering school and it was expected that we would marry. I planned to work as a secretary to help support him. We were going to live in a tiny little house across the street from campus. I drove by it with my girlfriends and I remember the house number to this day: 1815 Blue Bonnet Drive."

"What happened?" I asked, completely sucked into this woman's story.

Annette sighed and turned over her ring, a simple band of channel-set diamonds. "The summer we got engaged, I met a young man who worked in my father's office. Jim was handsome and funny and before long, I started to wonder if I was missing something. After all, Lee was the only boy I had ever kissed. It didn't take long for my fear of the future to make a mess of things with my fiancé. I gave Lee back his ring, and Jim and I later married. Within days I knew I had made a huge mistake. We stayed together thirty-five years and had two children."

"How did you and Lee get back together?" I asked, my hand clenched around the ceramic coffee mug.

"I was planning to attend my high school reunion—the big five-oh—when the phone rang. It was Lee, calling to see if I would be at the reunion. He had hired a private investigator to find me. I was thrilled."

"Did Lee get married?"

"Yes. He and Phyllis lived happily for almost forty-six years. She died of lung cancer. They had three boys together. Lee told me that he thought of me from time to time, but that he assumed I had moved on that day so long ago. I told him I never had."

Hot tears rolled out of my eyes. "That is a beautiful story, Annette. I would be proud to help you marry your sweetheart."

And here we are, in a sunlit grassy field, every stalk of wildflower wet with dew and a towering balloon on the crest of the hill. Annette claps her hands together and hugs me tightly to her chest. "It's magnificent! Just like I pictured."

Tony shakes Lee's hand from inside the gondola and asks, "Are you ready for this?"

Lee's laugh is a hearty one. "If I can get married again at my age, I reckon a hot air balloon ride is nothing I can't handle."

"Well, let's get your bride in here."

Almost as if we had planned it, Lee's three sons step forward and gently lift Annette into the gondola. She kisses them as the basket shifts under her feet. Annette's daughter and son step forward to kiss their mother. Grasping the edge of the basket, Lee swings his legs over one at a time. The couple kisses once, shyly, and then again as their families cheer.

"We love you! All of you!" Annette says, her hand firmly holding Lee's arm.

"Bye, Grandma!"

"Here're your flowers!"

"Don't fall!"

"Where will you land?" the children call out.

With a nod to his crew, Tony takes a gloved hand to the burner, heating the envelope and causing the balloon to rise from the ground. The tether cables drop and my bride sails into her happily ever after as the sun paints the field a bright pink and yellow. When the balloon is about twenty feet above us, Annette tosses her bouquet. The flowers stream to the field, much to the delight of the little girls, who scream and rush for the fresh blooms.

I arrive home early, happy to have the rest of the day off. I reflexively check the machine and my watch. Avery flew back to Atlanta last night after spending more time in the Virgin Islands with his father than he had initially planned.

He called when he landed, and asked if I wanted to see him this weekend. I said yes, but I was nervous after so much time apart. Would he expect a completely different fiancée? Is this when he would mention the prenuptial agreement? Or maybe, we would look into each other's eyes and decide sadly that things just did not work anymore.

I am brushing my teeth and examining a small mole on my cheek that produces a wiry black hair at all the wrong times when the doorbell rings. I use the peephole to peer into the hallway but no one is there.

Opening the door slowly, I glance down the empty hall. At my feet sits a waxy, white cardboard box with Cake Cake's logo stamped on the side. Attached to the top is a note in familiar handwriting. It reads, "Don't let the little man be all alone. Do what needs to be done."

Curious, I carry the box inside, relock the door, and place the strange package on the kitchen counter. I wonder what Iris has sent and why she did not stay to see me open it.

The box opens from the top, but the sides fold down to allow a cake to be picked up and moved without damage. I have seen it done a hundred times, so I use a fingernail to flip open the wings of the box. When I do, I laugh out loud.

Iris has sent me my very own wedding cake. It is in miniature, with all the trimmings. A tiny topper stands above the main base. Butter-cream icing coats the surface flawlessly and little polka dots run up and down the sides. Delicate fondant bows roll over the edges and a light dusting of white sugar makes the entire cake shimmer. It is delightful.

But the topper is the best part. Iris has affixed a solitary groom. The stiff, little ceramic man is dressed in a black-and-white tux, his frozen grin masking his distress at standing there all by his lonesome. I reread her note, loving Iris all the more.

She is right, of course. It is time I make some sort of decision. As I plan weddings for brides all over Atlanta and beyond, it is only fair that I think seriously about my own. Avery has been understanding, but it is not right to make him stand on the cake alone. On the other hand, if Avery has been hiding his secret ideas about our marriage, then I figure he can eat his cake, and say good-bye to Macie Fuller. I won't want anything else to do with him.

I dress quickly, knowing Avery is probably finishing up with his tennis lessons with the boys. Maybe he'll want to grab brunch at Tang when he's through. The boys have not had a lesson for two weeks, so Avery was eager to see if they practiced like they promised. By the end of the summer, if Antwon and Damon did well at Saturday practices and got along with each other, Avery had promised the boys brand-new rackets to replace their secondhand ones.

I select a pair of linen shorts and a sleeveless blouse. If we go to Tang, we will probably sit on the terrace, so I make sure to spray my ankles with bug repellant. I am fastening the silver shell necklace around my neck when the doorbell rings.

Curious, I open the door slowly. Did Iris send something else? Instead of a cake, a deliveryman hands me a large bouquet of daisies. I must have a look of complete surprise on my face because the man laughs.

"Yep, they're for you. If you are Macie Fuller, that is."

I nod, embarrassed, and dig up a couple of dollars for a tip. When the door is shut and locked again, I search for a card in the mass of white, yellow, and purple daisies. Surely Avery sent these. Who else would?

The small, white card reads, "Be generous in love."

I've never been good with short sayings, haiku, or Chinese fortune cookies. I like long endings, overblown messages, and drawn-out good-byes. So this concise message puzzles me. Be generous in love. Who in the world sent this?

I sit on the futon and think of my bride and her groom, sailing into the sun in a perfect four-mile-an-hour wind. Annette is generous—with her love, her grandchildren, and Lee. If you put aside the money and the uncertainty about the legal things Mrs. Leland told me, Avery is Avery. He is funny, loyal, loving, and a good sport. He makes me laugh, does not hold grudges, and has the sweetest smile of anyone I have ever known. I miss him, and I miss our closeness. But the weight of the future still hangs over me.

Speaking of Avery, I wonder if his lesson is done and if he will want to go to brunch. I try his cell once and then again a few minutes later. His voice is breathless; I hear the sounds of boys yelling in the background.

"Are you still at the park?" I ask.

"Yeah. We've had a great lesson. You'll never guess what just happened. Antwon and Damon's dad, Louis, you remember him?"

"Yes, he works at Chattahoochee Chocolates."

"Right. Well, he and another father came down to the park today and asked me to teach a few other boys and girls. They want a sort of tennis academy for their kids."

I am proud of him and put aside all of my dark thoughts about our relationship. "That's great, really great. What do you think about it?"

Avery pauses to holler encouragement to one of the kids. "I want to do it. It is perfect—I love to teach these guys, and with some girls added to the mix, things should get interesting around here. They are already so competitive. Let's get some young ladies to give them a run for their money."

I take a deep breath. I feel like if I don't talk to him now, I'll lose the chance forever. Life seems stretched out before us like a fancy, embroidered quilt.

"Avery, when your lessons are over, we really need to talk. I've done a lot of thinking while you were gone. Iris made a cake for me—well, for us, really—to kind of help me realize some things. Then your mother had stuff to say. And Annette—"

"You talked to my mother?" Avery asks, lowering his voice.

"And it was terrible. But after talking to Annette, I see that if I let you go, I—"

"Macie, I've got to get back to the boys, and then the dads want to have a meeting. Can you do an early dinner?"

I feel numb, but I tell Avery we will meet up later today. I can't blame him for not dropping everything and rushing over. I am the one who flaked out on him even after I said I was ready for a commitment. If anyone had told me I would be thrown for such a loop by a proposal, I would have said they were crazy. Looking back, I thought I was ready, but I can see now that maybe I was not.

Hunger propels me out of the apartment and onto Highland Avenue. I stroll slowly, moving out of the way of happy-looking couples walking briskly toward brunch or coffee. Because of my job, it is natural for me to glance at ring fingers. When I see the glimmer of gold or platinum on the hands of the people walking past me, I get a little pinch in my chest. I need to figure things out with Avery now. Waiting until tonight seems impossible.

I stop into a bagel and biscuit shop. Mindlessly scanning the menu, my eyes fill with tears. I would rather be doing anything with Avery than eating an egg and cheese biscuit alone. Does he want the things his wacky mother talked about? If they are so important, why hasn't he mentioned them to me? I sip a bottle of organic orange juice at a corner table.

"Is this seat taken?" A couple stands above me, peering down at the empty chair across from mine. They hold newspapers and a tray of drinks and scones.

I nod that they can take it. After the chair is moved, the extra space at the table mocks me. I toss my trash and head outside. I pick a side street beside the shop and walk in the opposite direction from my apartment.

Along the way, my thoughts return to Avery and this whole wedding mess. I have such fears about marrying him. Or maybe it's not Avery at all, I think as I walk past a row of 1920s bungalows. Maybe I just fear the situation that marrying Avery will put me in.

It's like my weirdness about Avery's wads of money. It's not Avery's fault he's rich. But I do fear being a part of that money, since we'll be combining our lives together. Will I have less of a say in what we do with our money because I bring less of it to the marriage?

The big question, of course, is the prenup. In reality, I just can't imagine Avery putting those words on paper and then handing me a pen to sign. Besides, thinking about it makes my head hurt.

The houses on the street are tidy, with tiny front yards boasting petunias, roses, and wide front porches. I pass two little girls swinging in a hammock. They giggle when I walk near, sharing secrets with each other. A few houses down, a sturdy bungalow with a blue door is for sale. Without even thinking, I bend down to take a flyer from the information box staked into the green grass.

The price is outrageous, but I notice the interior pictures of the home show a gracious living space with hardwood and built-in bookshelves. Avery would love the kitchen. Stainless-steel appliances and natural pine cabinets are right up his alley. I am peering at the picture of the master bedroom when it hits me that I am mentally moving into this home with my husband. I do not see us choosing some halfway measure like living together or renting this house. I imagine us unloading a truck with our own two hands—hands that sport matching bands. We unpack wedding gifts and pieces of old furniture we both could not bear to part with, and in my imagination, we are laughing.

I am lost in this little picture for a few moments. Then I remember I am standing on a sidewalk in front of a stranger's house. I am sure they are nice people, but all the same, I decide to get moving. Before I do, I tuck the flyer into my pocket. This little bungalow will always remind me of an important few minutes in my life. Maybe Avery will want to take a look at it later.

Walking a few feet, I take mental stock of my little house fantasy. My heart does not pound, I do not have drumming in my head—all good signs. Maybe I can mature a smidge and consider that just because I work with the most vain and selfish women in Atlanta, their disease does not have to rub off on me. Avery and I are special and different. At least that is what I tell myself.

My route takes a fork in the road and the sidewalk runs alongside a neighborhood park. Blooming crepe myrtles grow in a line next to a gentle slope of shade trees. As I walk closer, I spy all the familiar trappings of a Saturday morning wedding: gardenia garland, portable fern stands, and a sweating wedding party. The air is humid and I feel for the groomsmen in their jackets and vests. The ceremony must be over. Guests are milling about, and a photographer wriggles through the throng, snapping shots of the bride and her groom.

I am almost past the park when I hear a voice shriek out over the crowd noise. I wince, almost like the insult was directed to me.

"Carl, I told you not to step on my train! Do you need me to say it again? Are you dense?"

The bride, a tiny speck of a woman wearing a satin A-line, addresses her new husband with the fury of a hornet. Poor Carl looks caught between nervously laughing and choking on pure fear. A few women wearing large hats shake their heads. Former brides themselves, they silently berate Carl in a show of unity.

I walk past the park before I can witness another ugly display. I am so afraid that will be me—the curled hair, the rosy red lips, the mean heart. Even though things might be fine between Avery and me one day, what happens if I become that bride? Chill bumps pop up on my arms, even though I am sweating and the sun is high.

A new thought emerges. Maybe if I do everything backward or opposite, I will not transform into a mean bride. If I do not have any showers or parties, maybe greed will not sweep over me like a monsoon. An even stricter idea: not registering for gifts! If I don't go to the trouble to register, I won't have piles of presents to open. I would make a bet that in pioneer days the women were glad if someone tossed them a bag of sugar or a fresh beet. Those women were tough. If they needed a frying pan, they traded for one. No crystal and china registry for them, no sir.

I continue on my walk, totally dispirited. Weddings float through my head like a current of bad memories. Devin, Carolina, Darby. The names of some brides I have trouble recalling, but I can see their faces in my head. Other thoughts are just snippets of bad behavior. At the end of this sad parade is a lone, little bride who just wants to marry and live happily ever after. It has to have happened to someone out there, I am sure.

Suddenly, as I round the corner to my apartment, I think of Gwen, my sweet pink-haired bride. She seemed so content and ready to marry her fiancé, Jake. That I even remember his name is amazing because we never know the fiancé's name. Rule number one: The day is all about the bride.

I will call Gwen. Hopefully, she won't think it weird that her former wedding planner is calling for love and marriage advice. From what I know about Gwen, my questions will fit right in with her freewheeling, slightly offbeat sense of things. I feverishly hope that she is in town and able to take my call. I sprint up the stairs to the apartment, almost tripping on the last, uneven stair.

I have deleted Gwen's phone number from my cell, but I still have her file. It is pink, of course. I added a few pictures after the event and I reminisce for a moment with the glossy prints. There is the tiny park next to the church where we moved the wedding. This picture shows the wilted fancy flowers so out of place in the outdoors. The last photo is of Gwen and me at the Fox during the reception. She looks beautiful and I wear a huge smile. It was one of our best weddings, but boy, I was nervous down to the wire.

I dial nervously, but when Gwen hears my voice, she acts like we just spoke yesterday. She even invites me over to her loft for tea and "whatever else I can dig up." I tell her that I will be right over. I turn to replace Gwen's file in my desk drawer, but then I stop. I remove the picture of the two of us and I place it on the bulletin board, where it will give me hope.

Gwen and Jake live in a trendy, developing area of Midtown near Tenth Street. I have driven past their glass-and-metal tower before and even eaten in the restaurants on the ground level, but I have never been inside. I take the ultracool metal-and-blond-wood elevator to the eighth floor, sharing the ride with a tattooed mother and her little boy.

Gwen meets me at the door and gives me a big hug. Her hair is strawberry blond now, and she still wears the cutest clothes. Complimenting her on her striped skirt and matching belt, Gwen just smiles. I know that means she designed it. Oh well, I grimace to myself, there are other things I do well like create color-coded files.

Gwen gives me a tour of the loft, mentioning that Jake is at his studio working on a new series of paintings. The loft is warmer than most I have visited. A honey-blond wood covers the floor and some of the walls. There are the prerequisite floor-to-ceiling columns and metal accents, but the entire place feels comfy. I try to picture living here with Avery, but I have my heart set on something with a backyard for a future dog.

After the tour, I ask Gwen about her clothing business.

"I have a lot of orders for my wedding dress, would you believe?" she says as we curl up on the modern blue sofa that sits on a natural jute rug. "It's been in a few magazines, and I am sort of leaning toward doing just dresses for now."

"Does that mean your store opening has been postponed?"

Gwen nods. "I think I should go with what is big, for now. I can always do retail later, you know?"

I picture Gwen's dresses adorning movie stars at award shows. Having an obvious talent like hers makes me wonder if life is any easier for her. I have seen it with Maurice and Iris—once they found what they liked to do, they seemed happier. Avery, too, perked up a million degrees when he stumbled onto Chattahoochee Chocolates and his tennis lessons. Feeling a bit down, I decide to focus on Gwen and try to forget about my problems.

"Can I see your wedding album?" I ask.

"I know every bride likes to show off her pictures, but I can tell something is bothering you, Macie. I can always bore you with my pictures some other time." Gwen walks over to the kitchen and grabs two bottled teas out of the refrigerator.

Now that I have come all the way over to Gwen's loft, bothered her in the middle of a Saturday, and made myself at home on her couch, I have a sudden case of shyness. Maybe I could have figured this thing out on my own.

By just looking at the facts, it is entirely possible that Avery and I do not belong together. We grew up on different rungs of the socioeconomic ladder. I had a dog, he had a pony. My family went to flea markets, his went to antique fairs.

"I guess it all starts with my fiancé's proposal," I begin. "Well, he was my boyfriend at the time, but now we're getting married. Or not. I don't know—it's just so confusing. And I don't know what to do."

Laughing, Gwen says, "Take it easy! Just start at the end. Or the middle. Just pick a place."

And so I tell her all about wanting to get married, but then realizing a whole lot of things went with it—finances, moving, in-laws, Avery himself. I don't know how to share toothpaste with someone. I have no idea how to be a daughter-in-law. The worst part is, Avery seems unbothered by all of these day-to-day worries.

I tell Gwen my entire tale, up to and including today's conversation with my fiancé. Although, to tell the truth, he does not even feel like a fiancé, and that is not Avery's fault, it's mine.

"I don't have dreams anymore about our life together," I say quietly.

Sitting still, Gwen looks out her wide windows that offer views of downtown and the hazy, late-summer day. Traffic sounds are muffled at this height.

"Why did you call me? You've mentioned your best friend, Iris. Why not her?"

"She's heard all of this before. Her advice was to figure out what I was really afraid of. I did that."

"And?"

I throw out my hands. "Here I am!"

We both laugh, but I know I owe Gwen the truth. "Actually," I say, "I always admired you among all our brides. You were funny, kind, and you seemed to love your husband-to-be more than a ceremony or expensive reception."

"Thank you, Macie. That is a really big compliment."

I place my tea on a glass coffee table. "So, if I follow Iris's advice and figure out what I am afraid of, and if one of those things is becoming a mean ol' bride, I figure a good place to start is with a bride who was different."

Reaching for a striped pillow, Gwen says, "If you asked Jake, he would tell you I have my bad days. Several of them in a row, he would argue helpfully."

"Avery would chime in there, too."

"I don't know, Macie. I think Avery is getting quite a catch. The fact that you are trying so hard to really commit to him instead of just fantasizing about a wedding speaks volumes. If what you say about the brides you work with is true, then I would say you are miles above their level."

I let this sink in. Maybe I do have my heart in the right place. Avery has not run from me—yet—and my best friend still likes me. "I am just so scared all of the time. What did you think about before you were married?"

"Mostly, how I could not wait to be married to Jake. I just wanted our life together to start. I knew the wedding planning was going to be hard, no offense, and I wanted to get through it unscathed. My mother, I'm sure you remember, was responsible for a lot of those feelings."

I nod. "But when I think of our happily-ever-after life, I panic. In my mind, it's all about money or picking a house that suits us both or my strange mother-in-law to be. I want to dream about the future, I really do, but it just gets clouded over with all of this junk."

Gwen stands and walks back toward the front door. She takes down from the wall a small framed picture and brings it back to me. Placing it in my hands, she says, "This was taken the day I knew I wanted to marry Jake."

The photo shows the couple leaning jokingly over a body of water. Jake's tanned arms are wrapped around Gwen's back. She is safe; she's not going anywhere. Their faces wear expressions of mock horror at the prospect of falling into the water. I wonder where they are. Tahiti? Costa Rica?

Gwen smiles mischievously. "If you look closer, you might just recognize a famous Atlanta park."

I peer at the small photo. "Is that Lake Clara Meer?" The small lake in Piedmont Park is a tranquil spot to read a book or enjoy a picnic lunch.

"The very one. We were sitting on the dock one afternoon, legs dangling just above the water, talking about what we wanted to do with our lives. We had been dating about a year."

I smile, picturing the scene. I love the dock. It is wide enough for several groups of people to watch the sun setting over the city, the tall buildings behind the park a scattered palette of lighted windows. Cicadas and crickets keep up a summertime chorus to compete with deep-throated bullfrog calls.

"As we were sitting there," Gwen says, "I thought about how we were going to get dinner and maybe dessert, and then the next day we were attending a brunch for something—I've forgotten what—but it just hit me all of a sudden that I was looking forward to all of these little events with Jake. I saw us going about our lives, together."

I nod. I've had that feeling about Avery. It occurs to me that a happy moment does not have to end, but can keep going in spite of an unknown future. "I know what you mean, I really do, Gwen. I have had the same moments with Avery."

Gwen takes the picture back to its place on the wall. "Then you have already answered the big questions. Is Avery the one? Can I see myself with him for the rest of my life? The rest of this stuff is all just sticks and stones that get in the way."

"Even my fears of becoming a bad, bad bride?"

Gwen sits back down on the couch. "I think that's just a side effect of your job. I'll bet caterers worry endlessly about the food for their own weddings. Wedding gown designers kill themselves with last-minute redesigns. It's all part of the gig."

I feel happy, almost giddy. "Did you really worry about your gown? It was beautiful."

"Whipping stitches into it until the night before, I confess."

Gwen and I hug good-bye. She is going to take lunch over to Jake at his studio and I do not want to keep her any longer. When I ride the elevator down to Peachtree Street, I feel as if I am leaving a heavy burden up in the sky, or at the very least, up on the eighth floor of a glass-and-metal tower in Midtown.

Avery has a funny thing about parking his car. If we parallel park on the street, the car has to be placed with mathematical precision between the other two vehicles. All parking signs must be clearly marked. No rusty or deformed signs can be trusted. If he has even a foggy notion that the car might be towed, we lurch the car out of the space and try again somewhere else. Valet parking is a nightmare with Avery. "Is it just me, or are they letting eighth-graders park cars these days?" he grumbles when we arrive at Tang for an early dinner.

Once we are seated on the outdoor patio, Avery bubbles over with excitement about the lessons with the boys. He and the two fathers sketched out some rough ideas about the tennis academy, including gathering community support. Avery thinks he could get Ted at Chattahoochee Chocolates to help sponsor a junior tournament right in the neighborhood.

"And with my father's connections, just think, I could raise some serious money," Avery says, twisting his napkin in his lap. The air on the patio is heavy as the day's heat falls away.

"I am really excited for you. A lot of things are going your way lately."

Avery looks up. His green eyes are sad. "Not everything."

"Listen, Avery, there's something I need to know." Brushing a fly away from the bread basket, I try to line up everything I want to say in my head.

"I can guess what you are about to say. That we're not ready for marriage. That we should take it slowly," Avery says through tight lips. "Well, I think you're not giving us a fair chance. After all, we've made it this far, and we are happy. At least we were until I put that stupid ring on your finger."

Self-consciously, I look down at the engagement ring. "It's not stupid, it's a beautiful ring."

"Nothing has been the same since you put it on," Avery says, tossing back a piece of bread.

"Okay, Mr. Romance, how about your little legal paper? Nothing's been the same since I heard about that."

Our waitress stops by to tell us the specials in a singsongy voice. Avery asks for a few more minutes. We have not even opened our menus. My stomach growls, but probably more from nervousness than hunger.

"What are you talking about, Macie?"

"Remember I told you that I spoke with your mother? She called and asked me to come by the house."

Avery leans forward. His eyes look into mine. "She told you about the prenuptial agreement, didn't she?"

I nod slowly. Avery reaches for my hand, but I pull it away.

Speaking quietly so the other diners cannot hear him, Avery says, "I have an insane uncle. I've told you about him. Remember Uncle Len? He's my dad's uncle, so he's more like a great uncle to me, but that's not really the point."

Avery continues, his voice low. I have to strain to hear his words.

"Uncle Len is obsessed with the family money. There is loads to go around, but he has appointed himself sort of an unofficial guardian of the gold, so to speak. I really think the man counts his money all day long. It must be very lonely. When I was a kid, I never liked visiting him up in Virginia."

"What does Uncle Len have to do with your mother and me?" I am getting angry and the heat is making me cranky.

"I'm getting to that. About three months ago, Uncle Len showed up at the house for a dinner party or something. I made the mistake of telling him I was getting serious with a girl and that I was thinking about making it official."

"Three months ago? I thought our trip was a spur-of-the-moment thing. You've been sitting on my proposal for three months?"

Avery waves the waitress away. She shoots us a bored look and goes back to refilling water pitchers. "Anyway, right after we get back from our trip, I'm visited by one of Uncle Len's lawyers. The man had a prenuptial agreement a mile long."

"What did you do?"

"I hit the roof. I practically tossed the guy into those prize rose-bushes my mother is always fawning over near the porch. My father was pretty upset, too. He called Uncle Len and told him to stay out of my business. Len said it was my father's job to stick his nose into family affairs and protect our assets."

"Why is he so scared of a wedding planner from Cutter?" I was starting to feel compassion for Avery. I would have never heard about the prenup if it hadn't been for Babs.

Avery sighs. "Who knows? I just think that Uncle Len sees life as a game to accumulate as much money as you can and not share a penny of it. I'm sorry to have to tell you this. Please don't judge my family on this one incident—my father had nothing to do with it."

"Why was your mother pushing me to sign it?"

Avery rubs his hands together and leans back. "That is a more troubling question. I never told her I was going to show it to you, let alone ask you to sign something like that."

Nibbling on a piece of bread, I ask Avery, "What do you think of our chances? People sign things like that prenup because they want to hold something back, I suppose."

To my surprise, Avery stands up and walks around to my chair. He squats and puts his arm around me. A woman next to us whispers to her companion, "Oh look, he's going to propose."

Avery smiles up at me. "Macie, when I asked for your hand, it was because I had already thought of the what if's and maybe's and all that other junk. I was ready—and I still am—to be with you forever. I'm just not sure you feel the same way. Do you?"

Taking a deep breath, I feel my answer with every quiet and joyful part of my heart, my mind. "Yes, Avery, I do. I really, really do."

At this moment, our dim-witted waitress makes her third attempt to wring an order from us. Avery stands, takes my hand, and tells her that our plans have changed for dinner. He tosses a five on the table and we walk out of Tang hand in hand as the woman seated next to us remarks to her friend, "Oh, that didn't go well at all, poor dear."

We find ourselves strolling down Piedmont Avenue, walking with traffic on its one-way approach to Piedmont Park. Avery takes the outside of the cracked and broken sidewalks fronting million-dollar homes. I lean slightly on his shoulder, feeling a deep and soft part of me return to happiness.

As we walk, I tell Avery my fears. I retrace my steps to the moment I said "yes" and then into the few weeks of confusion and worry. I fill him in on my attempts at figuring things out with the help of Iris and Gwen.

"Iris sent me the best cake today, or did I already tell you? And I got the prettiest bouquet of daisies but with a weird, unsigned message."

"Did you say 'cake'?"

"It's amazing. You'll have to see it."

Avery pulls me closer. "I don't have any dessert plans. How about you?"

Thinking of dessert reminds me of Gwen and her breakthrough moment with Jake by the dock when she realized she wanted to marry him. I am having that moment with Avery again, and it is right. I know it with everything that is good and pure.

We return to the car, and as we get settled, I tell Avery about the house for sale near my apartment. He looks surprised but does not say anything.

"Do you want to? I mean, we could just drive by. We don't have to stop or anything," I add. Maybe it is too early to talk houses. I don't want to push him.

Avery's smile is my answer. He slips the car into traffic and instructs me to reach into the glove box. My fingers find a stack of house flyers wadded up next to an old bottle of sunscreen. I reach into my pocket and pull out the flyer for the house with the blue door. Avery glances at the flyer and then back to my face. He leans over and gives me a fleeting kiss while keeping one eye on the road.

"There's a great bungalow on Argonne Avenue, and you should see the Tudor on Morningside. You'll love it," Avery says, driving a little too fast. "And this house you've found looks really nice, too."

As we speed down the street toward a parade of homes, I have to laugh. It is good to have a stack of house flyers on my lap and my fiancé in the seat beside me. The air has turned a bit cooler, thankfully, and I reach for Avery's hand. If I snapped our picture at this very moment, the image would be of eyes and mouths, our faces lifting toward the sky and the space between us blurring as we race to fill it.

14

The Happy Bride

An audible hum lingers in the air wherever a bride walks on her wedding day. I have heard it with my own ears and even contributed to it as I buzzed past the bride du jour, peppering her with this question or that. Florists, hairdressers, makeup people zoom in and out of her field of vision, offering their wares. Studied closely, this last-minute activity either terrifies the bride as her natural habitat is disturbed or it excites her and she adapts, even thrives.

It is my wedding day, and I am falling solidly in the middle.

The entire two months we were putting this day together, I never had a sense of a clock in my head. Of course, I had my files and Maurice's steady hand. But it was not until last night's rehearsal dinner at Tang that it hit me: Go to sleep tonight, and tomorrow you'll get married.

I was up until midnight, packing for the surprise honeymoon. I was tempted to stay up all night, to welcome the sunrise on this most special of days. But sleep eventually came for me and I went to bed, arms wrapped around the pillow. When I awoke, it took me a few moments to realize the day—Avery and me! Our wedding!—

and then I flopped back into bed and smiled just because I felt so wonderful.

My parents are staying at the Lelands' house in one of their luscious guest suites. Avery has been living at our new home for the past three weeks, so he spent last night there, surrounded by mounds of wedding presents. He seems bewildered by all of the silver-and-white boxes dropped at his door daily, but I tell him that's what he gets for letting his mother have too much control over the guest list. "Think of it this way," I said the other day, "We'll never have to buy a crystal vase again in our lives."

"That's a huge relief," Avery said, rolling his eyes.

Iris will be stopping by soon to take me to the salon. Babs wanted to spring for a hairdresser and makeup person to come to the house, but the cost of something like that is ridiculous. Even though the Lelands are footing most of the wedding bill—my parents paid for flowers and the dress—I still do not want to spend money frivolously. Besides, it gives me a chance to be with my maid of honor.

Iris spent the past few days working on our wedding cake. I cannot wait to see it. The four-tier cake will be delivered to the reception by her staff so that Iris can be with me today and not worry about setting up. Avery's mother sniffed at this plan, and wondered out loud if we should have gone with the pastry chef from their club. I sweetly told her that Iris was our choice. I have never spoken with her about the things she said that awful day, and Babs has been fairly nice through this entire wedding planning event, so I have decided to let it go. I am learning how to be a daughter-in-law already, and the first lesson is: Some people do things differently. I am rolling with it.

Surveying my messy bedroom, I take stock of everything I will need today. Honeymoon bag, packed. Personal bag, packed. I wear a button-up shirt so I can take it off without messing up my styled hair. The veil hangs on a hook, covered in plastic. My shoes are in the personal bag, along with the strapless bra and pretty under-wear Babs insisted on buying. I have to admit it is beautiful, but the price was crazy for what amounts to a few inches of white lace. I do not think I will ever feel comfortable spending money like she does.

Lastly, I gaze at my dress that waits patiently, hanging from the door frame. Slipping a hand inside the garment bag, I once again feel the supple fabric. It gives me goose bumps. I cannot wait to wear this dress. It's funny, but I already miss it. You only get to wear these things once, and that makes them all the more special.

The phone rings. Maurice sounds completely in control and I realize for the first time that today will be a little strange for him. Even though he is cool, calm Maurice, it will be sort of strange to toss a bride he cares for—even if it is an employee.

Leaning forward into the mirror, I apply a little moisturizer and correct myself. "Partner" is the new word I must get used to saying. I am Maurice's business partner. Last week, after we wrapped up some last-minute shopping, Maurice asked me to dinner. Over a tasty plate of souvlaki, he told me he had been impressed by how I handled myself in all sorts of tough situations. Would I be interested in taking on a share of the business and working as the "special weddings" coordinator?

"We'll toss all the weirdos your way, it will be fun," he said.

"Maurice, they are not weirdos—these women just have different styles," I started to protest.

"Kidding! I'm kidding. Some people just can't take a joke around here." Maurice examined his fingernails. "You know I secretly admire freewheeling souls like you and Avery. I realize I'm not the best person to dispense advice, given my recent behavior, but I do have one thing to say: be generous with each other."

I stared at Maurice. "You're the one who sent the flowers a couple of months ago! I could not figure it out. Why didn't you say anything?"

"Things were so bad with Evelyn, I didn't think you would listen to me. But I could tell you and Avery were going through something tough. I figured it might make you think."

"It did. Thanks. I want to always be generous with Avery, in everything I do."

Maurice wore an emotional expression, something not often seen on his face. I was tempted to reach over and hug him, but he quickly composed himself and talk turned back to business.

With my change in status to Maurice's partner, we will both need to hire assistants. While we are on our two-week honeymoon, Maurice is going to sift through résumés and set up some interviews. He seems excited to have a new challenge. While I court the "different bride," he can go after the top-shelf money brides who want things a little more traditional. Maurice will also work less because he can trust me to handle my weddings. I know that working fewer hours—and staying out of a certain café—are two of the conditions that Evelyn has set for Maurice to move back home. He has been living in one of those extended-stay motels and is desperate to make things right again with his wife.

Iris breezes into the apartment a few minutes later, shaking me out of thoughts about work. She picks up my bag and bursts into tears. Startled, I ask what is wrong.

"Oh, I'm just so emotional today. I am happy for you, the sky is bright blue, it's a perfect October day, you're finally taking this huge step—everything!"

I hug Iris. "I would have never gotten to this day without you. How many calories did you feed me while I wailed on and on about my love life?"

"Too many, I'm sure. But I was happy to do it. Now, get out there, marry that man, and send lots of his cute friends my way."

On the drive over to the salon, I sit quietly in the passenger seat. A little song plays in my head: *Today you are getting married, today you are getting married.* We pass the street where I will live after today. I think of Annette, my golden bride. She always remembered the street address of the house she was supposed to live in with her sweetheart. I know that I will also cherish the sound of our new address: 1411 Adair Street.

The past two months have been a whirlwind. We had Baker Land's wedding and all of the media hoopla surrounding marrying off a celebrity. She was pretty fun to work with, but by the end, I really did not feel like she got the wedding of her dreams. There were just so many people butting in with their opinions and changing Baker's wishes behind her back.

After all of our starts and stops in the engagement department, Avery and I decided to just go ahead and get married. Neither one of us wanted something huge or fancy. We wanted to keep the guest list small—something that failed to happen, thanks to Babs—and the wedding simple. I think our guests will enjoy themselves. As for me, I am looking forward to tomorrow, when I wake up as Avery's wife. That will be a good day.

While my hair is twisted and prodded into a sleek pile on top of my head, Iris snaps a dozen pictures until her stylist sits her down and goes to work. I feel so lucky to have a good friend with me during these crazy hours before the wedding. I spent about three or four days at the Lelands' house this week working on wedding stuff and visiting with my parents and in-laws-to-be. I love them all, but the bridal buzz was killing me. I could not take a step without someone saying, "Macie, come look at the wedding favors. They were just delivered!" Or, "Macie, the caterer called. Do you want the silk bows tied tightly on the chair covers or sort of loosely?" For my mother's part, I have been really proud of her. She jumped right in, even though the Lelands can be a handful. My dad and Mr. Leland mainly steered clear of wedding madness. They took a classic car out for a spin or played golf.

After the makeup artist finishes up, we grab a quick bite to eat at a little sidewalk café. Iris remarks that with our casual clothes and overdone makeup and hair, we could be taken for a couple of out-of-place hookers. This makes me spit out a mouthful of water, which only makes Iris laugh harder.

"Can you believe we have to be dressed and at the botanical gardens in one hour?" Iris glances at her watch.

My heart bangs in my chest. One hour until I am with Avery again, this time for good. Rather than have our photos taken after the ceremony, we will be taking them before. Avery and I are not too worried about the "don't see the bride" rule. This way, we can go straight to the reception without having to wait. I think we will look a little fresher, too, for the pictures. After everything is said and done, I am still a girlie girl, and I want to have a fabulous wedding album.

The hour passes quickly. All of a sudden, Iris is lifting the wedding gown out of its bag. Gwen's design is stunning. The candlelight satin creates a slim shape, offering a square neck and a deep back. Tiny pearls crisscross the garment. A detachable train of matte satin gathers at the waist and is held in place by three delicate rosettes. I am near tears. I cannot believe this beautiful dress is mine to wear.

"Let's get this thing on, Cinderella."

While Iris holds up the folds of fabric, I step into the dress, feeling the heavy fabric move against my skin. It is a garment unlike any other. When she zips up the back panel and pats down the buttons on top of the seam, I get a little shiver. *Today I am getting married, today I am getting married, today I am getting married.*

"Absolutely beautiful," Iris says, near tears again. She shakes her head back and forth. "You look like a bride."

"Your dress is gorgeous, too," I say. "Gwen is amazing, don't you think?"

Iris wears a scarlet tea-length dress of matte satin with a matching silk band at the bust and hem. Strappy heels, and a gemstone necklace I gave her as a gift, complete the ensemble.

"It's time to go get you married," my best friend says.

And then, just like that, the minutes slip away like before. But this time, I welcome the tick tock of the hours. Avery's dad sends a car, whisking us away to the Atlanta Botanical Garden and the rose garden, where the outdoor ceremony will take place. My mom and dad see me for the first time, and we have a special family minute, just holding hands and talking. Iris walks up to us with my veil. With more than a tear or two, my mother gently nestles the veil into my hair at the back of my head.

I feel like such a fairy princess. Although our part of the garden is sectioned off with tasteful white ropes, visitors can still see our party coming and going. "Ooh, Mommy, a bride!" I hear one little girl squeal. The photographer walks in between the empty white chairs, taking shots of family members. The heady scent of blooming roses fills the air. Mr. and Mrs. Leland arrive with more of their family. I look back toward the garden entrance. Where is Avery?

Maurice appears at my elbow. He whispers, "You'd better come with me."

I do not like the look on his face. I turn red and follow Maurice away from the rose garden. He leads me down a short path until we stand beside the walled Japanese garden.

"Your groom would like a minute alone with his bride," Maurice says. He makes a little bow and then disappears.

Avery steps through a small opening in the wall. He looks so handsome in his tuxedo that I gasp and feel nervous, excited, scared, happy—all at once. I finger the smooth lapel of his jacket and smile up at my almost-husband.

"Can you believe we're doing this?" he asks me.

"I know. It seems so right but so very strange."

"You're beautiful, Macie," Avery says, his eyes filling with tears. "You look very lovely."

I spin around to show off my gown, but catch a heel on the gravel pathway. I stumble toward Avery, who stops my fall and then hugs me to his chest. "Let me be the first one to kiss the bride," he says.

And that is how Maurice finds us a few minutes later. "Okay, people, plenty of time for that later. Macie, you'll need lipstick. See Iris. We have to get these pictures made, let's get moving!"

The rest is pretty basic for anyone who attends as many weddings as I do. There are violins and flowers and well-wishers. Women in big hats sigh as they remember their own weddings years earlier. I listen to the minister, who urges us to love and forgive, laugh and trust. Avery cries and so do I. When it is over, trolleys decorated with white ribbons ferry guests next door to the dock in Piedmont Park. Beneath strands of white lights strung in the trees, guests mingle in the early night air to the sounds of big band music. I dance and laugh with friends from Cutter. My parents slow dance like champs—who knew they could waltz?

Avery finally tells me about our wedding trip. We will be having the journey of a lifetime—two weeks in Australia and New Zealand. I am beyond thrilled. I knew we were going somewhere a passport was needed, but the other side of the world? Iris squeals when I tell her. We munch on slices of her magnificent cake. Once again, I am overwhelmed by how much goodness there is to life. Everyone I love dances or stands within a few yards of me. Avery twirls around the wooden dock flooring with two young, giggling second cousins.

Every bride remembers her wedding as a blur, and I am no exception. Through it all, the platters of shrimp and salmon, the toasts and dancing, the kisses from family and friends, I always feel Avery's eyes on me. We touch hands once, near the end of the reception. Little clumps of people still sit around tables talking under a clear, moonless night.

"Nice ring," I say, turning Avery's hand over to catch a glimpse of the plain, platinum band.

"You, too. Are you ready to head home? I feel the need to carry someone across the threshold."

I smile, reaching for my new husband. In my mind, we fast-forward another hour until we climb the steps to our new home. If anyone is out and about on this late evening, they would see a bride and groom stepping across the wide front porch where many an after work conversation and Saturday morning brunch will take place in the years to come.

If our anonymous neighbor watches a few seconds more, he or she would witness the groom gather his bride into his arms and push open the old blue door. Then the scene goes dark and the neighbor walks on, perhaps remembering something from long ago. A few yards down, a dog barks just to be heard. Our new home, our new street, goes to sleep on this quiet night in October.